Violet Promises

A RETURN TO COAL HAVEN NOVEL

MARIE JOHNSTON

LE PUBLISHING

Copyright © 2024 by Marie Johnston

Editing by Dawn Alexander and Midnight Wanderings Publishing LLC

Proofing by MBE, Judy's Proofreading, and Deaton Author Services

Cover by Okay Creations

All rights reserved.

No part of this book may be reproduced in any form or by any electronic or mechanical means, including information storage and retrieval systems, without written permission from the author, except for the use of brief quotations in a book review.

The characters, places, and events in this story are fictional. Any similarities to real people, places, or events are coincidental and unintentional.

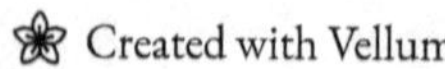 Created with Vellum

It was supposed to be one night to feel alive after getting out of a dud of a relationship. Now I'm having a baby, and I only have the soon-to-be dad's first name.

After my breakup, I need to find a job and place to live, but I can't move into the house my grandma left me unless I'm married. Fortunately, the guy renting the place doesn't know that, so I stop by and find out if he can move at the end of his lease.

Only when the door opens, it's him. My one-night stand. I do the only reasonable thing possible. I tell him we're going to have a baby and promptly puke over the railing of the porch. Next thing I know, I'm on his couch, and he's demanding a paternity test.

Except he doesn't just want the test. He wants to make sure I don't tamper with the results. He doesn't believe me. Apparently showing up jobless and homeless to persuade him to move doesn't make me trustworthy. Guess I'm not the only one with a dating history that leaves me jaded.

He insists I stay in the house that should be mine, right where he can monitor me. And the longer I'm around him, the more I can see that below his gruff exterior is a softie who planted acres of pumpkins for his cousin. A guy who wants to reconnect with his family. A man who makes me want to be more to him than violet promises.

Chapter One

Violet

One of the happiest days of my sister's life was just another crap day in mine.

I turned off the highway down the dirt road to the small farmhouse that was my destination, but I pulled to a stop by the ditch, the tall grasses brushing against the bottom of the car.

My stomach roiled. I sucked in a deep breath and let it out. I could control my body's reactions. I wasn't going to puke on the side of the road. The wild roses in the ditch wouldn't be covered with my ick.

My second fortifying breath was interrupted by the buzzing of my phone. I blew out the calming air with a frustrated growl.

My ex's name scrawled across the display in my car. Willis Hanson. What now?

Don't answer.

I didn't need this right now.

Don't answer.

Fatigue hung over my head and shoulders, and I just wanted to nap. I'd need a nap to talk to Willis. Would a logical approach work for him? When he wasn't irritated, he was more reasonable. But he was always needy. Somehow, that hadn't changed in the three months since we'd broken up. It was my punishment for being unhappy with him.

I scrubbed my face. No, I wouldn't answer. He'd phone again. Or text.

Willis was having trouble moving on. I'd left him bereft when he'd thought our future was together. If only he had acted like it. If only he'd understood that I expected equality in our future. A partnership. If only he'd been the man he had told me he was.

Now I was alone, driving to meet with some guy who had no idea I'd be showing up. I had left Willis. I had left my job. I had left California.

My life was like the road. I sort of knew the destination, but everything about getting there had changed. All thanks to a couple of impulsive, un-Violet-like decisions. The first had been the breakup.

After a few months of living with my parents in Billings, Montana, I had yet to find a job and an affordable place to rent. To distract myself, I had visited my littlest sister. Seeing Lily find love, *real* love, and then witnessing how my new brother-in-law, Eliot, treated her, I saw my life through a new lens. The lovesick look in my brother-in-law's eyes? I wanted that—from a real partner.

It had to be why I'd made impulsive decision number two.

During that visit with Lily and Eliot, I'd met a

stranger and had the best sex of my life. I couldn't return to California or Willis after that. It would've felt like too much of a betrayal, though to me or to him, I wasn't sure. I just knew I was no longer the same Violet who could pretend to be happy among Willis's pretentious friend group.

I was Violet Duke. The girl who wanted to forge a new path.

I was also Violet Duke, with the rapidly dwindling funds because, holy heck, how did anyone live off one income nowadays?

First, I needed a job and a place to live. I loved this little town of Coal Haven in the center of North Dakota. It was very un-California, with a whole lot fewer Willises. Lily lived less than ten miles away, and I had job options —hopefully. I just had to secure the place to live. Which was the task at hand.

I pulled back onto the road. My stomach would have to settle until this trip was over.

My grandma hadn't left me ugly jewelry when she died like Willis's grandmother had done. Nor had she bequeathed any money. Technically, she had left me a house and land. There were stipulations with the inheritance I didn't want to think about. Rules for how I'd get the property that could come in really damn handy right now.

I couldn't get my hands on the house because of those bizarre clauses, but I'd never backed down from a challenge. Lily had secured her inheritance. I could too. Aside from the stipulations my grandma might've thought were romantic, there was a renter in the place. A guy. No wife. No kids. No idea how long he planned to rent the place.

Aunt Linda was the executor. She rented the properties until we qualified to receive them, and she seemed staunchly supportive and weirdly timid about the renter. *He's quiet, Violet. He's been fixing up the place on his own dime, and he always pays on time.* I didn't understand her hesitation before she said *He's a Barron.*

The Barrons had a lot of land in Coal Haven, about ten miles from Crocus Valley, where Lily lived. Much of the property Grandma Annie Duke had left behind, including mine, was located in Coal Haven.

I remembered some of the Barrons. My family had lived in Coal Haven when I was a kid, before my parents moved me and my five siblings to Billings. The Barrons were a large family with lots of cousins close to my age. One had been in my class, but many of them were older. Aunt Linda wouldn't tell me much, only asked if I was married and ready to move into the house yet.

No.

If she wouldn't share what she knew of the renter or his plans, it was up to me.

I'd go to a house I hadn't been to for years, a place I'd done little more than ride by on horseback with my siblings when we were visiting our grandparents, and I'd talk to a man I had never met, in the middle of nowhere.

My sisters said I was the level-headed one. They'd have *opinions* if I told them my plan.

I had to do it. Just in case this mystery Barron said he was moving out tomorrow. If he wasn't, then I'd insinuate that he needed to move. Soon. Then I'd find a guy to marry me. Since Willis had dragged his feet for years.

It was now or never. My sister's anniversary party had been a good enough excuse to come to Coal Haven. I didn't know when another opportunity would arrive, and I still had a long drive to Billings.

I put the car into gear, and within minutes, the place came into view. A rectangular, two-story farmhouse that was strong but also weathered. Very, very rustic.

The landscape around it was some of the most beautiful I'd ever seen, but then I was biased. I missed my time in Coal Haven. I hadn't wanted to move when my parents broke the news that we'd be leaving.

Rolling green hills were broken up by small copses of trees and bushes. The occasional butte jutted proudly in the midst of the countryside, squat with a squared-off top. Every so often, the wink of blue from lakes or stock ponds popped against the green.

My stomach didn't find the scenery as calming. I pressed a hand against my belly. When would this feeling go away?

There was a big, beat-up silver pickup in the driveway.

Was this a really bad idea?

Of course it was, but I had to know. I had to know what to plan for.

I parked behind the pickup. It'd be easy enough to jump in the car and back out if things went south. My car wouldn't be blocked in.

This would be fine. The renter would be a nice guy. Even better, he'd tell me that he'd like to cut his lease early and I was solving a problem for him. He'd move immediately, and I'd have a place I could afford.

Right. Yes. *Let's do this.*

I got out and faced what could be an adorable porch with a little sanding and a fresh coat of stain. A few of the slats in the railing needed to be replaced, but the way it wrapped around the house would capture both the sunrise and the sunset. The front door was more inviting than the side entrance. Both were weathered, with screen doors that had a multitude of holes in the screens.

The steps creaked as I crested them. Those should get repaired.

The list of tasks added up in my mind, both in time and money. The wood siding was more than eroded. It was warped in some areas and should be replaced with a more modern, sturdier type. All the windows were old. The roof needed new shingles. What was left of my retirement would not go far. All I needed was for it to get me through to gainful employment and hopefully the winter. Because right smack in the middle of January, I needed both time and money.

My stomach heaved. There were still the stipulations. Did I think I needed to be getting married and moving in here? Finding a guy to marry—real quick—and taking on everything when—

The door squeaked open before I could knock.

My heart thudded behind my sternum, and I was faced with a big man. He wore wrinkled and well-used tan cargo pants over old cowboy boots, and his black T-shirt hugged a barrel of a chest. He was squinting against the sunlight, his head cocked. The gleam on his shaved head made my palms itch.

Because I knew what that stubble felt like. I knew what he looked like with every stitch of clothing off and how thick those thighs really were. I knew what he felt like thrusting inside of me for longer than I'd ever thought possible.

My gut roiled, and all the stress in the last three months of my life reached a crescendo. I opened my mouth to suck in fresh air, but words formed instead, and I shut my brain off. They had to be said. "I'm pregnant. It's yours."

Just as his brows drew together, I spun. I rushed to the railing and heaved all the contents of my stomach up into a patch of purple irises.

Chapter Two

Violet

Three months ago...

Have you come to your senses yet?

Come on, it's just a house.

Seriously, what do you want that you don't already have?

Everyone says you must've gone nuts.

The last text from my now ex-boyfriend slapped me to my senses. Willis had given me a lot, and for too many years, I didn't realize he gave me only enough to keep me hanging on. He probably nodded along when the question of my good sense came up with his family or his cultured friends.

I took a drink of the...I peered at my glass of craft beer. The crowd at the local brewery, Reservoir Barrel, maintained a constant din around me with the occasional burst of laughter. I didn't know anyone. Or maybe I did, and I didn't recognize them from when I was in elementary school.

Why was I here?

Because the place was irresistible. And it was away from my happy-as-a-clam littlest sister and her new, handsome husband. I loved them, and I couldn't be more thrilled for them, but when I was fresh off a breakup of a stagnant relationship, being surrounded by everything I had wanted and didn't get only made me more frantic about what really was in my future.

Here, I could get lost in the ambiance. I was surrounded by large windows, arching ceilings, and giant silver fermenting tanks of beer. Reservoir Barrel used to be a train foundry and repair shop. The area by the bar was where the train parts were made. On the other side, according to the bartender who'd worked here for a few years, was where the locomotives were housed for repairs.

The brewery was cool as hell and somehow soothing on my nerves.

"Isla around?" a deep voice asked from next to me.

I peeked at him from the corner of my eye. He leaned on the bar, his profile sharp. In a place where a lot of burly men frequented, he stood out. When I'd chatted with the server about the heavily male clientele, she said they got workers from the nearby refinery, gasification plant, and the coal mine. Coal Haven was an energy-rich area, but blue-collar men weren't the only customers.

Cowboy boots were a popular footwear choice. No surprise with the sweeping ranches and farms canvassing the surrounding area. Men and women were either dressed casually or looked like they jumped off a horse and strode in.

Willis would hate this place. My ex didn't do rugged. The trips to my parents' house in Billings had taxed him. He loved California too much to be comfortable anywhere else. And frankly, after a couple of trips to Montana with him, I was sick of hearing how nothing lived up to California.

"Isla doesn't tend bar much anymore," the girl said. She rested a hand on her hip and looked him up and down.

What'd she see? Without staring, I could only tell that he was a big guy. He loomed over me, and he wasn't even trying. His shoulders were wide, and his head was shaved. He should be intimidating, but my increased heart rate wasn't because I wanted to hop away like a terrified bunny. Nor was it from the beer. Heat curled through me, sinking further down, waking a long, dormant part of me that had gone unsatisfied for too long. That part of me liked this guy being close enough for me to smell his fresh linen scent.

Willis's cologne could get cloying. I could still smell it on my luggage. The items stored at my parents' should air out in the corner of the garage we'd stuffed them in.

The bartender tapped her fingers against her hip. "Who should I tell her is looking for her?"

"I'll catch her later," the guy said. "She mentioned she might stop in."

"You missed her by an hour." The bartender gave him an apologetic smile. "I can give her a call? She or her husband, McCoy, might be able to swing by."

"She's got my number." The guy slid onto a stool next to me and bumped my hip. "Sorry."

He glanced over, and his gaze traveled down my side

to where my hip flared out, the part he'd nudged when sitting.

"No problem." Oh, god. Did I sound breathless?

He was...a *man*. So was Willis, but my ex didn't have the presence of this guy. My pulse fluttered. I'd only drank half my glass of beer, but the warmth flushing me was like I was on my fourth.

He lifted his amber gaze to mine. Interest swirled in his eyes, and my breathing stalled, but he only nodded. When he shifted his attention off me, I could pull in air.

Had he checked me out? Was that interest for me or remnants from talking to the pretty young bartender?

"What can I getcha?" the bartender asked him.

He scanned the row of taps across from us. "Can I get a Reservoir Harvest? Tall."

"Coming right up." She looked at me. "Can I get you another?"

"No, thanks." I'd love to order a tall, just like the sexy guy seated next to me. Even more, I'd love to order a flight and try different flavors, but I was driving. One drink was my limit, but I liked the atmosphere. The beer was cold, and the crowd was accepting. I never felt this way when Willis dragged me to his preferred establishments. Only polos and sport coats were found in those places.

When she turned to fill his order, the man propped his elbows on the counter and glanced at me.

Another flash of heat hit me. Did he give me another once-over? I wore a striped violet and cream knit sweater and jeans, and I'd kept my hair in its curly, untamed state. I wasn't dressed to attract. I wasn't polished. I used to joke that if I could, I'd wear pajamas to work every day. Willis would've had a coronary. He already thought what I did for a living was uncouth.

Resentment stoked hotter. I took a long pull of my drink. The night out was having its intended effect. I had done the right thing breaking up with Willis and moving back to Montana. I might just be in a rental with no real address and no job, but I'd get there.

If I ever second-guessed myself again, I'd just have to watch my sister and her husband. Lily was stupid in love with Eliot. Had a boyfriend ever looked at me with hearts in his eyes?

My heart certainly didn't race around Willis. Had it ever? Seven years was a long time. I must've forgotten.

The raspberry sour played over my tongue. I made an appreciative hum.

He nodded to the girl when she slid a frothy beer in front of him before darting away to check on another customer. "If it's that good, why don't you order another?"

I looked around. Was he speaking to me? Men didn't do that. I wasn't the type of woman this guy seemed like he would be interested in. Blatantly sexual. Flirty. Confident in how men perceived them. "Me?"

He lifted a brow as if to ask *who else?* The stunning whiskey color of his hazel eyes pierced right through me. When his attention was on a person, they were captivated. At least I was.

"Yeah. You." He took a drink. "You're chugging it like it's ambrosia."

"It is." I tapped the side. "It's got raspberry in it. Tart Barrel is the name."

Humor lit his eyes. "Mine's got pumpkins."

"I thought about trying that one, but I'm a sucker for sours."

He slid the glass over. "Have a taste."

The responsible woman in me said absolutely not. He could've spiked it. He might see me as an easy target. My ex said I was a simple girl who could use some complexity.

Right now, I wanted to be compliant. I took a tentative drink. An ice-cold, sweet beer with only a hint of a fruity tang flowed over my tongue. "Mm. That's really good." I licked the foamy head off my upper lip.

His gaze zeroed in on my mouth. "Yeah. It is."

"You haven't tried it yet."

He held my gaze and took a long drink, his thick throat working over the swallow. He was...a lot. Overpowering. I craved more.

"Yeah, it's good," he said, wiping his mouth with a big hand.

I slid my glass over. "Try it."

He gave me a sidelong look. "I used to tell my soldiers not to drink out of something they didn't open themselves and haven't had control of all night."

I sputtered. "You offered me your mug."

The corner of his mouth kicked up. "I know I'm trustworthy."

I laughed, my head dropping back. "I'll take your word for it."

He took a drink out of my glass and considered the liquid inside. "Not my taste, but it fits you."

Defensiveness rose inside me. Did he think I'd pick a cheap beer? A weak one? No beer had been quality enough for my ex. "How?"

"Too trusting."

Surprise and relief prompted a laugh. How little had I been laughing the last few weeks? The last seven years? I swiveled toward him just a little. "So? Army?"

He took another drink, from his own glass this time, and smacked his lips. "Retired."

I could see it. He had the gruffness, an edge, that I didn't normally see in others. Military folks weren't the people my ex had wanted to hang out with. "What's your name, soldier?"

Did that come out of my mouth? I didn't flirt.

He studied me for a moment. "You from here?" he asked.

Had I overstepped by asking for his name? Was I reading our exchange incorrectly? I floundered in the dating world. Was that why I had tolerated Willis so long?

Regardless, I wanted the conversation to keep going. I wasn't from Coal Haven anymore, but I also didn't know where I was from. My future employment would determine that. "Just passing through."

His eyes continued to glitter, but he looked around. "Evan," he finally said.

His hesitance with his name was almost amusing. "You sure?"

"You'll take my drink, but you won't trust me about my name?"

"You didn't close up when you offered me your drink."

A gruff laugh left him. "You?"

"Me what?"

"You got a name?"

So his name was a touchy subject. Fair enough. I didn't want to run into any kids I used to play with on the playground. Then we'd have to catch up, and I'd have to tell them what I'd done with my life. I was tired of faking how much my career didn't suck the life out of me.

"I do have a name." I rested my chin in my hand. "My

sisters and I are all named after flowers. Want to take any guesses?"

He turned toward me, and our legs fully intertwined. He studied my eyes, then lazily lowered his gaze, caressing it over my mouth, down my neck to my sweater, then to the juncture of my thighs.

My breath caught. I liked his attention there. He was forward in the most discreet way.

"Violet."

I jerked when he got my name right. "How'd you know?"

Should I be worried? Was he stalking me?

Would I mind if he was? The idea of a guy who knew what he wanted, and that was me, sounded nice at this point in my life.

He dragged a fingertip over my sleeve. "The lines on this. And your eyes. They're violet."

"My eyes are blue."

"Not right now."

He said it so matter-of-factly I would've believed everyone had been wrong my entire life, that my eyes were, in fact, not blue but violet. Like my name. I suddenly wanted this man's insight on everything. I wanted to know if he wanted me. I wanted to know if that desire was real and what else he was so confident about. I didn't want to waste my time talking and learn later that he was only bored and I was convenient. Or rather, not convenient enough.

I really had to know if the way this man made me feel was worth it. I needed him to help me confirm that I hadn't made an epic mistake leaving a seven-year relationship because I was unfulfilled.

I finished the beer I'd been nursing since I'd arrived.

"Evan, I'm going back to my motel room at the little place on the edge of town."

Disappointment crossed his expression, and he nodded.

I slid off my stool. "If you'd like to do more than talk about beer and names, you can stop by. Room five."

Surprise flashed through his gaze, but I spun. I couldn't listen to a rejection. I'd go to my room and wait. If I fell asleep and no one knocked on my door, then maybe I should return to my senses and fly back to California.

My nerves scraped over my skin as I left the brewery. The drive to town only took minutes before I was pulling into the parking spot in front of the door to my room. Inside, I rubbed my sweaty palms up and down my jeans.

This was ridiculous. I wasn't having a one-night stand with some stranger, was I?

I didn't do that. I was responsible. I was the second oldest of six and the oldest girl. I was a role model. I was sensible, dammit.

Closing my eyes, I took a deep inhale. No. He wouldn't come. I was being impulsive. I hadn't thought out my breakup. I walked away from a man and a career I should love. I could still get them both back. Maybe not the job, but there were a hell of a lot more choices to be a chemist in California than Billings or North Dakota. They weren't in the specialty I was interested in, but I couldn't have it all.

I licked my dry lips. Heat seared the backs of my eyes. Had I been wrong to leave?

Tomorrow, should I return to Willis?

There was a knock at the door.

Chapter Three

Evander

Present day...

A raccoon-eyed Violet sat huddled on the couch I'd bought when I moved in six months ago. Whatever light makeup she'd had around her eyes had smeared in the wake of the tears and shaking that had come after her vomiting.

My mind reeled.

I'm pregnant. It's yours.

I didn't know this woman, and she said she was having my kid.

She took a drink from the glass of water I gave her. Her hand trembled, and she hadn't looked at me since she'd tossed her cookies in my yard. Afterward, she'd sobbed her apologies and asked where the bathroom was. When she'd emerged from the bathroom, her face had been wan, and she'd drooped like she was ready to tip over.

She was still cute, though.

She set the glass on the coffee table. She hadn't learned a thing from what little talking we'd done the one night we'd been together. I knew I was trustworthy. She didn't. And I didn't know if she was full of shit or not, but I knew what the odds were.

I brushed a hand down my face. I had spent the whole morning in the field, checking on my goddamn pumpkin patch for Isla and weeding through the raspberries and the giant fucking mosquitoes who thought I was breakfast, lunch, and dinner.

Pumpkins and raspberries. What would my former soldiers say? At least pumpkins wouldn't call me in the middle of the night because they'd gotten thrown in jail. I'd just come inside to clean up and be ready to give a pumpkin tour to Isla later this evening, and then Violet had happened.

Violet had happened once before. A nice goddamn way to spend a night, then I'd gone on my way. She'd gone hers. I had assumed. I sure as fuck didn't expect to see her again.

I might've hoped. A little. But not like this. Never like this. Never again.

A shudder racked Violet's lush body. Her curves hadn't been my imagination, and that fucker was vivid when it came to her. How'd she find me?

Coal Haven was a small damn town, and I was a Barron. My arrival had been, and still was, the highlight of gossip hour. Even after being back for six months, no one was used to seeing me around. Likewise, I wasn't familiar with much around Coal Haven anymore.

I should've asked her what "just passing through" meant when we hooked up. Did she live close by? Have a second family somewhere? I knew fuck all about this woman claiming to be carrying my baby.

"Care to tell me why you think the baby's mine?" I asked to get a move on things. My tone came out harsher than intended. I doubled down and crossed my arms. I stayed on the far side of the living room, close to the kitchen.

She flinched and swallowed. Shit. Was she going to puke again? "Uh... I know we used condoms." Some color returned to her face. Was she embarrassed to bring up that night? "But, um, I'm not on birth control. My ex had a vasectomy he didn't tell me about until right before I broke up with him, even though he knew I wanted a family."

What an asshole, but I couldn't look like I was on her side. Had her ex been an ex when we hooked up? Was he even an ex? I'd been taken by that schtick before.

I shrugged. "Okay? And the vasectomy was for sure effective, and I'm the only guy you've been with otherwise?" Derision crept into my voice. I'd heard all these excuses over the years. Whether it was my exes spewing lies or other soldiers' experiences—been there and done that.

To be fair, a lot of those instances had turned out to be true. Not mine.

She nodded. "Yeah, that's pretty much it."

Her nervous gaze flicked over the room, from my slate gray furniture to the generic pictures I bought to keep the walls from being bare. Then her attention fell to the maple hardwood floor.

This was the homiest place I'd ever had, but it wasn't

mine. The house was old. The bones were good, but the flesh needed a major upgrade. I had started on this room. My landlord told me it wasn't necessary, but I was bored spitless. I needed something to do until I figured out what my next phase in life was.

Which brought me to my next question. "How'd you find me?"

I'd been targeted during my time in the army. Girls outside the gate looking for a naive soldier with a steady paycheck and benefits. Bonus points if he was deployed several times so she could collect the paychecks and do what she wanted.

Cynical? Hell yes.

"I own this place," she said, unable to meet my eyes.

I let out a laugh. "And Linda is pretending?"

"She's my aunt."

I sobered. A little too much truth for my liking resonated from Violet. Her captivating eyes were dull today, and that didn't sit well with me. I also didn't care for the way her shoulders sagged, like she'd given up. The uninhibited passion she'd unleashed the night we spent together was nowhere to be seen.

"I should clarify," she said hoarsely. "Linda manages the properties my grandma left behind. Grandma split them all up between me and my siblings. This house and the section it's on are mine."

Yet I was renting it. "So you want me out?"

She winced. "Yes and no."

I wasn't prepared for her honesty. A small part of me softened toward her. No, I couldn't. This was the Kandi situation all over again. My ex had stripped my blinders right off to women like her—and Violet.

She picked at her nails. "I'm in a transition period in my life."

Because she was pregnant. "The baby could be your fiancé's."

Thank fuck for my religious use of protection.

But there was always a chance...

I pushed the thought out of my head.

"It's not." She closed those beautiful eyes and inhaled. "He had the procedure done two years before we were together. Apparently." Bitterness dripped off the last word. "And between the breakup and you, I had a cycle, so..." Pink tinted her cheeks.

Didn't mean she hadn't been with anyone else right before or right after. I'd buy stock in paternity tests before I believed her.

She waved her hands. "Don't worry, we can do a paternity test and all that," she said as if reading my mind. "I'm well past seven weeks, and that's the minimum for the test. All I'd need from you is a cheek swab. I'm actually relieved to run into you. I wasn't looking forward to calling the brewery and asking if anyone happened to know an Evan."

"Evander," I said gruffly.

"Hmm?"

"My name. I said Evan because I'm...I've been gone for a long time. I wanted to stay under the radar."

She closed her eyes, looking more dejected than before. "Right. Linda said you're a Barron." Just when I was about to ask why that mattered, she pinned me with that bright gaze. "I don't remember you. You're, like, ten years older than me."

"Why would you remember me? You said you were

just passing through town." How much had she lied? We didn't talk enough for her to tell that many fibs.

"I was," she said. "My family lived here when I was a kid. We moved to Billings when I was in high school. My sister moved to our grandma's old house last year."

Her phone buzzed. She dug it out of the linen shorts she wore that could be a few inches shorter if I had my way, but when she checked the screen, she deflated. She rested it on her lap, face down. "I'm in between homes. Right before I met you, I quit my job in San Diego and broke up with my long-term boyfriend. I moved to Montana, and I've been job hunting. I always liked Coal Haven."

I hadn't ever liked this town. I wasn't sure I could. "What's your last name?"

"Duke."

Violet Duke. Sisters are all named after flowers and her brothers are plants. I had little more than a vague recollection of the Dukes. "Do you have older siblings?"

"Alder's two years older than me."

No wonder I didn't know them. I had been in my own world, trying to break out. Now, I was in my midforties with roots and nowhere to put them.

She was homeless and jobless, and she claimed I was her baby daddy, and, oh, by the way, this house was hers too.

Was I in that different of a position? I wasn't exactly homeless. Nor was I jobless. I was growing goddamn pumpkins. "Let me get this straight. You want to move to Coal Haven. Ideally, you'd like to move in here. And now you're pregnant. But you think it's mine?"

"There's only been you."

A possessive *fuck yeah, there's only me* went through my mind.

"But like I said, we can do a paternity test. I don't mind. I would want to if I was in your place."

"And what place is that?" I had to hear her say it in her matter-of-fact way. Make this sound less crazy.

I couldn't be a fucking dad.

I was too damn old.

And I didn't know what the hell to do about my own dad.

Violet rubbed her temples, and the pallor from when I'd opened the door returned to her face. She groaned.

I pushed off the wall but ordered my feet to stay planted. The urge to sit next to her, tug her to my lap, and let her nap against me grew until my muscles twitched.

Holding her wasn't all I wanted to do. My dick knew exactly what she felt like, those little needy noises she made, and how fucking responsive she was.

I searched her face. This had to be a scam. I couldn't figure my way around the rules, but I would. The routine was usually the same. Baby trap the guy, then get his money and benefits. Only Coal Haven wasn't by an army post. Did the guys who worked at the plants and mines in the nearby area have issues like soldiers often did?

I didn't know. I'd followed Violet to the little motel because I couldn't *not* follow her. I went against my better judgment for the first time in years and had a one-nighter.

A night I hadn't wanted to end.

But it did. And she was pregnant.

Oh, and she wanted me to move out of the place I was renting.

Surprise, surprise.

Fuck. What if the baby was mine? All these years, despite all my best efforts, I had a kid.

My mom would...

She'd fucking love it. I'd have to see the joy of the news on her face and the crestfallen disappointment when I told her I was going to have nothing to do with seemingly sweet, clever Violet.

"You need to go." I felt like shit as soon as I said it. What kind of monster kicks a sick, pregnant lady out? "I've got six months left on my lease. You might want to live here, but then you shouldn't have rented it to me."

She closed her eyes, and all the air leaked out of her. Didn't she get enough sleep? Under that runny mascara, how much of the dark smudges were from the shadows under her eyes?

She inhaled and squared her shoulders. "Yeah. Okay." She opened her eyelids and listed to the side like she was ready to drop. "I'll order the test when I get back to Billings. It'll be late, but I'll get online tomorrow. We'll need a sample from you, but I can drive back from Billings to—"

"Billings is a six-hour drive." It was already late afternoon. She'd be driving until late, and she already looked haggard as fuck. Cute but ragged.

She nodded, uncaring of the trip. "Long drive, but it's peaceful."

She shrugged the blanket off. Did the fabric smell like a pasture full of wildflowers in the middle of summer like she did?

The woman had been worse than a ghost. Her scent had haunted me for three months. Too bad she'd turned out like the others.

The phone on her lap buzzed again. She went stiff

and dropped her gaze to it, only to immediately lift her focus back to me. "I need to get back to keep up the job hunt."

She'd driven that far just to kick me out? Why wouldn't a phone call do?

Would I have recognized her curt voice? Would she have figured out it was me? She might've eventually tracked me down with the help of Reservoir Barrel. A crusty guy named Evan? I would've been hunted down. Especially if she needed money.

"How long have you been out of a job?" Didn't she say she quit before she met me? Three months ago?

"The whole employment thing has been taking longer than I anticipated." She waved at her stomach. Her phone continued to vibrate. Without looking, she silenced it. "I can't get through an interview without puking, so I might have to find something part-time. I think it's the stress amping up the morning sickness. I used to be good at interviews, but that was before I had to ambush a future employer with maternity leave."

A pang of sympathy hit me in the middle of my stomach. No, I could not fall for it. My kid or not, she was most likely a user.

Been there; done that.

She hadn't known my last name, and she hadn't known I was fully retired. I wouldn't become a millionaire from my benefits, but I did okay. Well enough to do whatever the fuck I wanted.

Unless I had a kid.

Goddammit.

She jumped when her phone started buzzing again. Again, without looking, like she'd done it a zillion times, she pushed the button to silence it. "I'll just need your phone number." Only then did she look at her screen. Her right eye twitched.

My curiosity got the better of me. "You sure you can program my digits in between whoever keeps calling you?"

Her jaw went tight. "Yes. That'll work."

So she was cagey about the calls? Interesting. I rattled off my number. She was midpunching it in when her damn phone vibrated again.

She punched the screen, and then her eyes widened. "Shit."

She fumbled the device and pressed a red button. Red colored her cheeks deeper, thanks to the fucknut who wouldn't leave her alone.

After abandoning the phone on her thigh again, she wiped under her eyes. When she saw the makeup remnants on her fingertips, she blanched and continued swiping at the smudges. "So. Yeah. I'll call you. We'll do the test. You can figure out what you want to do with your rights when the results come back. As for the house, you're right. You're renting. Uh..." She sucked in another breath, and her gaze jumped away. "The lease won't be up for renewal."

Six months. At least I'd get those goddamn pumpkins harvested.

She rose and primly straightened her skirt and the blouse that was the light blue of a winter sky. Did she dress up to try to kick me out of the house and tell me I'd be a daddy?

I'd see her to the door and that'd be the end of it until I had to prove her right or wrong about the baby.

She trudged to the door. "So, um. Thanks."

I yanked my gaze off her round ass. Dammit, I'd been

staring. And what the hell was she thanking me for? For kicking her out or for being the dumbass who couldn't resist going to her motel room that night?

I could at least make sure she got to her car without vomiting. I wasn't heartless, and while I might be tossing her out for good reason, my mom would hate how I treated her. Mom would hate how ruthlessly I shot down a lot of women over the years.

And I detested how I didn't want Violet to leave when that was absolutely what she had to do.

"I'll walk you out."

Violet opened the screen door and stopped. "You have company."

I looked over her head, her wildflower scent floating up around me. My gut fell to my feet. I had missed the sound of the engine coming down the drive. All my focus had been on the wan pixie on my couch.

My cousin Isla and her brother Stetson were coming up the steps. They were near the stairs, looking at the gorgeous land around the house.

How was I going to explain Violet's presence? *Hey, I just learned her last name, and she says she's having my kid? Speaking of kids, how are yours who I've never met?*

Isla's eyes went wide when her gaze landed on Violet. A grin spread across her face.

Shit. With Violet's arrival, I'd forgotten Isla said she'd stop by with official contracts I told her I didn't give a crap about. She could screw me over. Growing goddamn pumpkins kept me busy while I figured out what the hell I should do about my aging parents.

How the hell was I going to explain Violet?

Chapter Four

Violet

"Hi!" A woman who looked vaguely familiar crested the stairs. She was tall and willowy, with blond hair pulled up in a messy bun. The jean shorts she wore only highlighted her long legs, and her yellow Reservoir Barrel T-shirt was tied at the waist. She probably hadn't puked over any railings.

My gaze flew to the side where the crime had happened. The irises in the flower bed glistened with droplets of water. Had he cleaned up my mess while I'd been in the bathroom?

Evan—*Evander*—Barron was hard to get a read on, but one thing I gathered was that he was intensely private. He also wasn't my biggest fan, and after dealing with Willis's calls, it would've been nice to have a guy look at me the interested way Evander had when we met at the bar.

Aunt Linda's mystery renter was my one-night stand.

Evander Barron? Small damn world. Most of my shock had been evacuated with the contents of my stomach, and I was left trying to untangle the mess my life had become. Now I had to deal with him as a renter and the dad of my baby when I would've been driving away to figure my shit out by myself if he'd been a stranger.

The new arrival smiled at me. The giant man next to her could almost make Evander seem dainty, but not quite. While he had an inch or two on Evander, he didn't outmuscle the man standing just behind me. Streaks of gray dusted his temples, and his gaze was assessing, but his mouth was tilted up as he glanced from me to Evander.

Oh. What must this look like? I was opening the door to a house I didn't yet own with a guy I'd only known for one night.

"Sorry to intrude, Evander. We're a little early." The woman stretched out a hand to me. "I'm Isla, and this is my brother, Stetson."

Isla. We used to go to school together. She was Evander's cousin. Now I recognized her brother. Like Evander, he was older than me. He hadn't changed a lot since school. Still a big guy, just with laugh lines and twinkling eyes. I struggled to recall Evander, but he'd left town so quickly after graduation, and of course, he hadn't given Isla rides to and from school like Stetson had.

"V-Violet." I tentatively accepted the shake. My phone buzzed. Willis. I released her hand and stuffed my hand in my pocket to hit the silence button. "We went to school together," I blurted out. Way to be smooth. But between Willis and his pestering texts and Evander and his intensity, my brain was fried. "Until my family moved."

A triumphant grin spread across her lips. "Yes! I

thought you looked familiar. Violet Duke, right?" When I nodded, her smile widened. "Wow—it's been years. How are your parents?"

"Good." Should I ask the same? *Do your parents still swallow children's souls?* That was how it had felt when I was younger and Cameron and Naomi Barron were around. I remember little more than wondering why Dad would work for him for so long. Dad had said he was a better boss than he was anything else.

Evander's heat soaked into my side. He was crowding me at the doorway. The shame of telling him he couldn't renew his lease still burned into my soul. I was a horrible person. Dammit, Grandma! I could really use this place. If I didn't have to worry about a roof over my head, I'd worry less about the whole job issue.

Mom and Dad would always let me live with them if my money ran out. I hadn't told them I was pregnant yet. It hadn't felt right when the dad hadn't known, and I also hadn't figured out what to do about that.

At least that problem was solved. Didn't mean I wanted to leave a disappointing relationship and live with my parents to have a baby. I was in my midthirties, and I'd given up too much life for Willis.

Isla was smiling at me. Stetson had a twinkle in his eye. Right. Evander and I looked like a thing, but his distance after I told him I was pregnant suggested that'd never happen. It could've been the vomit.

Was my mascara still running rampant across my face? I forced a weak smile. "I'm sorry to intrude. I was just leaving."

Isla's expression fell. "Oh no. I didn't mean to interrupt anything." Her hopeful gaze passed from me to Evander. "We can always talk another time."

"It's no problem." If my nerves cranked up higher, the irises on the other side of the porch would get a sick blast too. "I was just stopping by to talk about the lease." Guilt looped through my stomach and pulled tight. I skated around a lie, but my conscience didn't like it.

"That's right." Stetson nodded. "I forgot a Duke owned this place."

"The old renters were here so long, we all did," Isla added.

The previous tenants were the original owners of the old farmhouse. They had fallen on hard times and had to sell. My grandparents bought the place and gave them a steep discount to rent. Had she suspected the trouble her damn trust would cause?

My smile this time had to look more like a grimace. "It was nice to see you again."

I edged out of the door, and the siblings stepped back.

Evander's heat followed me. "I'll be right back," he said to his cousins.

"Hope to see you again," Isla said to me. "We might cross paths more if you come to town to see Lily. Eliot has a sister that's married to one of our cousins."

Curiosity got me to stop. Lily had mentioned how close the Knights were, and I'd probably met that cousin. Eliot only had one sister, Aggie. "Ansen?"

Stetson hooked a thumb in his belt loop. "Archer and Ansen were raised in Texas, but now they're back, and so is their dad. One Barron from each generation seems to take off and never communicate."

He wasn't looking at Evander, but we all knew who he was talking about.

With the attention off me, a yawn snuck out. I tried

to stifle it. Evander and Isla were shooting dirty looks toward Stetson, but Evander switched his attention to me.

My belly flipped, but the reaction wasn't from morning sickness and anxiety. His piercing whiskey gaze was a spark to my libido, striking the tinder and making it ignite.

"You're tired," he said.

"It's been a long few months," I murmured. I gave Isla and Stetson a little wave. "Before I make this a Midwest goodbye—"

"Guys, can we do this another night?" Evander asked. Did he wish to avoid them? Or to make sure I drove out of city limits? He curled his hand around my elbow, and I almost moaned from the strong, hot grip. "I'll call you."

Stetson snorted. "Sure 'bout that?" His tone was good-natured, but the intent behind his statement was not. *One Barron from each generation seems to take off and never communicate.*

"I don't give a crap about contracts," Evander retorted. "Isla needs pumpkins; I'll grow them."

"I just need to set the rate with you," Isla said. "We can do it over email, but I wanted to be nosy." She nudged her brother. "It was Stetson's idea."

Stetson grunted. "I'd turn into a skeleton before I got an invite."

The wall that was Evander softened. Did Stetson's words bother him? "You already told me the rate. I told you I'd grow them for free. I don't care."

"I need the write-off." Isla shrugged. "And I need to be by the book just because. Anyway, we'll let you two be." She tossed her arms around Evander for a lightning-quick hug that made him release me and left him stiff and blinking and caused Stetson to smirk at him.

Evander shot Stetson a promising glare.

Whatever had happened between Evander and his family left hard feelings.

Had the fallout been Evander's fault? Or had it been a slow dive into isolation? Was he the type to burn bridges and that was why he wasn't interested in me beyond whether the baby was his or not?

Would he give up parental rights? And the house?

Isla and Stetson left. The tension they had brought was gone from Evander's shoulders, but his scowl remained in place. It was likely permanent.

I propped a hip against the railing. A caffeine stop would be necessary before I left town. I didn't want to sleep at the motel. I'd come into town last night for Lily and Eliot's party, but I'd been given room five again. Nothing like trying to fall asleep with a roiling stomach and the memories of the most intense sexual experience of my life. That night would hold the record forever.

I folded my arms. I'd done more than I had set out to do today, and I had no other reason to be in Coal Haven.

I rubbed between my eyes. "What do you need?"

"You're too tired to drive all the way to Billings."

I exhaled a gusty breath. "And you know what? I'm tired of men who think they know better than me."

A dark brow quirked. "Are they taking paternity tests too?"

My nausea vacated with a spike of anger. I'd been patient. I'd been understanding. I'd been respectful. The irises might disagree. But the last of my patience snapped. "Trust me, I want nothing more than for you to sign away your parental rights and move out so I can have a nice, quiet place that's mine to raise this kid. No pretentious, domineering men allowed."

Evander hadn't been pretentious. But he could be! He was also domineering in the most titillating way, but I could not afford to romanticize a one-night stand. I no longer had just me to consider. This baby was part of the future I had envisioned for myself. The path to this point —no. But I had wanted to be a mom and would do right by this kid.

"Why do you think I'll sign away rights?" he asked evenly.

The pitching stomach made a resurgence. Same with the buzzing of my phone. Dammit, Willis! I squeezed the damn button through my shorts. "I said I'd like nothing more. I don't know if you will, but I don't know you. I don't know if you'd make a shitty dad or if time spent with you would corrupt the kid." His eyes narrowed. He might not like to hear it, but I'd gotten a vaguely insulting vibe from him. If he could dish it out, he had to take it. "I don't know if you think car seats are a marketing ploy or if you think boys will be boys." His brows drew together. "No. I don't know the gender, and I don't want to find out. Everything about this kid has been a surprise. Why not that too?"

My phone started vibrating again. I huffed and dragged it out of my pocket. "I'm just going to shut it off."

"Who is it?"

I scanned the litany of texts from Willis. **The diamond ring was four-point-five carats. Kaitlyn remembers a platinum-set, sustainably-farmed pearl necklace. She has the insurance papers for each item. Do we need to file a report with the police?**

Frustration burned away some of the nausea. He was still going on about the stupid jewelry? I'd been fielding messages all day about his grandmother's gaudy costume jewelry. I didn't care how much money he claimed they were worth. I wouldn't pay five dollars for them.

"My ex," I explained. "Out of nowhere, he thinks I took his grandma's ugly costume jewelry." I let the phone continue buzzing in my hand. "I didn't, for the record. I didn't work a job I hated to pay off my student loans only to sit on a fortune I planned to steal later. But I think he's threatening me with going to the police." I prodded my temples. "I've had too many other important things to worry about than that ugly jewelry."

Evander plucked the phone out of my hand. Horror dawned cold along my flesh as he answered. "File a police report or leave her the fuck alone." He hung up on Willis and calmly passed the phone back.

It was warm from his grip. I just gazed at the dark screen, astonished. What did Willis think about Evander answering? That I'd moved on so quickly after years with him?

I had, but not like that.

Should I care what Willis thought? He was the one who'd dragged his feet.

"At least we know where each other stands," Evander continued like he hadn't intercepted a call from my ex. "But you can't drive to Billings tonight."

"Who says?"

"The bags under your eyes."

Ouch. I palpated the puffy spots above my cheeks. My sleep had been horrible. I'd been too sick to find a job in Billings. Since I was coming to Coal Haven, I had looked at openings in the area. There were two chemist positions at the refinery my dad used to work at. If Evander moved out at the end of his lease, I'd only have six months to rent a place. A home and a job.

I might not get the position, but between the vacancies and the house that should be mine—I couldn't not try. It'd also take the planets lining up and some deception, which I hated myself for. But I had a kid to take care of and no income or benefits.

Because of that kid, I wouldn't make the long drive. Lily and Eliot would be leaving for their honeymoon, but I didn't want to stay with them anyway. They had a full family and a rambunctious house. I needed a little quiet to think about everything.

I could stay another night and check out rentals and the job openings. "I can get a room in Dickinson. I think my brother is staying there tonight."

Somehow, Evander managed to look even grumpier. "You went to talk to a male tenant alone instead of asking Linda and her husband or your brother to come with you?"

Definitely not my aunt and uncle. Alder would've required an explanation. "I was in town for my sister's anniversary party. I left early, and they don't know I'm pregnant." When he cast a sharp look in my direction, I shrugged. "I've had a lot to juggle, and their reactions weren't one of them."

He propped his hands on his hips and glowered at the horizon. His strong jaw worked back and forth, then I was pinned again by his direct gaze. "Stay here."

Evander

"*Here* here?" Her big blue eyes were saucers. Buried deep in them was wistfulness. She coveted this house, and my rental agreement tampered with her plans.

Did she know who I was when I had hit on her at the refinery? I tried to figure out a way the information would've been useful to her then.

Did she need an escape from that jackass who kept calling her? I'd only heard a partial word in a whiny voice and that'd almost been enough for me to go full asshole on him. But I also didn't know what he was capable of, and I didn't need more trouble that came with the short, sexy whirlwind who'd entered my life.

"There's more than one bedroom." We'd shared a bed before, but we sure as hell hadn't been sleeping, and I'd been gone before morning. "We'll order the paternity test, get the samples, send it back in, and get the results. Then you can go."

"Then I can go?" She almost sounded like she was going to laugh, and yeah, I heard how it came out.

If she wasn't trying to use me, then she'd have serious reservations about living with a guy she barely knew. If she was conning me, then I didn't want her hours away, plotting.

"I need to oversee every part of this test process." I ground my molars together. "You're not the first woman to claim I'm the father of her baby."

A mix of emotions played through those expressive eyes. Surprise, curiosity, hurt. "Really?" She shook her head. "Sorry. None of my business. I take it your experience wasn't a good one."

I dipped my head once. The scam had ripped my heart out.

Violet folded her arms. "I do have some business in town, but what if your family stops by again? What do we tell them?"

"That you're checking the place out, making sure I'm a good tenant."

She screwed her face up. "You think that'll work?"

Did she care? Shouldn't I be the one who was poking holes in the story? I should be the guy shoving her out the door and not caring how far she drove while she was drooping and yawning. Yet I'd made the stupid demand that she stay here. It made sense. Given what Kandi had tried to do.

If my mom showed up, would she believe that a pretty young woman was in my house because she was making sure I wasn't living in filth?

I was an idiot. "We can say we're dating. Then, when you leave, we broke up. Simple as that."

Her expression remained impassive. Yeah, I hadn't alluded to the baby actually being mine.

"We can order the test now." I ticked a finger up. "When it arrives, do not open it." I put up a second finger. "When we collect the samples, we do it together." A third finger. "When the kit gets packaged to mail, I'm there." I added a fourth finger. "I watch you drop it off." I might even squat by the mailbox until the postal carrier emptied the damn thing. "And I'll be the only one checking the mail."

Her mouth dropped open farther with each demand. She shook herself, and I braced for a tirade.

"Okay," she said. "But the results will be emailed, or they'll have their own account to log in to."

My brain whirled like my tires were spinning to keep up. She was way ahead of me, but I had my past to lean on. Technology had updated. Of course it had, but it worked out for me. Harder for Violet to alter results. The obstacle didn't faze her.

Damn. Was I really going to be a dad? "You sure you're okay with that?"

She tipped her head. "What am I supposed to say? I didn't steal Willis's grandma's jewelry, and I'm not conning you. But just like he has to rant to his sister and paint me as the villain until she remembers that she has it —" A gasp left her. "Oh my god."

She yanked her phone out, and her fingers flew over the screen. She punched one last button that must've been send. "There. I bet his perfect sister's delinquent teen sold the ugly jewels. But Willis was with me when we gave it to her because she nagged so much about which pieces actually went to her. As if I'd put up a fight over them. He must've forgotten. He hadn't cared about the damn things until now."

Violet really hated that jewelry. I almost laughed.

No softening around her. She'd kick me out if I didn't have a rental agreement. As it was, I'd have to watch her to try to figure out her game. But the thought of her staying under my roof loosened a knot behind my sternum.

I didn't want to be behind an accident caused by fatigue. That was it. It had nothing to do with the satisfaction I got from picturing her in my bed. *Guest* bed. In a guest room. Until she left. Then Violet Duke would never be in my bed, or under my roof, again.

Chapter Five

Violet

It was morning. The blankets were pulled up to my chest, and I was dressed in my sleep shorts and top. My tender breasts were unbound. For a brief moment last night, I had debated about wearing a bra while I slept. I didn't know Evander, not really. This wasn't a hotel, and if I had run into him when I went to the bathroom, I didn't want to poke his eyes out with a nipple. I should look like I had my shit together.

But the soreness had won out, and I had taken it off. My stomach had quit pitching. For once, I didn't feel so off-kilter. Most mornings, I woke and the worry started. Half the time, the stress was what had woken me.

Not today. California was two hours behind, and Willis had left me alone since Evander answered his call. My ex hadn't even replied after I told him that we'd given his sister all the jewelry two Christmases ago.

Closing my eyes, I enjoyed the silence and the quiet phone. My stomach rumbled. I had real hunger pangs for the first time in months. I rolled to sit up and stared at the closed door.

An enigma was on the other side.

Evander Barron. A guy who had some undetermined family drama, yet he grew pumpkins for Isla on at least half the acres of land he was renting. He didn't trust me, that was apparent enough, but he was giving me the spare bedroom. Hopefully, for free. I could pay him. I would.

I would make my own way. I was the oldest Duke sister. If my youngest sibling could pick herself up off the dirt her ex had tossed her in, so could I.

I hadn't heard any noise from the rest of the house, and I needed to get ready for the day. Would Evander let me use his computer to apply for jobs? Using my phone was too tedious. He was on his laptop last night when he searched for paternity tests and ordered one.

If I was going to be staying for two or three weeks, I could use a computer. I had a few outfits packed, but eventually I'd need maternity clothing. I'd also need something to do to keep me sane while worrying about getting hired. The blanket I started crocheting last month was at my rental in Billings. I was using it to learn the stitches again, and the unevenness around the edges stretched the whole length. I could buy more yarn. Grandma Annie taught me how to crochet. I'd have that from her at least.

A little anxiety piped into my stomach. What would Evander say if I came back from town with new yarn and hooks? Willis had thought the hobby was for old women. I told him that Hollywood stars were known to knit, but he'd sneered and said crocheting was a waste of time. It'd been easier to just leave the hobby behind.

My rental in Billings was up at the end of July, but I'd keep my things there until I knew for sure where I'd land. The place was little more than a vacation rental, expensive, but I didn't dare lose it in case Evander decided we couldn't cohabitate.

If I showed up at my parents' with more stuff to store, they'd have questions I wasn't ready to answer. Just like I had news for them I wasn't ready to tell. I'd feel better spilling the news if I also had information on where exactly I'd be living and where I'd be working.

I hoped it was in Coal Haven. I had liked growing up here, and now with a baby on the way, the attachment was stronger. I had at least one sibling within ten miles. The only niece and nephew in the Duke family were Lily's kids. I could go anywhere, but I wished to stay here. Just so happened, Coal Haven was also where my baby's father was. Until his lease ran out anyway.

Was Evander home? Was he still sleeping, or was he working outside?

I gathered my clothes and toiletry bag. Then I cracked the door open and listened. Nothing. Wait—

Was that a meow?

Did he have a cat?

I waited for a heartbeat. Must've been my imagination. I rushed into the bathroom. The decor was as tasteful as the living room and the guest room. Done in grays, like his furniture, it was all bold lines but managed to be bright. It fit him. He might wear wrinkled cargo pants and boots, but he was all planes and angles. Even his shaved head had definition. My fingers tingled with the memory of his scalp under my palms while his head was between my thighs.

The things that man could do with his tongue.

A stroke of longing traveled around my heart. He'd never touch me again. No, my news hadn't been welcome.

I left the bathroom. In the guest bedroom, I folded my pajamas for tonight. Another meow reached me. The sound was muffled. I got closer to the door and the mews got quieter.

Hmm. I crossed to the window and waited. Another mew. Did Evander have cats? I hadn't seen food or water bowls. I loved cats.

I scurried out the door and down the hallway. The floor shifted beneath my feet, and I put my hand on the wall. Food and water. I could not find a kitty without sustenance.

In the kitchen, I found the bananas by the new stainless steel fridge. All the appliances had been replaced. By Evander? I couldn't see my aunt and uncle pumping money into a house that'd either go to me or be sold in six years.

I opened a cupboard. It was cleaned out. I checked another. Also empty. I finally found one cabinet with canned goods, rice, and packets of taco seasoning. Another was full of glasses and plates. I took out a glass.

The fridge was full of fresh produce, lunchmeat, and ground beef. Since I was snooping, I checked the freezer. Packages wrapped in white butcher paper filled the inside. Meat, meat, and more meat.

I gobbled my banana, downed a glass of water, and went in search of the cat. I had nothing else to do until

Evander returned and, hopefully, let me use his computer.

Before I left the kitchen, I went to the filled cupboard and grabbed a packet of tuna just in case Evander hadn't fed the cat yet and if I couldn't find the cat food.

Outside, a light breeze ruffled my hair. I'd put on a pair of jean shorts that I wouldn't be able to wear much longer. My shirt was an old one I'd gotten at my last job. It said Oswell Labs on the front and was an obnoxious yellow as a nod to the work done there.

"Kitty, kitty, kitty."

A tiny mew was barely audible, but it came from the same side of the house my window was on. The corner of the deck stopped under the window while the other side wrapped under the side door. I squatted down.

Another mew.

The grass was damp, but I ignored it and got on my hands and knees. I flicked the flashlight of my phone on and peered under the deck. A couple of feet of clearance spanned underneath, with a slight opening between the bushes as access.

"Kitty, kitty, kitty." I slowly swept the light until I landed on a pair of eyes. "Hey, baby."

The black-and-white kitten meowed, its little whiskers glinting white in the light, making it look like a wizened feline.

Another little head appeared and mewed.

"Oh my goodness, there are two of you."

I tore the top of the tuna packet off with my teeth. I used the end of the flap to dip into the tuna and waved it around.

The kittens' noses twitched, and they both meowed.

They were scared but hungry. I might not have to body-surf under the porch.

"It's all for you. Come on." I brandished the tuna pouch a few times. I sank lower, my ass in the air and my upper body almost flush with the cool ground. "It's so good. Come on."

I kept my voice light, nonthreatening. It'd been ages since I'd coaxed a cat. Willis had been allergic to everything, mostly the idea of a pet that would get attention over him.

I kept the light trained on the kittens and put my head as low as possible to see them.

"What are you doing?"

Startled, I pushed up and peered behind me. Evander's hot gaze was stuck on my ass, a contradiction to his perplexed tone. The seam of my jean shorts dug into my groin, and the hem was tight around my thighs. I hadn't thought when I packed that I should've given elastic waistbands priority. With as much as I'd been sick, it was amazing I was increasing in size.

I puffed a curl out of my eyes. Evander was in a gray T-shirt, soaked with sweat that covered the tattooed chest I had distinctly wanted more time to explore, and black workout shorts that had him displaying as much leg as I was. He was muscled from head to toe.

Good thing he was tall, or my butt would be in his face. Which, if memory served, was something he liked.

A flush swamped my body until I was afraid the remaining dew around me would turn to steam. "I'm trying to feed your cats."

He lifted his gaze off my backside. "I don't have cats."

I didn't get up. The kittens were hungry and somewhat used to people since they didn't scatter, but they were scared. "These kittens say otherwise."

His brows drew together. He walked to stand next to me, squatted, and peered where I aimed the light. "They weren't here yesterday."

"Good thing, or I might've thrown up on them."

The corner of his mouth tipped up. "Someone must've dumped them. Growing up, we used to have a ton of barn cats. My dad used to say few things are free in life, and kittens are one of them." His lips pulled into a frown.

Was that a bad memory? Or did he realize he was almost conversational with me? "My sister is a vet tech. I can take them to the clinic in Crocus Valley where she works and make sure they're okay."

"I can't keep them." He straightened but stayed in a squat. "You're kicking me out in six months."

Oh. The banana in my stomach turned into a lump. A little panic sprinkled in. Aunt Linda would demand a marriage license before I could move in. One thing at a time. "I mean, I can take over as their owner. I'll cover all the expenses." Thankfully, kittens didn't eat much.

His mouth tightened. "Not if they're mine until then. Think they're feral?"

"I don't think so. They haven't hissed once."

He flattened out on the ground and belly-crawled under the deck. A minute later, he emerged with two furry bundles half-heartedly struggling in his hands.

"Ohmigosh, I think they're only a couple of months old." I sat on my butt, heedless of the dampness or the itchy grass, and shook some tuna onto a spot that I had flattened when I was crouching.

Evander set the kittens next to the food, and they started gobbling the tuna down.

I scratched the tops of their heads and around their ears. They were pretty well taken care of. Whether they'd escaped from their mom and couldn't get back or they were dumped, they probably just needed a deworming and some shots.

I took out my phone to call Lily.

She answered with a "Hi, Violet."

"Hey. I know it's Sunday, but do you know if there's an opening at the clinic tomorrow? I found two kittens. They seem healthy."

"Uh, maybe? Were they outside the motel? In the parking lot?"

I lifted my wide gaze to Evander. He must've heard her question. The corners of his jaw were flexing. I didn't think before I dialed. How did I explain this to Lily? "Yeah, I can explain later. I'm...kind of staying in the area for a few weeks." I pressed the back of my other hand to my forehead. The scent of tuna washed over me, and my stomach roiled. Before, it wasn't strong, but I hadn't put the smell right by my overly sensitive nose. "I'm bothering you. It's your honeymoon."

She laughed. "We haven't left yet. I can text one of the vets and see if they can fit you in."

"No hurry."

"Are you taking them back to Billings?"

This phone call was a bad idea. I shouldn't have bothered her. Then I wouldn't have to lie. "I think I have a place for them. I'll explain all that. Later."

"Now you've got me curious."

My sisters would love this story. I'd rather know more

about my future before I told them. "Go. Have fun with your new old husband."

"Trust me. I have been." She snickered.

I smiled despite the spear of envy piercing my chest. "Nobody likes a braggart."

"But you love me."

"I was told I have to when you were born."

She laughed. "Goodbye, Violet. I'll let you know what I find out."

I hung up. Instead of meeting Evander's gaze, I shook as much tuna out as I could and pried the edges of the pouch open. It was obvious I'd been evading my sister's questions.

Evander sat on his ass and propped his arms on his bent legs. "I was going to have that for breakfast."

"Oh crap, I'm sorry." I gave him an apologetic smile.

A twinkle lit his eye. "It's fine."

Was he...joking? He had a sense of humor, but I hadn't seen it since he'd opened the door yesterday.

"I thought your sister had an anniversary party?" he said.

Why did I get the feeling he was trying to catch me in a lie? Maybe because I was withholding a lot of truth. "She did. They married a year ago but can only take a honeymoon now. She was a new mom, and he ranched in eastern Montana. But he found a manager and lives with her now."

I kept my focus on the kittens. The man was intense, and I was still not telling the whole truth. His gaze burned into my face.

"The kid his?"

"No." I smiled sweetly. "But he knew that when he met her. She has an older girl too. Her ex's daughter, who she adopted. He was a douche." I snuck a peek, but he didn't look fazed. "She got divorced when she was pregnant and got custody of both kids. He gave up his rights. He's a real loser. Then she met Eliot and got married, but he had to figure out how to keep his business going while he's living in another state."

Evander's expression was still impassive.

"You don't seem surprised by any of it."

"You'd be shocked at the living situations I've run into during my years in the army." He shrugged. "Whatever works for people."

He seemed like an accepting guy. Unless a woman showed up on his doorstep and told him he was a dad.

I will still be on his doorstep, at least until he moves out. Either way, I'd need a job. I also needed a husband to live in the house, but I'd gladly worry about that later. "Can I use your computer?"

His gaze sharpened. "Why?"

"So I can apply for jobs." Look for places to rent until he kicked me out. Find a guy to marry.

Would Evander ever—

No. He didn't seem like someone who played to others' demands. He wouldn't care that this place would go up for sale. Hell, he could probably buy it. And after I informed him I was kicking him out when his lease was up, I doubted he'd say an enthusiastic yes.

He rubbed his lower lip between his thumb and forefinger.

Frustrated, I picked up the tuna packet remains. The kittens were sniffing his running shoes. "Never mind. I'll run to Bismarck and buy one."

"You can afford a computer with no job?"

"I'm living off my investment money." Technically, it

was what I'd taken from my retirement. I rose and looked around. There was an old shop that had one big sliding door hanging cockeyed. "Do you mind if I make them a spot in the corner of the shop?"

"The shed would be better."

I spun to study the shed. The roof sagged, and the door was perpetually cracked open. "It's a piece of shit."

"Most buildings around here are, but I can fix up the shed faster than the shop. I'll get some lumber to reinforce the roof."

"I'm tempted to lock these guys up until I get back, but maybe if I leave more food out, they'll stay until I return." Evander likely wouldn't cat-sit.

"I only have so much tuna." He rose in one fluid motion, but his knee cracked and he winced. At my *are you okay?* expression, he lifted a burly shoulder like it was nothing. "I didn't stretch after I ran. You fed them. They won't go anywhere, or if they do, they'll be back for more food."

"Oh." He seemed to have more stray barn cat knowledge than I did. I picked up one. It struggled but also started purring. I stroked its little head. "Should I go get you some yummies and a cozy place to sleep?" I folded its furry body into both hands and stroked it along my cheek. "I think we can tell if they're male or female this early."

"Two females."

Oh. He was on top of things. I admired a guy who could take care of shit. Bonus points for no whining.

"Let me clean up, and we can ride together," he said. "Get some cat supplies and groceries."

"I don't think I can get a computer anywhere in Coal Haven or Crocus Valley."

He clenched his jaw once. "You can use mine." Then he stalked away.

⁂

Evander

I let the warm shower spray wash over me.

Why couldn't I keep any distance between me and the sexy kitten whisperer?

It'd taken inhumane effort not to drop to my knees behind her and palm her ripe ass through those tight jean shorts. To tell her that I couldn't fucking sleep last night because she was in the room next to me and I know how tightly that pussy of hers clenched around me.

My persistent erection roared back. How many times had I jacked off to the memory of that night?

Add one more.

I gripped the base of my dick and pumped. *Fuck.*

She'd been so needy that night. Shy and reserved, until she wasn't.

I stroked myself and let my head tip back.

She had made those little moans when I had her legs wrapped around my ears. My climax was building at record speed.

She was on the other side of the door. Only, instead of imagining the past, I saw her round ass in the air, her face down. Like she was presenting it just for me.

I cut off a groan.

I had to jack off quietly.

Then she'd done a little wiggle, and I could've come in my shorts.

I didn't then, but I was now. The storm that had raged inside me since she'd appeared on my doorstep had an outlet. Energy zipped down my spine and put a noose around my balls. My load shot from me. I gritted my teeth together and grunted through the pleasure. Goddammit. This was nothing like coming inside of her.

The small release I got was fleeting. I opened my eyes and stared at the drain. I'd come inside her and that was causing all the issues. Condoms failed. I knew that. But women lied. I knew that even better.

Yet I got out of the shower almost salivating that Violet would be with me all day.

Stay fucking strong.

It'd been years since I'd been swayed by some pussy. It'd been forever since I had a woman under the same roof. And it'd been even longer since there was one face I thought of when I jacked off.

I dried off and hooked the towel around my waist. I didn't bring in a change of clothes, but then she'd already seen all of me. Maybe she'd be encouraged to walk around in nothing but a towel.

I shook my head. This would be easier if my attraction to Violet Duke wasn't at an astronomical level. Ever since I'd seen the back of her sitting at the bar that night in the brewery, she'd been dead center in my brain.

In the hallway, I stopped when keys jingled. Violet was opening the front door. "Where are you going?"

She looked over her shoulder, and her eyes flared. Her gaze stuck on my chest, brushing from side to side like she had to decide if she had a favorite pec. "I'm moving my car. Since you're getting lumber, I figured we're taking your pickup."

I relaxed. She wasn't sneaking out. Why would she? She had a free place to stay and two kittens.

I had two kittens. For as long as I was here. They could catch the mice in the shop and shed. I was at war with the ground squirrels, and the cats could help with that too. "I'll be right out."

By the time I was dressed and went outside, she was sitting on the steps of the porch, two kittens in her lap. One was already asleep, and the other had the most blissful look on her face.

I had gotten the same way when Violet had stroked me.

I rubbed my temples. "Ready?"

"Yeah. I hope you don't mind. I used your second tuna pouch and put it under the porch swing. I'll buy replacements in town."

I minded a lot when it came to her, but seeing her take care of the two kittens nudged its way into my heart. Still, she could be a good human and a shit girlfriend.

She scooped the kittens up and put them closer to the food. She'd also taken one of my plastic food storage containers and filled it with water.

"Let me wash my hands, and I'll be right there."

I loaded up and pulled to the edge of the walk that went from the driveway to the front door. Then I inched ahead until I was far enough along that I could watch Violet out of the mirrors without obviously staring at her.

When the sun glinted off her hair, my fingers itched to brush through her curly strands. Were they warm from the sun? Was her skin?

I ground my molars together. The answer to any of

those questions didn't matter. Back to the task at hand. I'd pick up lumber after we were done getting more groceries and cat supplies.

How did I go from living alone to having a woman and two cats on my property?

I pulled into the farm supply store. Violet hadn't spoken for the short trip, but the silence hadn't been awkward. She looked at the window, and when I snuck glances, her expression had been mostly content. Just a slight pinch in her brow like she carried stress. But then she was homeless and jobless and I hadn't been enthusiastic about being a supposed dad.

It wasn't that I didn't want to be a dad. I just didn't want to be tricked into it.

When we got out, I kept track of her out of the corner of my eye. She had an ease that wasn't there when I'd first met her. In the brewery, she'd joked around with me, but there'd been an undercurrent of tension. Supposedly, she'd just broken off a long-term relationship with Vasectomy Willis.

She pushed her hair back, but the wind caught it and threw it into her face. Instead of getting frustrated, she smiled. A secret smile meant for no one other than herself. She couldn't know my focus was all on her.

In the store, I let her take the lead. She was going straight for the pet section. But also—her ass. She couldn't see me ogling it.

She found the feline aisle and picked out toys, treats, cans of cat food, a cozy bed that would get disgusting in a few months, flea and tick treatment, and little collars.

Those cats had found a home whether they liked it or not.

"What are you naming them?" I asked.

She was inspecting litter boxes. Was she moving them inside as soon as I moved out?

"What do you think?" She straightened. "I've never named a pet."

"You haven't had any?"

She smiled. "I have five siblings. It was a fight to get any time with a new pet." Her gaze turned curious. "I don't recall. Do you have siblings? It's Isla and Stetson, and then there are the two cousins from Texas—"

"No." I swallowed past the sudden lump in my throat.

She flinched and probably wondered why I'd answered like an asshole, but I didn't need to be telling her in the middle of the farm supply store.

"I'll have to think on it," she finally said. "Maybe it'll come to me when I'm playing with them."

Her voice rang with so much damn excitement. She looked forward to playing with cats?

She spun the cart around and pushed it to the end of the aisle. I followed.

She was about to turn when she stopped. "Sorry. Go ahead."

Another shopping cart came into view. Aw hell.

The woman pushing the other cart smiled sweetly at Violet. "Thank you." Her eyes lifted to mine, and her smile widened. Genuine joy filled her face, and the pool of guilt inside of me spilled over. "Evander."

Shit. "Hey, Mom."

Violet whipped her head around, her eyes wide.

Mom abandoned her cart and engulfed me in a giant hug. Each time she put her arms around me, she held on like I would disintegrate into dust and be gone forever. Her hugs were part of the reason I stayed away. The reminder of why she hugged like that had been too painful for too long.

Yet I returned her embrace just as tightly. She wouldn't be around forever, either, and I'd given up decades of time with her.

"Fancy meeting you here," she gushed when she finally released me. Her interested gaze landed on Violet.

Crap. We'd talked about this, but I wanted more time to prepare, to form a plan of attack and anticipate all the questions. "Mom, this is Violet. She's—We're—"

"Seeing each other." Violet stuck her hand out. "Hi, I'm Violet. I'm in town for a long vacation, and he's seeing how long he can tolerate me."

Mom melted more with each word out of Violet's mouth. She clutched Violet's hand. "Oh, my. *So* nice to meet you." She glanced between us, beaming. "How'd you meet?"

"At Reservoir Barrel," Violet continued, able to tell a half-truth like no one's business.

I should be growing more suspicious, but I was too grateful she knew how to answer without making things uncomfortable. I was tired of discomfort around my parents.

"I'm a Duke," Violet continued, "so I'm familiar with the area, but I hadn't been to the new brewery."

Pure joy radiated from Mom's face. "Duke? Weston and Magnolia?" When Violet nodded, I feared Mom would collapse from the delight vibrating from her. "What a small world." Mom's gaze shone when she aimed it at me.

"Yeah," I said roughly, remorse tugging at my chest. There was no stronger sign that I'd let down this woman than her reaction to meeting a date. The last twenty years slaked off her face, making her look more like the mom crying in my rearview mirror. She still wore the same loose slacks and sensible shoes, but at this moment, she was the mom I'd grown up with.

"I'd appreciate it if you kept this quiet," Violet said, a friendly smile in place. "My parents would get so excited at the connection, but it's so new."

"I see. Of course. I understand. News like that tends to travel fast." Mom wrung her hands together. "You two have to come over for dinner."

The relief from Violet's quick intervention about us turned to dread that curdled the acid in my belly. Mom was at peak happiness. How did I crash her entire day? Week? If I turned her down—

"We'd love to." Violet twined her warm fingers through mine, and I jerked. A current of electricity passed between us. Pure heat that went straight to my dick and to hell if I was in public. "I'm sure we've got a free night." She tilted her face up to level me with a steady gaze.

At least one of us wasn't unbalanced. Violet was a rock. She was too good at this. "Yeah. Whenever."

Her fingers tightened around mine.

"How about tomorrow?" Mom's eyes creased at the corners. Her smile hadn't faded. "Bruce is going to be so pleased."

Dad was always something, and pleased was not it.

"Is there anything you're allergic to, honey?" Mom asked Violet.

Violet shook her head. "No, and I'm not picky, so don't worry about me."

"Oh, that's perfect. Kennedy and Liam would just love you."

I flinched, but thankfully Mom's gaze was on Violet.

Fucking great. More people to lie to. More people I never expected to have much to do with.

Violet beamed like she was soaking up the attention.

Mom waved her hands. "Don't worry. I'm not going to throw all kinds of family at you. I wouldn't want to scare anyone off." Her grin faltered.

Yeah. I'd caught the jab. Between that comment and the family bit when it came to Liam and Kennedy, this encounter was another reminder I didn't belong.

Violet might be doing me a favor. I'd stick it out for six months, and then I'd be gone again.

Chapter Six

Violet

The afternoon was hot, but the porch was shaded, and I had the kittens sitting on my lap. Their bellies were full of the food Evander and I had picked up yesterday. They were sleeping, and I was gazing at the green pastures around the property. A mix of Black and Red Angus milled across the rolling green hills. Occasionally, a *moo* would cut through the air.

Sounds of pounding came from the shed. Evander was adding support beams for the roof and muttered something about how that'd do, but I'd have to eventually replace the shed. I'd asked if he wanted help, and he'd given me an *are you serious?* look and stomped out of the house.

If I thought he had been in a shitty mood after I arrived, it was nothing compared to the last twenty-four hours. Pretty much right after we ran into his sweet, almost timid mother.

I didn't expect an explanation of the awkwardness in the air between them, but it would've helped me understand him. His mother clearly loved him, and Evander had been uncomfortable with the attention. He'd closed up since then. It wasn't what he said, it was that he said even less. He became a storm that raged within the confines of the wall cloud. He didn't lash out verbally, and he wasn't physical. Evander put himself to work as if he could out manual labor whatever feelings were roaring inside of him.

He had family issues. Clearly.

I ran my finger over one kitten's head and along its fuzzy little body. I had used Evander's computer to update my resume and check out the other requirements for working at the refinery.

The application window closed soon, but I hadn't applied yet. I had to make sure I crossed each *t* and dotted every *i*. I was stalling, just a tiny bit. Every job had its own environment. How was the refinery lab to work in?

My job at Oswell was enough to show me that I might love the science, but it was the people and the environment that were critical to actually liking work. Some of my former coworkers were good friends. I'd miss them. But too many were like Willis—arrogant to the point of insulting. I had loved my now ex-boyfriend, but I had changed careers from education to a private lab after working with him for two years. All that aside from the fact that I had always planned to work in the oil and gas industry.

Willis had scoffed at the field. If it wasn't academia, it wasn't respectable.

I liked my fellow quirky chemists. The ones who could talk my ear off about the grapes they grew for their

DIY wine, their family, or all the different types of guitars and how their construction changed the sound. But one Willis type in the workplace was one too many. And it seemed that no matter what lab I was in, there was always a Willis type.

I closed my eyes and drew in a slow breath. I had no idea if I'd get the job in the first place. Honestly, my stress was more about showing up to a new job pregnant and losing credibility than it was with dealing with smug coworkers. Besides, I wouldn't be going home to the same attitude with my next job.

I'd look at other openings in the area tomorrow. I needed some cat cuddles to fortify myself. After I applied, whether I stayed or left wouldn't be up to me, and my nerves balanced on edge. I wouldn't get any support from the cranky man in the shed.

We were set to go to his parents' place in an hour. Nerves had begun circling in my belly, but we wouldn't be lying to them that much. Evander and I weren't seeing each other, but I was sort of on a long vacation. This time together would help us determine how well we could co-parent together—not that they'd know that yet.

Evander had never said that he was willing to co-parent. Not even after I told him I'd rather he gave up his rights.

Did I want him to? No. It wouldn't be easy for a kid to grow up wondering why a parent voluntarily agreed to stay out of their life. But it'd be easier. I could do as I wanted. I'd have the freedom I often felt I lacked when I lived with Willis.

"Goddammit!" Evander's shout rang across the lawn.

I gently set the cats down. Their tired protests didn't keep them from being tiny gobs of gelatin. Once they were off me, I jogged to the shed. The door was propped open, and Evander's big back faced me.

He looked fine—so *fine*—but I couldn't see an issue. "You okay?"

He spun around, nearly knocking his head on the sagging plywood of the ceiling. "Don't come in here. It's not safe."

I stayed where I was. The shed was empty, except for his tools, and was nothing but worn wood and a saggy ceiling. "I thought you said it was safe enough for the cats."

"They're so tiny they won't get crushed."

I cocked a brow. "You were willing to risk it?" He was right, but I was irritated with him. He shut down in the store after meeting his sweetheart of a mom. He'd been absent from the house all last night and today, but he hadn't gone anywhere. Had he hand-weeded each and every pumpkin plant?

I didn't have a right to any of what was going on in his life, but the hurt didn't listen to reason. I was nothing to him when that night together, he'd made me feel like everything.

He fully turned, cradling his hand. "The cats would've been fine if the roof collapsed. They'd have skedaddled after the first creak. You wouldn't have been fine, and I haven't seen you run, but I wasn't going to gamble that you could sprint as fast as them."

A tiny tendril of warmth looped around my heart. He was worried about me?

He was a good human, at least.

I took a couple of steps back and waved at him. "What happened? I can take a look."

He clutched his hand tighter to himself. "I'm fine."

Stubborn man. "Then what happened?"

His teeth were going to turn to nubs from the way he ground them together. "I got a sliver."

A laugh sputtered out. He wouldn't react like this from a sliver. "I can still help."

His eyes narrowed. "I'm fine."

"You obviously have shit going on with your family— the ones we're meeting in less than an hour—and you've been quieter than a church mouse. But you get a sliver and yell so loud the whole county can hear? You're not fine, and I happen to have a lot of experience removing slivers from my siblings."

We faced off for several moments. His gaze was flat, but deep down, emotions swirled. Did he ever let them out?

Why wasn't I backing down? He didn't want my help.

Yet on some level, I sensed that he needed it. Or it was just wishful thinking. I hated feeling like a freeloader. I was using his computer, living in his house, and eating his food. I didn't mind Billings, but I'd rather be jobless here than surrounded by neighbors who were gone all day and hated me for my California license plates.

Every time I ran into one, I said, "Hi, I'm Violet. I'm *moving back* to Billings."

It'd helped a little. Not as much as my new Montana plates.

"Fine." He stomped out of the shed. The only way he could walk today.

"Fine is a third of your vocabulary. Be careful you don't use it up."

He stopped and gawked at me.

I smirked and strode past him. "I have tweezers, but

depending on how embedded it is, I might need a pin." I squinted at the partly cloudy sky. "Why don't you sit on the steps? The light is better outside."

I waited at the top of the stairs to see if he'd actually listen. To my surprise, he plopped his ass on the top step and kept his hand cradled to his chest. The militant expression was still in place. I could work with that.

Pleased, I went to the front door. "I'll be right back."

I grabbed my nail kit and found a bottle of spray antiseptic in a small white box in the bathroom. Inside was antiseptic with a label I didn't recognize, wipes, and bandages. Just in case, I brought the whole thing with me.

The kittens were snoozing in a sunbeam, oblivious to us.

"Where'd you get this stuff, or did it come with the house?" It looked old enough.

"From a medic's kit."

"Were you a medic?"

"No. Infantry. But we had plenty of kits around to raid."

I gestured for his hand. When he opened his fist, a giant chunk of wood fell out, and a few drops of blood hit the boards.

"Oh my god." I stuffed a tissue in his hand and closed his fingers back over them. I couldn't see any other wooden shards. "That wasn't a sliver."

"Compared to the whole two-by-four, it's a sliver."

I nudged him. "Stop it. I might think you have a sense of humor."

"I have a sense of humor."

As much as I wanted to hang on every word, I feared he might quit talking if he noticed I cared. I took his hand

and gently uncurled his fingers. I put the tissue on the floorboards next to me. There wasn't much new blood welling up.

I propped his hand on my lap and opened the kit on the step between our feet. When I leaned over for an antiseptic wipe, my belly brushed his hand. A small touch, but my body lit up, remembering how good he was with his hands.

Focus, Violet.

He was quiet while I dabbed at the drying blood and angled his hand to get a good view. There must be a few slivers left behind.

"Everything's changed," he said quietly.

I held in an encouraging smile. He didn't strike me as a guy who opened up to people. I kept quiet to prompt him to keep talking and continued to clean off his skin. He had two good-sized slivers and a smaller one I might need a needle for.

"My dad and I...we didn't get along. Mom and I fought a lot. They were servants to my uncle and my grandparents. I got tired of calling it out and getting told to keep my mouth shut and do as they said."

I paused and peered at him. His gaze was glued to his hand. Had he ever shared this with anyone, or was it the upcoming visit with his parents that was bringing it up? "You wouldn't do as you were told, so you left and joined the *army*?"

The corner of his mouth ghosted up. "That's what —" His jaw went rigid, and he tore his attention away from his hand to stare down his driveway. "It's ironic."

Curiosity tore at me. What had he been going to say?

I used the tweezers to get the first sliver. "And now? You said everything is different."

"My uncle is an asshole. Was? Fuck, I don't know. People seem to like him now. God help me if people talk highly of Aunt Naomi."

I snickered. "She scared me."

"She scared everyone. Cameron bullied everyone. My dad did whatever he was told. My grandparents." He let out a derisive snort. "Uncle Cameron learned it from somewhere."

I tugged at the second big sliver. It was proving more challenging, but Evander didn't flinch. "My dad used to say the only bad part about working for Cameron was that he would never retire. That's why Dad took the job at King Oil when the owner retired. But Dad and Cameron never hung out as buddies."

"All the land. All the oil money. It just gave them an excuse to behave badly." He shook his head.

"Them" must be Cameron and Evander's grandparents. "Was your dad in a tight spot?"

"Yes, but it shouldn't have mattered. Then there's Aunt Kira, but I guess she's always on some tropical vacation with a different guy."

"So you left when there was *Yellowstone*-type drama and came back to a Hallmark movie?"

He blinked at me. I was rewarded with a small smile. "Yeah, but I don't trust it. They probably forced everyone right where they wanted them, and now they're happy."

My family was chaotic but mellow. I couldn't fathom going home to a drama-filled house. "So you're nervous about tonight?"

"The last time didn't go so well."

"When was that?" The second sliver came out. "Yes!"

He did a double take, but I buried myself back into tackling the last sliver. Squinting, I moved his hand in different directions. A tiny portion was sticking out. I dabbed at the tiny bit of seepage from where the larger shard pierced him.

"The night we met."

I stopped what I was doing. "Really?"

"I probably wouldn't have hooked up with you if I wasn't so pissed at them."

Hurt cooled off that lasso of warmth around my chest. "Swoon."

He lifted his other shoulder. "It's why I agreed to grow goddamn pumpkins for Isla."

A one-night stand that resulted in a baby was on the same level as pumpkins? "You were told not to?" I stuffed my feelings away and continued to attack the last bit of wood.

"He said it was a waste to rent land. He asked what'd happen if I planted a crop and then got my lease yanked out from under me."

Shame crept up my cheeks. Good for me for not trying to run him off sooner. I'd been so focused on me and the baby, but Evander was in the same boat. We could go anywhere, but something tied us to Coal Haven. He could afford this place, and I wasn't sure I could. I needed a husband to do it anyway. So why was I trying to get him to move out when his lease was done?

I retrieved the last sliver. Triumphant, I wiped off his hand again. "Want a bandage?"

"Nah. It'll come off when I shower."

I checked my phone. "Better go do it. We have to leave in fifteen minutes."

He stared at me. We were sitting close enough I could count the speckles of amber in his whiskey eyes. His smell was comforting. Soap and fabric softener. Fresh linen.

This close, I caught a faint whiff of the woodsy aftershave he used—also mild smelling.

"I don't like being bossed around," he said, almost teasingly.

"Then you hooked up with the wrong woman." Defensiveness flared in his eyes despite the humor in my tone. He was prickly. I tossed the tweezers and gathered the dirty wipes and tissues. "Although you know very well there are times when I like to be told what to do."

At his sharp inhale, I left him at the top of the stairs.

⁂

Bruce and Willow Barron's place was a tall farmhouse, square with a steeply pitched roof and a cute, peaked overhang over the front door. The farmyard was tidy with two giant shops, one red and one tan. A barn almost as big as the shop loomed farther away from the house.

Evander hadn't said a word the entire way. I couldn't complain. I got to admire the green pastures and full fields of sunflowers, wheat, and corn. He didn't need to talk. I was content. But still, was this the guy who struck up a conversation with me?

Guys did a lot to get laid. All Evander had to do for me was open his mouth. He'd caught me at the right time. Would there have been a time I turned him down?

When he parked, I slipped out and met him around the front of the pickup.

Willow waved to us from the front door. "Come on in, guys. Bruce is still out in the field."

Entering the house was like going back in time to

when my mom used to cook for a family of eight every night. Savory smells filled the air, and pots clanged from the kitchen. Then as we got older and her writing career took off, Alder and I had to take over. For now, I reveled in the memory of good food and a cozy home.

The smell of roasting meat filled the air, and my stomach growled.

Evander maneuvered me toward the living room, a warm hand on the small of my back. "You need any help?"

Willow fanned her oven mitt at us. "No. I threw an elk roast in the oven. I hope you don't mind elk meat, Violet."

"It's been a while," I said, the hunger morphing into nausea in my stomach. My morning sickness said better late than never today. "Sounds delicious."

My stomach might've churned at the different species of food, but I'd suck it up. The scent in the air helped.

Evander didn't take his boots off, so I kept my sandals on and padded farther into the homey living room. There were two entrances, two exits and a set of stairs on one end. The windows were as squat as the rest of the room, but it was inviting. Crocheted blankets and throws draped over the couch and recliners. Pictures littered the walls and mantel.

I drifted closer. Familiar and unfamiliar faces smiled out from the photos. There was one of a much younger Evander, his hair cropped tightly to his head. He wore aviator sunglasses and less rumpled cargo pants. The younger guy next to him was grinning, and they had their arms slung around each other.

My mind worked over the face. "I recognize him, but I can't remember his name."

"That's Derek," he said, his voice rough as sandpaper. "My brother."

I frowned. "I thought you said—"

"He died."

I sucked in a breath. *Way to step in it, Violet.* Sympathy welled, and I wanted to embrace him. From the rigid way he was standing, it'd be like hugging a brick. "I'm sorry."

"Me too." He cleared his throat.

Our conversation from earlier ran through my head. "Did he give you a hard time about joining the army?" My brothers would give each other shit about a major life decision like that.

Evander nodded, his body rigid. "He always made smart-ass comments about me following someone else's orders."

I moved on to another photo, worry gnawing at me that I crapped on his day more by bringing up his brother.

"It was an aneurysm," he said. "While he was driving."

This time, I couldn't stop myself from comforting him. I gave his hand a brief squeeze. "I'm sorry."

He gripped my fingers back, so I didn't let go.

"Stetson and Isla," I muttered when I reached a picture of them with their parents. It had to be twenty years old. Isla was still a lanky young teen, and Stetson was a young man with a charming grin and serious eyes. Bordering that photo was one of each of their families. "Adorable."

I sidestepped, and he came with me, our fingers still intertwined.

"Holden and his wife Emery," he said at the next one.

"A lot of kids."

He grunted his agreement. He tipped his head to another couple with two little kids. "Holden's sister, Nora, and Colt. He used to work for Aunt Kira."

"From what you said about your family, can I guess that was a story?"

"You'd guess correctly."

Smiling, I moved to another one. "Oh, I recognize Ansen and Aggie. That must be Archer. Aggie is Eliot's sister."

"Small world," he said, not telling me that I was repeating myself. Willis would've been smug about it.

"It is. People don't understand how small of a world rural communities are."

"The army was like that."

His fingers twitched in mine. His troubled gaze was on another set of frames.

In it was a couple that was probably a little older than me, with two boys that were likely twins and two little girls. The man was familiar, but like with Derek, I couldn't come up with a name. "Who are they?"

"That's Kennedy. Derek's wife."

"Oh." Didn't his mom mention a Kennedy in the store with another guy's name? "And him?" I pointed to the man with her.

A muscle in his jaw popped. "Liam. Derek's best friend."

"Oh." I didn't know the timeline, but that had to have been hard. Was Evander upset Kennedy moved on with Liam?

"He's Cameron's kid. From an affair we weren't allowed to acknowledge even though it killed Liam's mom."

Shock ricocheted around my skull. "Seriously?" I was not prepared for this level of Barron drama. No wonder Evander had left it all behind.

He glanced behind us. A large truck with a flatbed loaded with round bales coasted past the window. Was that his dad? Would he be as critical of me as Evander said his dad had been about him? We were supposed to be pretending, but I didn't care to wither under a parent's disapproval like I had with my ex.

Dishes clanged in the kitchen, and Willow's humming reached us.

Evander must've determined the coast was clear because he leaned toward me. "Liam's mom got told off by Cameron. She was distraught and crashed, killing her instantly. Liam was raised right next door, and Cameron forbade us from having anything to do with him."

But Liam was Derek's best friend. "Derek didn't listen?"

He shook his head.

"Did you?"

"I didn't care, but I was older than them and had more responsibilities." His eyes flashed when he said the last part.

Poor Liam. That had to have been a hard upbringing in a small town like Coal Haven.

"Dad hated him." Evander's voice was so low I barely heard him. "Treated him like shit and told him he was worthless. Everything that went wrong was Liam's fault."

That was awful. I scanned the happy pictures on the mantel. "But their family photo is with all the rest of the cousins?"

"Like I said, everything's changed." He pulled his hand free from mine.

I clasped my hands together, needing something to do as my nerves slowly ramped up.

Willow appeared in the doorway. "Dinner is ready. Just in time. Bruce finally pulled in."

She untied her apron, her eyes bright. This was a woman who loved her son, but she was ramrod straight. Prim and proper. Was she afraid one wrong word would chase Evander away again?

She'd already lost one kid. Evander's absence must've been hard.

Evander returned to Coal Haven, and the life he'd known had been upended. The dynamics that had made up his family were different, and he struggled to adjust. Then I came along and changed it even more. No wonder he guarded himself from me.

Chapter Seven

Evander

When would this dinner be fucking over?

Mom's cooking was delicious. We were packed around a table that had seemed so much bigger when I was younger. Dad had given me a nod, but Mom had taken over after introductions were made with Violet.

"So, what do you do, dear?" Mom shoved the mashed potatoes closer to me.

I took a second helping. Mom made damn good mashed potatoes.

"I'm a chemist, analytical mostly, but I've done some organic work, and it's what I got my master's in."

Dad sat straighter. Hell, I did too. I had thought Violet might be cunning, trying to fool me. But she was legitimately smart. Dad had always been awed by smart people. Probably why he deferred to Cameron and got frustrated with me. "Say, that's impressive."

She shrugged. "Thanks. Chemistry works for me

because I can see it in images in my head, how the mole-cules go together and bond. It helps that I had a lot of 3D models to play with. If you asked me about investment funds and retirement plans, I'd be lost. I almost failed all my history courses."

"You must have an interesting job," Mom gushed.

Violet's expression froze. "I... It was—it *is* okay."

I shoved my fork into some potatoes and rested my free hand on her thigh.

Christ, I forgot she was wearing shorts. Warm, silky skin glided under my palm.

She gave me a grateful smile, but a pink tint lit her cheeks. "I developed, uh, develop novel fluorescent dyes that are used in flow cytometry." My parents stared at her, and I stroked her thigh to encourage her to continue. Her muscles flexed under my touch. "It's a procedure that counts lots of little particles or cells in a fluid." She shrugged again. She did that a lot when it came to her job. "I liked it, but I'm ready for a change."

I continued brushing my hand up and down her leg. She was doing fine, but I wasn't removing it. I stuffed another forkful of potatoes in my mouth.

"Can't retire yet though?" Dad said, his tone cynical. "Like Evander here."

I bristled. Why did he always make my accomplish-ments seem subpar? I could stay in my pajamas all day and make a full-time wage. My take-home pay wasn't high, and to be totally comfortable, I'd like to add a part-time income. But I was forty-four and retired.

"Not bad for a dumb grunt." I stabbed the last hunk of elk on my plate.

Violet blinked at me. "Why would you say that? Dumb grunt?"

"I was infantry."

She cocked her head, confusion still in her eyes.

"They call infantry grunts, and since that MOS—uh, job—doesn't need high test scores—dumb grunt."

Her brows drew together. "I don't like that one bit."

The spark of warmth in my blood was a new sensation. "It's one of those inside jokes. We can make it, but if anyone outside of the military tries to, then it's insulting."

She chuckled, and her thigh muscles relaxed under my hand. "I guess that's different than science humor."

"I wouldn't know. I don't have a sense of humor."

"You are very serious."

My lips twitched.

The weight of my parents' attention registered. Mom wasn't bothering to hide her grin. Dad's expression was unreadable.

Self-consciousness itched up my shoulders. I'd been flirting with Violet in front of them, and it wasn't for show. I tucked my chin down and kept eating. The girl would burrow so far under my skin I'd never be able to forget her, which was exactly what I needed to do if that baby wasn't mine.

But what if we had something real?

I flicked the thought away. If she set out to deceive me, then she would be out of my life for good.

Besides, she was too smart to stay with a guy like me.

"I hear your pumpkins are growing well," Dad said gruffly. His fluffy white mustache made him appear more like the diabetes and oatmeal guy I'd grown up seeing on commercials.

"Yeah, it's looking like a good crop. Could do with more rain."

Dad grunted his agreement. "You gotta plan in mind if it doesn't? Pumpkins need a lot of water."

"Yep," was all I said.

Dad's grip on his fork tightened. He was the expert in growing things, and he wanted me to know it. "You've gotta have a plan."

"I said I did." I was researching irrigation techniques. I hadn't gotten to the rank I had because I was an idiot, even if I was a dumb grunt.

Dad's jaw worked. "Isla said you're growing ten acres of pie pumpkins for her?"

"I'm overshooting it in case the crop doesn't have the yield she needs." The rest would be easy enough to sell or give away. Farmers' markets, food pantries, pumpkin patches, even the nearest pigpen. Extra produce wouldn't go to waste.

"Then what did you plant in the rest of the field? Doesn't that property have twenty acres?"

My inclination was not to answer. He wouldn't like my response. "Nothing."

His brows dropped, and his attention was on his plate. "Been thinking over what we talked about?"

"I told you no."

"It's not like it was," Dad said quietly.

"Does Stetson tell you what to plant, when to work cattle, what you're going to raise, and then take a generous cut?" I tired of this argument whenever I was with Dad. My cousin was fair, but I'd been bossed around my entire life. I didn't retire after twenty-six years in the army to lose my freedom to my family. Again.

"He's a fair man."

"I didn't say he wasn't." I put my fork down. "I

didn't come to get more reminders about why I'm not good enough to get any part of the Barron empire."

Red crept up Dad's face. He might've mellowed out over the years, but this topic was an instant trigger for him. And if there was one thing I was good at, it was aiming dead center of the target.

"That wasn't my decision," Dad gritted out.

The fuck it wasn't. He hadn't put up a fight. I had, and that was against family rules. No one argued with my grandfather about his totalitarian ways. He preached about respect, but he'd never shown it. I had called him on it several times, and he'd cut me out of his will. "And now?"

"It's all under one umbrella, Evander."

"Have you asked if it can be divided?"

"Have you decided to stay and take over?" he countered.

Frustration tore through my patience, shredding it like tissue paper. I scooted my chair back, and Mom let out a startled gasp.

"I have dessert," she said, her tone frantic.

"Sorry, Mom." I rose and helped a stunned Violet stand. "I'm not going over the same fight that's going to lead to the same bullshit insults."

Dad slammed his hand on the table. "I never insulted you."

"What about after Derek's funeral?"

Silence descended. Violet's head swung from my dad to me, her blue eyes fraught.

Dad couldn't meet my gaze. "I apologized for that."

"Yeah. You did." Didn't mend the damage done.

I nodded to Mom, barely meeting her stricken gaze. One more disappointment added to many I'd given her. I cupped Violet's elbow and led her out the door. My parents didn't chase us outside. They let me go like they always did.

The summer sun was still high and bright in the sky. I squinted against the glare and tried to keep from dragging her across the gravel to my pickup. Why did I expect tonight to turn out differently than before? I wasn't changing my behavior because of Violet. Perhaps it was best for her to see that giving birth to a kid in the Barron family didn't mean a damn thing.

I helped Violet into the passenger seat. She was buckled by the time I got in. I skidded down the drive before yanking my own seat belt across my body. Dirt kicked up behind me, thanks to the fucking lack of rain.

My hand was still clenched around the wheel when I turned down the long driveway to my place. Our route from my parents was like tracing a big square. In one direction was Liam and Kennedy's place. Go the other direction, and it went past this place.

Hell, maybe it was part of why I rented it. Close enough to say "fuck you" to everyone who thought I should settle for getting treated like a disgruntled employee.

The trip was quiet like usual, only this time discomfort radiated from my pretty passenger. Fuck if I knew what to do about it. I parked in front of the door so Violet wouldn't have to traverse over the uneven lawn to the porch.

Her hands were clutched on her lap. "That was intense."

Despite my guilt for putting her through that, I almost laughed. "It's like that."

"Every time?"

I nodded. Enclosed in the cab of the truck, with her wildflower smell surrounding me, I could pretend the dinner wasn't my special Groundhog Day hell. Except for the one memory that was on a loop in my head. "I found him almost catatonic after Derek's funeral. He kept saying Derek's death was a senseless waste." I ran my thumb and forefinger over my lower lip. "He said he feared for my life when I was deployed, but at least I fought for something. Then he, uh..." I had to clear my throat to get past the block in my windpipe. "He said, 'Isn't that funny? All along, I've been prepared to hear you've been killed, and sometimes I wondered if I'd even notice the difference.'"

I swallowed hard. The memory never failed to clog up every emotion I had. Derek had been their baby, and I'd never faulted my brother for it. He hadn't needed to put up with the bullshit I did. But to hear that I was almost nothing to Dad—after they'd lost one son already? Fuck me. My chest ached.

Her hand was on my hand. At some point, she'd unbuckled and twisted in her seat. "I'm so sorry, Evander. That's awful."

She was leaning as far over the console as she could. I'd never told anyone that. The only time I brought it up was to throw it in Dad's face. But I'd never repeated the words. I soaked up her comforting presence.

"You know why I joined the army?" I should shut the hell up, but in a way, she had to know more than anyone. If she was trying to cheat me, there wasn't much there. I had my retirement and little else. But if she was living off hers, then I still came out ahead. She needed money, and I was a target. I'd have to show her that she should've picked a different baby daddy. "My grandparents had a lot of oil money. We have wells on our land, and my grandfather was behind the refinery. It's why they can't sell out until Cameron retires. Each grandkid got a trust worth millions that they received on their twenty-fifth birthday. Stetson and Holden built houses and eventually bought their own land. Isla started Reservoir Barrel. Nora opened a couple of coffee shops. Derek's is going to Liam and Kennedy's kids. You know what happened to mine?"

She shook her head. Her touch was a balm, but it did nothing against the sweltering rage building like a storm cloud behind my eyes.

"Nothing. I didn't get one. I argued too much. I wasn't the obedient oldest, and it was almost like it was a punishment to have the audacity to be born before Cameron's first kid. And you know what sucks? No one knows. My cousins have made comments about me not using the trust fund money. 'You don't have to gut out twenty years when you're a millionaire already.' No one knows." I shook my head. Telling them would've made me feel even more pathetic. "Fuck 'em all." I captured her bright gaze. "But I thought you should know. If you came to get money out of me, there's nothing there."

Stunned sympathy morphed into instant hurt. "How could you think— Why would I—" Anger sparked in the blue depths of her eyes. "Well," she said sarcastically, her tone a whip to my conscience, "it's a good thing you didn't get your grandma's jewelry. I heard it's not safe around me."

She jumped out of the pickup.

Shit. She was getting away, and that notion flushed panic through my blood like a smoke bomb. "Violet."

She slammed the passenger door.

I scrambled out, almost tangling myself in the seat

belt. She was marching up the creaky stairs by the time my boots hit the dirt. Her ass was wiggling in the most delicious way, but I had no time to stop and admire.

"Violet, dammit."

She charged into the house. Why didn't I lock the damn door?

I rushed behind her. She beelined into the bathroom and started rummaging around, tossing her toothbrush and toothpaste into her toiletry bag.

"You can't leave. We haven't done the test yet."

"I don't care." She stuffed a hand through her hair, and some curls fell back into her eyes. "You know what I was most worried about? You missing out on time with this kid because I couldn't find you." She zipped her bag so hard the whole zipper should've torn off. "But it's clear you think I'm nothing but a crook. What I can't figure out"—she bunched the fingertips on one hand together and poked at the middle of her forehead—"is what you think I'm after. I can get a job for seventy thousand with benefits. I can build my retirement back, no problem. All my student loans are paid off. Just what do you think I'm after?"

The words "I'm sorry" danced on my tongue, but I didn't say them. I hadn't wanted to hurt her feelings, but I had to protect myself. I wasn't getting used again. "You want this house."

She shoved past me and went into the bedroom. "It's not worth it." She hauled her suitcase to the bed and threw it on top. "I can go anywhere. I can probably get a job anywhere there's an oil refinery. That opens up a ton of states. Minneapolis has all types of labs. I can go there." She clamped her lips together like it was the last thing she wanted to do.

Good. Minneapolis was too goddamn far away. "You don't have to go."

"I'm not staying where I'm treated like I'm going to pick your pocket. It's a *baby*. My two concerns are taking care of it and myself." She kept trying to fit her toiletry bag inside her suitcase, but it tumbled out once, twice, three times. She let out an enraged snarl. "The bag can fuck right off, and so can you."

I had meant to make a point, but I'd pissed her the hell off. Would she leave like this if I wasn't the dad? "We have to take the test together."

"I said you don't need to be involved." She started zipping her luggage with half the toiletry bag sticking out.

"I'm not abandoning my kid."

"'I'm not abandoning my kid,'" she mocked in a deep voice. "If I wanted to get treated like what I want doesn't matter, I would've stayed in California."

I gently gripped her arm and urged her to turn toward me. She finally obliged. "I hope you aren't comparing me to that sniveling idiot who couldn't find his way out of a paper bag."

She stabbed a finger in the air. "You both accused me of trying to steal from you. I'm not having this kid exposed to a guy who thinks I'm—"

I kissed her, pulling her in tight and silencing her tirade with my mouth. I didn't want her to finish whatever that was. I had every right to be suspicious, but this woman managed to turn my entire world upside down. She made me want things I'd given up long ago. She made me think that maybe I should stick around somewhere, with someone.

I swiped my tongue against her lips, and she opened for me. She didn't shove me off, and she didn't pound at my chest. Instead, she fisted her hands in my shirt like she was afraid I'd be the one pushing her away.

When I licked my tongue against hers, a little whimper left her like she'd been wanting this, needing it. I sure as fuck did. The real woman in my arms was better than the memory of her when I was in the shower.

I ran a hand down her back, dipped in at her waist, and finally palmed that round ass I'd been obsessing over. Arousal built in my veins, clouding my thinking and blocking out the whole evening.

She groaned and skimmed her hands over my shoulders and hooked them around my neck.

I devoured her mouth, tasting the dinner we'd just had mixed with her own sweet flavor. It'd been too fucking long since I'd had her last. But I was content to taste her, licking and nibbling along her mouth, then down her long neck.

She tipped her head back. "Evander, you are so damn good with that mouth."

Fuck yeah, I was.

I pushed her to the edge of the bed. I was about to tumble her back and come down on top of her when I remembered the suitcase.

She was leaving.

She was leaving because I insulted her.

I insulted her because I didn't trust her.

She needed to stay. I had to figure this shit out. I had to know. Was Violet Duke everything she seemed?

I ditched her collarbone and rested my forehead against hers. "Don't go. I was an ass."

"You've been an ass for days."

"I've been an ass my entire life."

She caressed my cheek. "You've been hurt. I know

you don't trust me. I accept that. But my days of tolerating disrespect are done."

Chagrin doused some of my desire. We were still touching. I looked down the slope of her nose to her puffy red lips. I ran my thumb along the bottom one. "I'm sorry you missed Mom's dessert."

"It's fine. I was gutting through the elk."

I pulled back with a frown. How did I not notice she wasn't enjoying her meal?

I had been wrapped up in myself.

"Do you need something else to eat?" I did a quick log of my fridge. She'd bought her own food, and it wasn't like we sat at the table for meals. "We could go to town."

"No. My stomach's fine; it's more mental. Food outside my usual upsets my hormones." She dropped her arms from around my neck to my biceps. I restrained myself from hooking them back in place. "I just want to cuddle the cats and read a book."

My hands were still on her ass. The dark circles had made a return at some time today. From the stress of dinner? I should've known better. Mom meant well, but Dad and I couldn't stay off each other's throats. "So you're staying?"

She peered into my eyes for several moments. "Yeah. And you are too."

I was lost.

"The house. Renew your lease. I'm not stopping you. You're better for this place than I'll ever be, and...I just don't feel right."

My heart twisted at the thought that one day, she wouldn't be under this roof with me. "Where will you go?"

"Where I get a job, but I'd like to stay in this part of the state or go home. To Montana."

Montana was not her fucking home. She was born and almost fully raised in Coal Haven. But she'd been gone almost as long as me. Yet she and I were standing in the same room in Coal Haven, not far from where each of us had lived. "You can stay," I said, my voice thick. "For as long as you need to find a job. If we get the results and you haven't been hired, you don't have to leave." I wouldn't kick a pregnant woman out. She might have family nearby, but after insulting her earlier, I wanted to redeem myself. I wasn't a selfish piece of shit.

She smiled, and damn, I loved the pleased look in her eyes. "If you can put up with me for that long."

I was afraid I could put up with her for a lot longer. Forever was starting to feel too short.

Chapter Eight

Violet

The kittens were settled back at the house after their vet appointment. I meandered down the grocery store aisle. The place hadn't changed much from when I was younger. There'd been updates with the branding, but a grocery store was a grocery store. I had one choice unless I wanted to drive to Bismarck or Dickinson for more options.

I didn't care. I didn't need some gourmet, all-organic store. Maybe when I had my own place, I could have a garden.

My own place.

It wouldn't be Evander's home.

I'd read a lot into what had happened last week. Evander felt like an outcast. His family's love was condi-tional. Willow seemed like such a sweet woman and doting mother, but when she'd been younger and outnumbered? It'd probably been hard to be vocal.

My parents were like Bruce and Willow on the outside. Warm and concerned about their kids. But my parents were our champions.

Then there was Grandma and her trust. If Dad had known, it would've caused a giant argument between them. Same for Aunt Linda. She was left to handle it all, and she had to sign off on whether each Duke marriage was real or not. Dad had to agree. No, Linda and Dad would've fought with Grandma. Our family would've been ripped apart.

Instead, we'd sort of banded together to figure this trust stuff out. I'd have to tell Aunt Linda that I would let my property go unless I found someone to marry and Evander moved out. I wasn't going to be the one to displace him from somewhere that seemed to bring him peace, two new kittens and all.

Since he'd assured me that I could stay, I'd been looking for job openings. He'd been checking the mail each day, presumably searching for the paternity kit. It should arrive any day. We'd been roommates, speaking only when needed. I made my own meals; he made his. He worked outside all day; I went out to play with the cats and take a short walk. It'd been like a pleasant vacation.

No more kissing. He had returned to being distant but slightly less grumpy. I'd take it. I'd also take more kissing and what we'd done in the hotel room, but first things first. There was no written procedure for us, but I couldn't jump to the final reaction without going through the steps. Unlike the work I did, I had no idea what to expect at the end.

I wheeled the cart down the candy and cookie aisle. The elk might've brought back a resurgence of morning sickness, but my sweet tooth was unaffected and screaming for Oreos.

I grabbed a pack of Double Stuf and then perused my other options.

"Oh my god. Violet?"

I glanced up. A woman a little shorter than me with chin-length wavy blond hair looked back. Excitement rose inside me. Daisy was Alder's ex-wife, and before their divorce, she'd been one of my favorite people. Afterward, we'd lost touch. "Daisy? Hi."

She wrapped her arms around me, and I hugged her back.

"How are you?" she asked.

"Good." I would leave out being slightly queasy from being pregnant with a one-night stand's baby—and *oh, do you remember Evander Barron? It's his.* No, we would be keeping that down until the paternity results were back and my family was informed. All they knew was that I was job hunting in Coal Haven. "I'm no longer in California."

Her mouth dropped open. "Are you moving here?" She looked up and down the aisle like she was afraid my brother would pop up.

"Maybe. I saw the refinery had a few openings." I had applied.

She grinned. "That's where I am."

A thrill ran through me. Daisy was a medical technician, but she'd know enough of the standard lab policies and procedures and have a solid chemistry background to learn the rest. If chemists didn't grow on trees, then a med tech could do the job. And if my ex-sister-in-law, who didn't put up with bullshit, worked at the refinery, her insight would be valuable. "You're not with the state lab anymore?"

Her gray eyes flashed. "Not after three epidemiologists gave my data to the CDC for a paper to be published in the *New England Journal of Medicine* and didn't credit me as an author, only themselves."

"Oh no. Did they really?" That was dirty. Insulting and just plain unprofessional.

"Yep." Her lips went flat. "Epis act like we're just the help. Anyway, that was just some of the BS I put up with. I don't kiss enough ass to work for the state."

I laughed. I'd always admired Daisy for her strong convictions. She didn't put up with nonsense, and that had included my brother. He wouldn't be the man he was today if Daisy hadn't dumped him on his ass.

"Put in your application," she said. "I'll tell them all about how brilliant you are."

"I already did, and I really appreciate it." The excitement inside me grew. I'd put so much into my education, and while I'd been using it, I hadn't worked in the field of chemistry that had really interested me. I hadn't done a lot since finishing my master's degree that really interested me. The chance to work in the career I set out for was within my grasp.

I should've never lost touch with Daisy.

"How's your daughter?" A twinge of regret shadowed my mind, not for me, but for Daisy. Her daughter should've been my niece, but she'd gotten pregnant well after Alder. I'd heard she had a kid but never met her.

Fondness graced her smile. "Laila is full of attitude, and I can't believe how fast she's growing. How are you liking being back in Coal Haven?"

I fought the urge to tell her about my situation, to

share a brief moment of understanding. I thought I'd be married and pregnant with Willis's kid by now. Maybe even our second. Or third. Instead, I was having my first baby at thirty-five, and I only learned the dad's full name a few days ago. Would Daisy know how I felt? Waylaid plans and all that.

"Honestly, it's good to be back. I'm catching up on some reading." Something that wasn't a scientific paper or whatever would appease a social circle I hadn't really been a part of. "I might start crocheting again too." She wore a small diamond ring on her finger, but I couldn't tell if it was a full wedding set. "How are things with you?"

"Good, good," she said, her voice pitching up. "Wedding's planned for next summer."

"Congratulations."

From the speed she looked away, I wasn't sure I'd said the right thing.

"Thank you. It's stressful. Lots of planning."

"Big wedding?"

"No." She smiled brightly. "Just a wedding in general. Stressful."

I'd take her word for it. She probably didn't get a house just because she was getting married. She hadn't when she and Alder had married either. They'd had a small ceremony by the lake, then had a big bonfire at Grandma's old place after. Alder had worked in the oil fields while Daisy went to school in Bismarck. They hadn't had time for a big wedding.

"Well." She hooked her hands on the purse strap she wore bandolier style. "I need to get Jason his Dr Pepper. He gets cranky without it. Nice seeing you."

"Nice to see you again. I hope we're not strangers."

She started walking away and then turned. "Where are you staying?" She snapped her fingers. "With Lily? I heard she moved into your grandma's old place."

"No." Evander and I were pretending for his parents, and the news hadn't trickled back to my family yet, but it would. Bruce might not want to rock the boat with Evander more than he had. But Daisy had kept her distance from the Dukes since she divorced Alder. She'd needed a clean break, and we'd respected her wishes. Still, I wasn't rushing to keep up the pretense. "I'm staying with a friend outside of town."

If she read into what I said, she didn't show it. "Maybe I'll see you around. Maybe for an interview." She disappeared around the aisle.

Maybe she would see me around. Maybe it would be with Evander, and perhaps even when I could say he and I were the real thing.

<hr>

Evander

Goddamn pumpkins. I'd planted them out of spite toward my dad. He said I couldn't plant this much acreage without any major equipment. I had rented what I'd needed to work up the ground and plant the seeds.

Now I was in the patch every damn day, watching my leafy green plants grow. Getting a jolt of excitement every time I found a round little ball of fruit.

I'd overshot the amount I needed. There was no way

Isla was going to roast this many pumpkins for her beer. But it was midseason. Anything could happen. Hail. Wind. Tornado.

Anxiety crawled up my spine. All I had were ten acres of unnecessary pumpkins. Isla's brewery would survive without pumpkin beer in the fall. No one else was depending on my crop. But the stress of losing everything I'd worked for chewed through my stomach lining. Each place I'd been stationed, I had something to show for it. A new ribbon. A medal. A promotion. Something to display that I wasn't an unruly kid who left home and didn't come back when his parents needed him the most.

No wonder Dad had been a crab ass every year. I had chalked his attitude up to getting ordered around like a servant by his brother. Dad might own the land the farm and ranch operated on, but without those yields, he'd lose it all. Without income, he wouldn't have been able to support a family on the property he owned.

I leaned against an old wooden fence post. None of this was mine, and yet I worried. I worried about letting my cousin down. She'd been the first to recognize me. The first to greet me. The quiet little girl I'd known had turned into an inquisitive woman who'd asked about me and my experiences. She didn't look at me like I was the family disappointment. Like I was an outsider.

It was why I'd gone into Reservoir Barrel the night I had met Violet. Then Violet had flirted with me like I was a normal guy. She hadn't looked into my crevices, wondering what she could take before she left me behind. She accepted what I offered and hadn't asked for anything in return.

I pushed off the fence. Even now, with the paternity test sitting on the table, waiting for us to collect the samples and mail it off, she was in her own world. Tapping away at my laptop.

I scraped a hand over my scalp. The hot sun was beating down on my skin. I should be in the pickup, ready for her to hop in so we could go to the clinic. She'd get her blood drawn, and then I'd collect a cheek swab. From there, I'd hold the samples until we dropped them in the mail.

But my boots moved sluggishly.

A kitten popped out from the grass, batting at a bug. Flo. Right behind her was Poly. Violet joked that the names were short for polymer and fluorescent. A nod to her career.

In the house, the clicking of the keyboard filled the air. I washed my hands and walked into the kitchen. She was sitting with her back to me, paging through pictures of what looked like diagrams, headphones on.

Fruit filled the counter, a new dish towel I didn't buy rested next to it, and a little vase of flowers was in the middle of the table. The kitchen carried the most presence of her, but the same happened in the rest of the house. Tiny bits of her that made the place different, more welcoming, were scattered everywhere. A sweater hung over the arm of the couch so the living room didn't look so staged. Her robe was hooked on the back of the bathroom door.

She saw me and took her headphones off. "Are we ready?"

My chest grew tight. No. If this baby wasn't mine, was that it? Violet was out of my life as soon as she got a job?

It doesn't have to be that way.

What if I could have her—

No. I wasn't opposed to being a father figure to a kid that wasn't mine. It was the lying I detested. The selfish use of another person. Yet there was nothing about Violet that screamed self-absorbed.

I nodded toward what looked like boxy molecules or something filling the screen. "Helluva application?"

She flashed a quick smile, but a flush crept up her cheeks. She tucked a few curls behind her ear. "No. I have an interview in a few days."

She might have a job and be out of my hair before we even got the results.

Then what?

What if I asked her to stay? What if...

I hated what-ifs. Decisions were made, and I committed to them. Likewise, I walked away from those I didn't give my word to.

"I'm..." She hugged herself like she was sheepish. "I'm looking at cat sofa patterns." Her blush darkened.

"What's a cat sofa?" I pulled a table chair out. We had time before we went to the clinic, and I was apparently interested in cat sofas.

"Uh..." She freed one hand from her solo hug and circled it in the air. "It's crochet patterns for blocks that can be connected and stuffed." She opened her laptop and spun it toward me. "Cat couch."

A small sofa greeted me on the screen. An actual cat was perched on the one in the picture. "You can make that?"

"I think so. It's been a while since I've been a hooker." She grinned, but her blush got even brighter. "You know? Crochet hooks."

Well, that was a relief. More power to her, but

crocheting was safer. "Okay. What color are you going to make?"

"It's silly." She hastily closed the lid. Was she embarrassed?

"Why?"

"I just...it's useless." Her bottom lip puffed out like she was troubled.

Why would she be embarrassed about a hobby—Oh. "Vasectomy Willis?"

Her lips quirked. "That name—"

"Is accurate. So let me get this straight. A guy who didn't tell you he had a procedure to prevent kids when he knew you wanted kids says crocheting's for dummies and you think he's right?"

"He was...he's..." She blew out a hard breath, then nodded. "He's a pretentious dick. Anything that didn't prove his high intelligence was beneath him. You know what? I'm ordering hooks and yarn when we get back." She sat up and tapped her finger on the white paternity test box. "We'd better get going. I made my blood draw appointment for the afternoon, thinking that was when we'd be less likely to see anyone."

Disappointment settled deep into my gut. Parading a pregnant Violet around resonated somewhere deep inside me. Hiding her didn't.

"Let's go," I said roughly.

Once we were loaded into the car, she plastered her face to the window like usual.

"It's so beautiful here," she murmured.

Agreed. "I've lived in a lot of places, but there's nothing like it."

She smiled at me. "It's a simple beauty, isn't it? We don't have mountains, but the sunsets—"

"Stunning." I had perched on the front porch every night for a week, pondering life and watching the pink-and-purple sunset paint the sky.

"I missed those. Mom used to call us out of the house to look at them." She laughed. "I'd get so irritated because I was in the middle of my homework."

I could picture a studious Violet with her mouth set, getting pulled away from a science textbook.

The drive to the clinic didn't take more than ten minutes. We actually chatted this time. More about the scenery and who used to live where or what business had changed to another since we'd grown up here.

After I parked, we collected my sample in the pickup. She started giggling while I swirled the swab in my mouth. I cocked an eyebrow as I twirled it, and she giggled harder. Then she read the directions out loud, and we packed it away.

"Okay. Blood draw time."

The parking lot was quiet and only half filled. After she checked in, the receptionist told us to follow the signs to the lab.

I shoved my hands in my pockets and let Violet take the lead. Voices drifted down the hall until we reached a window. My stomach dropped to the tip of my boots.

Shit. Isla's best friend since childhood stared back at me. Lyric was grown now, the same age as Violet, but with a wildly different aesthetic. The collar of a maroon scrub top peeked out of her lab coat, and her hair was bunched on top of her head in two buns and tinged in pink.

She blinked, recognition sparking in her eyes. "Oh, hey, Evander. Stetson said you were back."

Stetson. Not Isla. Because Lyric was married to him.

They had kids together. The little girl I used to know had a whole-ass family with my cousin. Just another sign that shit was different. "Hey, Lyric."

Fuck me. Was she going to tell her husband I was here? Was she going to tell him all about the paternity test? He'd know the visitor I was playing off as nothing but my landlord had been in my bed instead?

Did I care?

Yes. News would reach Mom. Yet another letdown for her if the baby wasn't mine and that I hadn't told her first—or at all.

Violet stiffened next to me.

I handed Lyric the kit. Violet had obliged the insistence that I never had the thing out of my sight. Right now, she watched me with a wide gaze. Our secret was getting outed. Dammit. I'd been made a fool of before, but at least it hadn't been in my hometown. Dad would have a field day with this, claiming that I was old enough to know better.

Surprise flitted through Lyric's pale-blue eyes when she read the kit instructions. "Oh. Okay." She looked up, and recognition lit her eyes like it had in Isla's. "Violet? Violet Duke?"

Violet grabbed for my hand. Did she realize she'd done it? I gave her a reassuring squeeze.

"Hi, Lyric. It's been a while. Nice to see you again."

Lyric smiled, but her gaze jumped between me and the woman clinging to my hand. "Come on in and have a seat."

My footsteps hit heavy as I followed Violet into a little squared-off room with a chair and blood draw supplies organized neatly on a small counter.

I could see into the rest of the lab, but I didn't recognize the older woman who worked with her.

Violet sat and Lyric asked for her birthday, then jotted down some info.

"I feel like I should tell you," Lyric said as she wrote, "that everything's confidential. I won't be going home to tell Stetson, and I won't share this with Isla over drinks."

Violet's shoulders relaxed. "Thank you. We have some things to figure out first."

"I totally get it." Lyric started arranging the tube from the kit and a needle and bandages. She put her gloves on. "I was in the same chair for the same reason."

"Seriously?" I asked before I thought better of it.

Lyric pulled a face. "Oh, yeah. You think Cameron and Naomi approved of me?" She straightened Violet's arm and put the blue tourniquet on. "Our oldest, Marina, was definitely unplanned. You know, a one-night stand kind of thing."

Violet's lips quirked. "Right."

"Stetson got to where he didn't care if she was his or not, but his parents weren't going to let it go, so I made sure we did the test. Here's the poke." She drew the blood in just a few seconds, then slapped a bandage on Violet and labeled the tube. "The rest is history. I even get along with Naomi now." She scanned the directions and packed the tube.

"Everyone seems to get along with Cameron and Naomi now," I said bitterly.

"Not completely, but they've changed." Lyric handed the little box to me, all packaged and ready to go. "It's taken a lot of time, and they're still careful. They know there are hard feelings. They keep their distance, even around Liam and his family."

"Cameron talks to Liam?" How long was I gone? Hearing that my parents and the kid they blamed for all the world's problems were close was disorienting enough.

She shrugged. "They're cordial. Which was further than any of us thought they'd get. Stetson thinks Cameron might've even apologized. Not Naomi. But her apology is not trying to destroy someone's life, so..."

I snorted. Lyric knew my family.

"Anyway," she said. "Tell your parents I said hi." She paused. "Or don't. Just know I won't mention it."

"Thank you, Lyric," Violet said as she got up.

"Anytime." Lyric gave her a mischievous grin. "Don't be a stranger either. Us outlaws have to stick together when it comes to the Barrons."

I bristled. Her jab was meant to be humorous, but it was also truthful. Like she knew I was hanging on to the results of this test to be an asshole, just like I'd grown up seeing the men in my family behave.

I wasn't like them. I'd left because I was different.

Yet when I thought about how I treated Violet after she showed up on my doorstep, I couldn't find a difference.

Chapter Nine

Violet

I thought Evander would be logging into the account multiple times per day, even while the test was in transit. But I didn't see him buried in his phone or the laptop. He didn't mention checking for the results. In the two days since we'd mailed our samples, he acted the same as always. He worked outside all day, either with his plants or fixing up the shed he insisted needed replacing.

I was in the kitchen on the phone with my mom. "I talked to Daisy."

"How is she?" Mom asked, interest filling her voice.

I relayed everything Daisy had said. "It was nice talking to her again. It'd be really cool if I worked with her."

"I miss that girl," Mom said in a hushed tone like she was afraid Alder would hear from wherever he was in Billings. "You're really thinking of moving there?"

"Yeah, if I get the job." The interview had gone well.

"I'll be closer to Lily and the kids. Closer to you and Dad than I was in California." Closer to the father of my kid.

"I'm so glad—Anyway. It's nice to see you more."

"Were you going to say you're glad I broke up with Willis?"

"No. Yes. I did not like him. I'm sorry, honey."

Mom had been nothing but supportive. I owed her a little more of the truth. "He got a vasectomy before we met."

"What?"

"Vasectomy Willis." When she snorted, I grinned. I should not be using Evander's name for him. "We had the marriage-and-kids talk before we moved in together. He knew I wanted kids, and he never said anything. All those years, I put up with him because I thought...I don't know. I thought he was it." We'd met in grad school. He'd been flattering at first, and then I'd tried to keep up with his lifestyle. Tried to keep earning his approval. "It was easier than starting over."

Starting over was stressful, but I was doing it, and the freedom was worth it.

"There's still time for you to find someone who loves and respects you. Those babies will come."

I put a hand on my stomach. The urge to tell her everything fought against the need to have all the information first. My pragmatism won out. "I know."

"Tell me when you hear how the interview went."

"Will do. Love you guys." I hung up with her.

Easier than starting over. Wasn't that the truth?

My phone pinged with a notification. I frowned. It was the group text that had been quiet for months. Lacey Wilcox. What'd she want? She was one of the more insufferable people I'd gotten to know through Willis. She was a friend of his family.

An image loaded of her holding out her hand with a giant gaudy diamond flashing on her ring finger as she stood next to Willis.

"What the..." I enlarged the image. Yep. His grandmother's engagement ring. My indignant gasp rang through the kitchen. "It's been less than four months, you asshole."

I deleted the message.

Asshole!

Vindictive bitch. Years of cutting remarks. I should've just dumped wine on her head the many times I had fantasized about it. Had he cheated on me?

I crossed my arms and stared out the window. No. Willis was a liar, but he'd been too needy to cheat. I'd have noticed the change in him. He was so needy he'd rebounded to the first girl who took him and proved he could settle down.

Or he'd found something in her that I lacked. Fuck him. He wasn't married yet anyway.

An engine sounded outside. A minute later, Evander entered holding a box. "Yarn's here."

I squealed and rushed to grab it. Losing myself in a pattern would be the perfect way to take the sting off the picture. I tore into the box. Evander got himself a glass of water, but instead of leaving, he moved the packaging out of the way as I opened each container. It was filled with hooks and several skeins of yarn, mostly dark plum, and then another had baby blue and yellow yarn.

"It's going to be so pretty," I cooed. Excitement rang through me like a bell, loud and clear, more powerful when I knew how I'd been discouraged before. "I can't believe I'm geeking out over yarn."

I set my new supplies on the table. "I think I've got enough to make two." Wasn't one cat couch bad enough? Two? "Never mind. That's ridiculous."

"Why?"

"It's a waste of time." Making furniture for barn cats. The sparkly engagement ring filled my head. "And a silly idea. They'll probably get mouse-infested in two days."

"Brave mice to bunk down with a couple of cats." He picked up the hooks and glanced at the instructions I had printed at the library yesterday. "I've seen a lot worse hobbies, Violet. Make all the cat couches you want. It's not a waste of time if it makes you happy."

I fluttered my hands above my head. "I should be doing something."

He crossed his arms, and God help me, he was wearing a T-shirt that showed how much his biceps bulged. "Where is this coming from?"

"What?"

"The bullshit about a hobby that lights you up?" When I shook my head, he pulled out a chair and angled it so he faced me when he sat. "It's that pussy of an ex, isn't it?"

The photo was stained on the cells of my brain. No acid wash would get it out.

Evander took his ball cap off and tossed it on the table. He ran a hand over his head and scratched his fingers down his scruff the way I wanted to every day.

When did my hormones get so wanton? I didn't sit around thinking about touching and tasting a guy I was attracted to. Precisely one of the reasons why I was starting all over again. "I got a picture sent to me from someone I used to hang out with. It appears she and Willis are engaged."

He whistled low. "That was fast."

Shame and regret burned hot in my cheeks. "Seven years I wasted with that man." I closed my eyes. I couldn't keep that mantra in my head. "It was a long learning lesson that's hard not to regret." I screwed my face up. So damn hard not to regret. "I can't help but wonder what that makes me. I knew how he was. And I stayed."

"It makes you human."

"Sure."

"Violet, I've been around a lot of personalities in my time, and I had to be in charge of a lot. Like herding fucking cats. It might surprise you that I've been around a lot of guys like your ex." Disgust curled the corner of his lip. "I'd get a lot of commanders wanting me all up in my soldiers' business on their off time. Fuck that. If they're not breaking the law, I don't give a fuck if they game every second of every hour they're at home. We went through enough shit. Sure, I'd step in if I thought they needed mental help, but other than that? They should do what brings them joy—at the very least, peace. I just made sure I was there if they needed anything. If they wanted a book club when we were deployed, I found a place for them to have a book club. If they wanted to give swing dance lessons in the desert, fuck it. We're having swing dance lessons. What they didn't need to be doing was cleaning their weapon each second from watch duty to watch duty. Not everything you do needs to signal productivity or even be a gauge of your intelligence."

I'd been discouraged from joining a book club before. My coworkers weren't reading the next great American novel. They'd chosen a thriller that had sounded good. I'd settled for so little from a guy while Evander had made a book club happen just because it made his soldiers happy. "I never thought I'd find so many similarities between myself and soldiers." His expression went blank. Crap. I sounded like a Willis. "Not like that. Most of your soldiers were guys?"

He nodded. "For infantry, yes."

"I barely even hunted."

"Not many of my soldiers ever hunted either." He sat forward, propping those muscled and veined forearms on his knees. "Attitudes like Willis's weren't specific to a rank or gender. I had officers who trashed anyone they could, and I've had privates put down others with every word out of their mouths. I put a lid on that real quick. Shit's done to hurt others, not help them. Do what you love."

The warmth inside me spread farther out with every word. He was defending my hobby. More than that, he was encouraging me to have hobbies. "I once brought home a coloring book after I got my first big girl job, and Willis laughed like a donkey."

"Did you nut punch him?"

I grinned, but the humor faded quickly. "No. I never colored. He thought gardening was a waste of time, but he wanted our place to look nice. Keep up with the Joneses, you know."

"Mom weeded my flower beds. I give zero fucks about flowers, but she enjoys it. I'd never stop her. That'd be a dick move."

A knot tightened around my heart. He loved his mom. He hated feeling like he was hurting her, but the discourse between him and his father did just that. So he kept his distance. "What about you? Are you doing what you love?"

He scowled, his gaze boring into the floor.

"What do you do for fun?" I pressed, curious now why it was so hard to answer.

When he lifted his gaze, those dark irises burned into me. The temperature in the room ramped up, and an answering throb ignited between my thighs. I'd experienced what he liked to do for fun.

Then he blinked, and a wave of cool air washed over me. The AC had kicked on, but that wasn't it. His expression was carefully neutral. "I'm still finding out."

"Did you like the army?" He was talking, and I wanted him to continue. I had enjoyed the Evander I had met at Reservoir Barrel. The brooding, dubious man I'd stayed with had layers. He had emotions he kept bottled up. I wanted to know him as much as possible. For the baby's sake.

Once, I'd dared peek into his bedroom when he went to town. The room was done in grays like the rest of the house and punctuated with thick, black blinds. He had a shadow box on his dresser with what looked like medals hanging inside, but I hadn't dared breach the threshold of his bedroom.

"Sometimes," he finally answered. "The deployments themselves could be real fucking hard."

"Could be? Not all the time?"

He lifted a shoulder. "Not all the time, but what sucked was a level of hell that overshadows it all." He ducked his head. "Same with life after deployment. Moments of hell that just...taint it all."

"You lost a lot of people?" I leaned closer, wanting to put a hand on his shoulder, even give him a hug. Would he accept the comfort or toss me off? He could run hot and cold, and I didn't want to risk it. I'd rather he kept talking.

"Yeah. One way or another," he said roughly. Shaking himself, he slapped his hands on his legs and rose. He tapped the top of the case of hooks. "Maybe it's why I think your ex is a piece of shit for trying to ruin the joy in your life. Make a cat couch, Violet. Then, if you want, make another. Fuck your ex and everyone else who thinks it's a waste of time."

"Thank you, Evander."

"Nothing to thank me for."

I stood and stepped in his way before he escaped out the door. "There is. You've...done a lot for me. I know you're doing it to protect yourself, but thank you."

His gaze stroked over my face, but he didn't move around me. "Wanna grab something to eat? Later?"

"Like at a restaurant?" Was he asking me out? I kept my delight at bay.

"I hear Rattler's is good. Or Purple Petal in Crocus Valley."

I repressed a wide smile. "I'd like that. I've never gone so long eating my own cooking."

"Whatever you make smells good."

"Cooking was never my strong point. Baking is. It's more precise and less art. Like chemistry."

A ghost of a smile played over his lips. This time, he did sidestep me, but he stopped and leaned close. "Don't underestimate your cooking. I've snuck a bite or two of your leftovers."

I was full-on grinning when he left the kitchen.

Evander

Violet tapped her fingers on her curvy thigh in the passenger seat. We'd decided to go to Purple Petal in Crocus Valley. Fewer relatives we might run into.

Whose bright idea was it to take the cute, pregnant woman I was living with on a date? And why was I so desperate to do it before the paternity result showed up?

The last week had been nice. Peaceful in a way I hadn't experienced. Ever. Violet did her thing. I did mine. When she spoke to me, she wasn't cutting, snide or demeaning. She didn't blame, and she didn't insult me. She'd started cooking more for dinners and mentioned that there was enough for me. We hadn't eaten together. But I'd devour her meals.

Since she didn't need to be waiting on my ass, I made extra for breakfast. I didn't know what she was into, but it wasn't tuna. I had learned that quick enough. I stuck to eggs in various forms—sandwiches, burritos, bakes. Each time, she thanked me. Something so simple but was like the goddamn sunrise, brightening my whole day.

I might not trust Violet, but she was showing me that I'd had poor as fuck taste in women before her. If she was untrustworthy, she was still better than anyone else I'd dated.

She listened. Probably why I couldn't keep my mouth shut around her when it came to my family or telling her why I had enlisted and what army life had been like. She was easy to talk to.

I'd miss her when she left. Or when I left. Whatever the hell happened.

I pulled into the parking lot. A giant crocus graced the logo on the sign. The same pretty purple flower was growing in the pastures when I'd rented the house.

"I love that they named the restaurant after a flower," Violet said. "My mom would take us out crocus hunting each April. Some years, they'd cover the hillside."

"My mom loves them too. She says their limited season makes them extra special."

"Mom used to say the same thing. Sometimes, we'd go to Sweet Briar Lake to fish in early summer just so she could find violets with me." Violet grinned, and it punched me right in the chest.

I wasn't a flower snob, I never thought twice about them, but violets were prettier than crocuses.

The parking lot was half full for a Friday, but it'd probably be packed before we left. It wasn't five yet. I had suggested we go earlier to beat the crowd. The desire to stay private for as long as possible was an unspoken agreement between us.

After I parked, she was out of the vehicle before me. We walked next to each other, though I was tempted to walk behind her. She hadn't worn her jean shorts again, but the linen shorts she preferred draped over her round ass cheeks, and the thinner fabric gave me a better show.

Today, she had on a sleeveless top with a pale-purple pattern. I could put her hand in the crook of my arm again, have her skin against mine, but I resisted. If anyone we knew saw us, they'd question if we were on a date or just friendly. I didn't care to lie to more people than my parents.

Inside, the hostess seated us in a booth in the back.

I ordered a Kona on tap, and Violet stuck with water. She pored over the menu. Her shirt was loose, but she'd be, what? Three and a half months along? Was she showing? When would I be able to tell?

Would I be around?

The young server returned with the water. "Your beer is on the way. What can I get you?"

Violet pushed her menu toward the end of the table. "Steak tortellini, please. I'll take the salad with ranch on the side."

I got a burger and fries. When the girl disappeared, Violet sipped her water and stared out the window.

The way her face had lit when she got her crocheting supplies would stay imprinted in my psyche forever. Joy and excitement in her eyes, then the sheepishness when she got self-conscious. She'd been radiant. Then her light had been dimmed.

Fuck that guy.

She crossed her arms on the table and drummed the fingers of one hand against her other arm. I looked around. The place was filling up with families and groups. A few other couples sat in the bar.

"Why'd you finally ask me out?" she asked.

I should've asked her about her crocheting before she could hit me with the tough questions again. I had told myself this wasn't a date, but it sure as fuck felt like one. "I don't know."

She nodded and turned her attention out the window. "I understand, you know. Why you don't trust me. I have my own baggage, and you have yours."

She understood. I didn't trust her, and she knew it and she understood. Hell of a woman. "When I was twenty and at my first post and living up life with my newfound freedom and my own money, I met a woman." Was I really going to tell this story? I hadn't spoken about it since it happened. Bad enough that my parents had known about it.

She smirked. "I bet you met a lot of women."

"In those early years? I met all the wrong ones. Then I felt like I was a magnet for the hot messes and kept my distance. I learned to be alone, to deal with my feelings without sex or substances."

"Then you met another mess in Reservoir Barrel."

"No, Violet. You're not a mess." She was smart and knew what she wanted. Mostly. I was starting to believe that if I truly didn't want a thing to do with this kid, Violet would walk away and forget about me, and I wouldn't know what the hell to do. "But this girl, she was, uh, a user. She lived by military posts and preyed on young soldiers."

"Was she older?"

I nodded. "Twenty-five."

Surprise flitted across her face. "That's not the most scandalous, but it's..."

"Suspicious." When she nodded, I continued. "The thought was intoxicating. Older woman. Flattering for a young guy competing with a shitload of idiots for a girl's attention." My beer was delivered, and I took a long pull. "Kandi seemed different. They all do at first. That might seem blunt, but it's what I've experienced."

"I can see why you thought the worst of me."

I couldn't bring myself to nod. Violet was nothing like them. I could see that now. "She treated me like I was more than a dumb kid. I guess for a guy who left home for that reason, it was intoxicating. Then she got pregnant. Results even said it was mine." My lungs constricted at the memory.

Violet's lips parted.

I cleared the thickness in my throat. "I was thrilled. My own family."

"Especially after the way you left home," she said, her voice soft.

"She pushed to get married, and I guess some part of me wasn't thinking with my dick. I'd seen other buddies get married only to have their relationship go down in flames. Guys my age, paying alimony or child support. Thank fuck for my intuition. I kept telling her that after the baby was born, we'd elope. She'd get pissed, demand to know why I loved staying in the barracks more than with her, threaten to break up, and that just fueled my gut feeling more." I let out a cynical laugh. "I guess my natural stubbornness saved me. I told my parents. My dad was...reserved. Mom was...excited."

Understanding filled Violet's face. My insistence to keep the baby quiet until I had irrefutable proof of paternity. No, it wasn't her fault, but she was catching my shit for it.

"I started ring shopping. I did plan to propose as soon as the baby was born. She was at the mall that day. With a guy. She didn't see me." The residual anger was nothing but a dull echo. It was the bitterness that lingered strong. "So the next time we were together, I checked her phone." Violet's brows went up. "Yeah, I know I should haven't snooped."

"It's a fine line when that's the only way to get the truth."

Yeah, I'd do it over again. Saved me a lot of heartache. "I saw all the texts between her and this guy. She was with him before me, but he was a broke fucker. No job. No benefits. I found the message to her best friend I never liked. Plans for how to fake results and how easy it was to fool me. Turned out she was two months further along than she told me. She got pregnant right before we met." More resentful laughter left me. "I might've been stubborn, but I was still a fucking idiot."

"That's awful. You weren't an idiot. Genuine paternity confusion happens, but she intentionally tricked you."

"I know. She hasn't been the only one to try to use me."

Violet's eyes went wide. "What?"

"Young soldiers away from home can be easy targets. We're impulsive, inexperienced, and have too many hormones to know how to handle them. The stress piled on us isn't traditional either. We aren't worried about paying rent. Our basic needs are being met, but we're still worried about survival. In the back of our minds, we're aware that in one deployment, we could lose everything and everyone. But we don't really talk about it like we should. Everyone acts like it's normal, and what's fucked up is that it is normal for the military. Yet how I handle it in my forties is vastly different than when I was in my twenties." I thought first and reacted later.

"I never thought about it that way." She dipped her head. "I'm sorry I brought everything back. I really didn't expect that night to leave me with more than an idea of what I'd been missing out on."

"And what is that?" I pushed my mug to the side,

intent on her response and grateful to be done reliving my past.

A flush crept up her neck. She got a full-body blush when she climaxed too. It'd been my goal to dust her body with pink when I'd been fucking her. The way she let go had been addicting, and I'd gone without for months, only to be teased by her presence for almost two weeks.

"True passion," she whispered and discreetly looked around. "Repeat orgasms. A guy who isn't selfish in every aspect of his life."

The last comment pulled me out of the moment. "In what aspects am I selfish?"

She ran a finger through the condensation on her water glass. "You're self-protective. You had to deal with a lot with your family. Then that woman. You basically had a kid taken away."

My chest twisted. Those months we'd been expecting had been some of the happiest of my life. I thought I had found something different. I had gone to the field, and Kandi had still been there, counting down the days to our baby.

The shock of being lied to never left me. For all my family's faults, they were forthright and unapologetic. Kandi had been my first direct exposure to lying and cheating.

I'd wanted to be a dad. Sure, I'd been young, and if circumstances had been ideal, I would've waited. The devastation of having it all ripped away had poured a hard resin shell over my emotions.

Violet reached across the booth to put her hand on mine. She didn't say anything, just offered her support. I let her warm touch sink in and unknot the tangle of my past.

That shell cracked, just a little. Violet was worming her way in, and she was doing so just by acting like she cared about me. Only time would tell if she was telling the truth. Or if she'd validate my suspicions, just like the others. And for once, I didn't want to be right.

Chapter Ten

Violet

My belly was happily full after the delicious meal we'd had. Instead of heading home, we drove out of town a few miles to Lake Sakakawea.

"It was the biggest argument they'd ever had," I said, giggling. My family could laugh about it now. "Mom refused to help Dad with the boat ever again. Alder had to start backing the boat trailer up."

The corners of his eyes crinkled at my story. "I heard my dad joke once that calving season and backing trailers up are the biggest cause of divorce in ranch families."

I laughed as he parked by a stretch of beach in Hazen Bay with spots for tent camping. Each small, square site had a little grill ready for charcoal. No campers were around, but boats dotted the bay. The dock on the other shore bustled with pickups loading and unloading boats that headed to the deeper water of the main lake.

I kept my shoes on as we walked the rocky beach. "I remember coming out here when I was little." I picked up a flat stone. The wind wasn't that strong today, and the land rose to a craggy bluff ahead of us, the natural shoreline when the water crested high. Across the water was a shorter bluff.

I skipped the rock but only got one skip in before the stone plopped under the surface. "My brother Alder used to love fishing."

"He doesn't anymore?" Evander toed the rocks, turning them over with the tip of his boot. He'd worn jeans to our date. Between his thick arms and the way the denim teased me with his powerful thighs, I might need to jump into the water to cool off.

"He's a workaholic. He used to be...less responsible. Then he swung in the other direction, and that's where he stuck." I toed the beach, hoping to uncover another skipping stone. "What about yours? Did Derek like to fish?"

He popped his head up, his eyes flashing with surprise and more than a little grief. "Yeah," he said roughly. "Little fucker was lucky too."

I smiled, relieved I hadn't overstepped. Who'd been there for him when his brother had died? "Alder would say it's not about luck; it's a science. But it's a science I never got."

"Derek had a sixth sense for where the fish were biting." He squatted and selected two flat rocks. He rose and skipped one across the water. Three skips before the rock sank. "He didn't need to use fish finders or anything."

"And you?"

"Fucking sucked." A gravelly laugh left him. "He used to say I got the hunting luck."

"Dad made us all take a hunter's safety course." I had almost failed. I hadn't been interested.

"Can never have too much education about hunting and firearms." He spread his feet apart, aimed, and let the second rock rip.

"Five skips! Nice." I peered harder at the rocks and found a small one that might work. I skipped it and got two bounces. "Damn."

"You got it."

Did he know he was a natural cheerleader? "You must've been a good leader."

He gave me a bemused look. "Why?"

"You're encouraging and supportive without being coddling. My parents are like that."

They'd like Evander. It'd taken too long for me to admit that my mom and dad had tolerated Willis. It wasn't until I saw how they were with Eliot that I could tell the obvious difference. Dad rushed to chat with Eliot. Mom was relaxed around him, and the hugs she gave him were no different than any of her other kids. With my ex, they'd been stiff. Stilted. Uncomfortable.

He squinted across the water. "I just acted how I wished my dad would've. A lot of the guys I served with needed that." He toed another rock up from the ground. The other side was flat. He picked it up and handed it to me. Our fingers brushed, and my belly clenched. "Try again."

The spark of heat stayed with me. I pictured the throw and carried out my vision. Four skips.

"Nice." He held out his fist for a fist bump.

Grinning, I touched my knuckles to his.

He captured my hand and tugged me toward him. "You're a fascinating lady, Violet Duke."

Warmth exploded through me, flowing over my mood and heating. "You're not bad yourself, Mr. Barron." I frowned. "Or do I have to address you by your rank?"

His deep chuckle reverberated through my body, a pleasing rumble that lit up every nerve ending under my skin. "No. I'm just Evander."

His hands slipped around my waist, and I rested mine on his hard chest.

He didn't lower his head to kiss me, and I didn't want him to let me go. So I kept him talking. "What were you? Your rank."

"I retired as a first sergeant."

"First sergeant?"

"Top."

"Top of what?"

The corner of his mouth quirked. "That's what they call first sergeant. Top. We're at the top of the company's enlisted soldiers."

It fit him. One syllable. Curt. Like he often was. "You were at the top?"

"No, only in one sense. Squads make up platoons, platoons make up companies, and companies make up battalions. Then you have brigades— Anyway, I had a lot of people above me, and I could've kept getting promoted."

"Why didn't you?"

The intensity in his eyes grew. I knew this look. He was speaking about things he kept to himself. Evander was a private man out of necessity. How many times had he wanted to share his life with someone only to be let down?

"I didn't mean to ask such a personal question." I should've known better. If anyone asked me why I quit Oswell, I couldn't give a simple answer. I could've moved out on my own and still worked at the lab. My decision hadn't been about promotion or location. I had just decided I was done for so many personal reasons, and any response would've been a glimpse into my personal life.

"No, it's fine." He spread his hands across my waist. "I was never good at politics, and the higher I got, the more I had to play a game and the less I was involved with the individual soldiers. More office work, less field work. It didn't appeal to me. It was time to get out."

He said it so simply that maybe my answer for why I quit at Oswell and moved out of California wasn't complicated. It had been time.

"So you're growing pumpkins."

His eyes darkened. "Goddamn pumpkins."

I giggled. "Why do you seem so disgruntled about the pumpkins when you dote on them?"

His lips flattened. "I do not dote on the pumpkins."

I patted his chest. "Sure you don't."

"It's not like wheat. I don't have crop insurance. They're just different. Pumpkins." He slipped his hands from around my waist and linked one of his hands with mine. He started leading me toward the pickup. "They weren't on my radar, that's for sure. And they tie me to Coal Haven until the crop is harvested."

"What about longer?"

"What about it?" He opened the passenger door but blocked the entrance.

"You know I'm not kicking you out, right?"

"That's what you said."

I licked my lower lip, and his gaze tracked my tongue. I hadn't been honest with him. The full truth would ruin the moment, but I had to clarify part of my story. I picked at the hem of my dress. "I can't kick you out. Only Linda can. Technically, she's the executor of the trust that the property is in."

He lifted my chin with two fingers. "But you wanted me out?" he asked quietly, his voice full of challenge. If I didn't answer honestly, I'd lose his trust completely.

"It would've been convenient, but I can't go through with it. You assumed, and I went along. She refused to ask you if you planned to move before your lease was up, so I thought I'd find out for myself."

His exhale was sort of a laugh and a little bit of a sigh.

"I can rent somewhere else easily enough," I rushed on. Did I ruin the mood for the whole night? I let him assume. He might've moved because of me. "There are a few houses open and some apartments. It'll be no problem to get another place."

Displeasure rippled through his features.

"Are you saying you might miss me?" I teased.

His fingers dug into my hips. "I'd miss..." He worked his jaw back and forth. "I'd miss seeing you and remembering all the things we did together that night."

Lust pumped through my veins, hot and smoky. "I've been having the same memories."

My body ached for him. His little confession hit all the right places in a way that should be wrong. I'd never been more turned on in my life. My breasts were full and tender, but if he got his big hands on them, all would be right in my world.

"Let's go home," he said in that low, rough voice.

I bit the inside of my cheek. Did he realize what he said? Would I ever be able to tell him how much I liked it?

***

Evander

The drive to the house took too damn long. I had to set the cruise from the lake to town, or I'd break all the speed limits. I didn't floor it while we circumvented town on the highway, but once I hit gravel, I got a little tougher with the accelerator.

I was all but fishtailing down the driveway. I had precious cargo, but I also had a turned-on Violet making idle chatter next to me.

I'd given her little more than grunts for answers.

What a beautiful night.

Grunt.

I've always loved the drive to the lake.

Grunt.

I still want to eat at Rattler's. We could always order takeout one day.

Grunt.

I parked next to her car, not bothering to pull into the garage. I got out and was around the pickup just as she was getting out. I took her hand and twirled her toward me.

"I can't wait until we get inside." I pressed her against the dusty pickup, hoped to fuck she didn't mind, and claimed that pretty pink mouth of hers.

She tasted as decadent as the steak tortellini she'd had for dinner. Rich and robust, she was a flavor that consumed me.

A little whimper left her, and she twined her arms around my neck. I invaded her mouth, taking everything I wanted, tired of holding back. I should keep not trusting her, but my brain had shut down. My dick had full control. Violet was the only thing on its mind.

I hefted her up. Her clothing scraped across the pick-up's paint, but I didn't fucking care. She could key this whole damn pickup. I wasn't thinking clearly until I could be buried in her one more time.

Just once. If only that was enough to get her out of my system.

She hooked a leg around my waist. Her other one slipped. I lifted it, and she clung to me, but every time I took a hand off of her, she dipped. I couldn't drop this woman. But I had to touch her all over.

I scooted us down the box. Keeping my mouth on hers, I hugged her to me with one arm and dropped the tailgate with the other. Then I set her on the edge.

She broke from me, sucking in a big breath. "Evander? Outside?"

"Afraid of a few mosquito bites?" I lifted the hem of her shirt. If she wanted to go inside, I'd take her in. Just a nibble first.

Last time we fucked in a small motel room. The idea of taking her under the wide-open sky was even more appealing. She could scream my name and no one would hear her. This time, my full goddamn name would leave her mouth.

She didn't answer. I flipped her shirt over her creamy tits. The mounds pushed over the edge of her bra cups. I thanked every power out there that I could witness this beautiful sight.

I tugged the lacy hem of her bra down until her nipples popped out. I caught her eye. She stared at me, her blue eyes wide with wonder, then she looked around like she was afraid someone would see us.

"There's no one for miles, Vi."

Her pupils dilated at the name. Did no one call her Vi? She'd probably corrected them all her life, but she wasn't telling me.

"I feel so exposed," she said breathlessly, but those black pupils of hers stayed wide. She liked it. A little exhibitionism just between us.

Need pounded at my temples, but I wouldn't rush this. Three months had been too damn long. "You have pretty fucking tits."

She took a deep breath, making her chest puff up. "You think so?"

I groaned. I could unhook her bra and get full access, but I liked the little peek. The way the band pushed her plump flesh up. "They're begging for me."

I dipped my head down and sucked a pearly nipple into my mouth. Her ragged moan drove right through me, ramping up the desire. It'd been too long since I'd had her.

"Oh my god, Evander. You and that tongue."

I released the nipple with a pop. "Say it again."

"You and that tongue?" The apples of her cheek were dusted in pink, and her lips were parted.

My desire stoked hotter. "No. My name."

Understanding lit her eyes. "Evander."

I licked across her tight peak. "You're going to yell that tonight."

"Promise?" She arched her back into me.

This woman. I ran my tongue around her nipple while kneading the other breast. Then I switched sides to give each one attention while Violet squirmed and moaned against me. My brain fogged with arousal.

She tipped her head back and skimmed a hand over my skull. Her legs widened, and I fit perfectly right in the juncture of her thighs.

I pulled back and trailed my fingers along her abdomen. She was fuller in the stomach than before, and the reason why made my caveman brain come alive. "How wet are you for me?"

Her eyes were glazed. She rolled her hips. "I think you need to find out."

Fuck yes, I would. Hooking my fingers over her waistband, I drew another nipple into my mouth. She started shifting from side to side to help me draw them down. Right when I reached the round of her ass, the drone of an engine reached my ears.

I snapped straight. The elastic of her shorts whacked her skin. I was tugging the cups of her bra up as I looked down the driveway. No car had come into view, but I could hear it.

Violet arranged her clothing until it didn't look like I'd been stripping her down. Her flushed face said I'd been doing just that.

Finally, a sedan turned down the drive. Who had the worst fucking timing in the world? "Linda."

Violet whipped her head around, and the color drained from her face.

"Why's she here?" She scooted off the tailgate. Her sandals hit the dirt, and she pulled the legs of her shorts down and brushed her hands over her shirt. Stress filled her eyes, and tension tugged at the edges of her mouth.

"She mentioned random visits to make sure everything was okay with the property." After being in the army so long, that didn't strike me as invasive. I'd told them anytime. They didn't have to call first.

"Uncle Darin's with her," Violet said with a groan. "Shit."

Her reaction sent up all kinds of warning flares. What was going on?

Darin parked behind me, then backed out to face down the driveway as if they planned to do their business and then dive into the car to speed away.

"Violet?" Darin said as he got out. "I didn't realize you knew Evander. We thought we'd do a halfway point check-in and make sure everything's okay with the property and see if you need anything from us."

Linda climbed out. Her long floral dress fluttered around her legs as she rounded the hood of the car. "What a surprise. Are you two getting married?"

Her words hit me like a shockwave. I barely wrapped my head around having a baby and entertaining the idea that I wanted to date Violet for real. Married? Wasn't that out of nowhere?

Violet crunched in on herself. "Actually, Aunt Linda—"

"You know you can't move in until you're married," Darin said.

I propped my hands on my hips and faced Violet. "Move in?"

My parents thought we were dating, but unless they told the whole town's population, what did Linda and

Darin think was going on? Who had Violet told, and what did she say?

"The trust," Linda said, her gaze jumping between us. "In order to get the house and property, Violet has to be married for a year before she inherits the place. And she can't move in until she's married."

What. The fuck.

Chapter Eleven

Violet

I'd had the best date of my life. It was everything I had ever wanted. Sweet and sexy. Fun. He was easy to talk to, and he'd opened up to me. Something he likely rarely did with anyone. I had felt special. The date had been about to end with fireworks, and then my aunt and uncle showed up and ruined it all.

Evander's walls slammed down before my eyes. His gaze grew as hard as his jaw. He'd break his molars if he ground his teeth any harder.

"I haven't told him about the trust," I said, my voice shaky. I sounded guilty. "Our business—" I winced. Business? Could that sound more emotionless? Emotionless had been my life before Evander. "The way we know each other isn't about the inheritance, exactly. I don't need to claim the house and property."

"Oh." Linda's mouth formed a confused line. She glanced at Darin, who was regarding us with his brows drawn together. An uncomfortable chuckle left her. "I'm sorry. I thought you two were dating."

"No," Evander said with a flinty tone.

I let my eyes fall shut. Ouch. "The house has nothing to do with what's going on between us," I said deliberately, trying to meet his gaze.

The yellow flecks in his eyes sparked. He didn't believe me. My heart sank. I was just another one of his exes who tried to use him.

"I see." Linda lifted her arms to encompass the property. "Your crop looks great, and I can see from here the work you've done on the shed. I imagine with the nicer weather, you're not working on the interior as much as before. Just let us know what you've done, and we'll take it off the rent like we discussed."

"You can inspect it if you want," Evander said. Everything about his mood was flat. Carefully restrained.

I swallowed the acid creeping up my throat. "The house has never looked better." As if I'd seen the inside before.

"Right," Darin said and cleared his throat. The discomfort between me and Evander had to be noticeable. "I heard you planted pumpkins."

"Ten acres," Evander said in that monotone voice. "After harvest, I'll move out."

I flinched. He'd just leave. Because he thought I was using him for what? After all we'd talked about tonight and in the kitchen, what did he think I was after?

No matter what I did, I was falling short of his expectations. The familiarity crawled over my skin. Wasn't this how I'd lived for the last seven years? Only to be replaced within months by someone who was nothing like me.

"You're not renewing your lease?" Linda sent me a beseeching look as if to ask if there was anything I could do. Like marry him and live here for a year until the house was mine? Was she worried about finding a new renter? Evander was a dream tenant. He'd leave the property better than when he'd moved in. He probably even downplayed what he'd spent on materials he'd used fixing up various rooms.

"No." He gave me a look and a blip of smoldering emotion showed through. He was enraged. Betrayed. Hurt. Let down. All the negatives because of me.

He was thinking about himself. Protecting himself.

I couldn't blame him. But all the same emotions were coursing through me. Where he'd made me feel so damn secure, now I ached. I was lonely and tired. I was tired of wanting one type of relationship with a man only to have it teased and yanked away.

I'd gotten my hopes up that there was something real between us. A foundation that could build into so much more. There hadn't been one with Willis, and I'd been an idiot to stay so long. I had teetered on doing the same with Evander.

"Perfect timing." The burning in my throat grew. "I can work on finding someone to marry by the time you move out." I was lashing out, but dammit. The pressure in my chest eased slightly.

Rage flared in his eyes, blazing hot. "What?"

I shrugged but smiled at my aunt and uncle, satisfied that I'd gotten to him. Evander thought I was playing games, so I'd play games. "I'd hate for you to find a new renter, and I guess since I'm looking for a place, all I have is what? Six months? That's enough time for a love connection."

I didn't need a love connection. I only needed to make a point to Evander.

"Yes. Sure." Linda squeezed Darin's arm, a signal I'd seen her use when I was younger. A way to say she was ready to go. "Keep us updated. Uh, both of you."

They got in their car and drove off. I waved, my smile as fake as the relationship I thought had been starting between me and Evander.

Once they disappeared down the road, I stuffed my hands on my hips and faced Evander.

He opened his mouth, but I talked over him. "I know what you're thinking. I lied. I'm just like the others. Blah, blah, blah." Surprise filled his face. Emboldened, I continued. "I really liked you. I liked you that night we met. And it's only grown since then." I barked out a sardonic laugh. "After dinner, I thought we were going to build something real. A cozy little family." Sadness threatened to creep in. Tears burned the backs of my eyes. "You're almost the perfect guy. Except for when you make me feel like crap."

He reared back like I'd slapped him.

He claimed to want the truth, but he didn't like hearing it. "You know what? I'm done feeling like I have to constantly prove myself, or I'll lose everything. You insist on leaving, then leave. Just know it's your decision. None of it has to do with me. But if I'm so easy to forget, then maybe I'll find someone who can help me get my trust." I stomped toward the house. "Then I'll get the house, and I can drop him after a year," I called over my shoulder.

I had no plans to find a man who'd marry me for a year. The thought of another guy brought a resurgence of the nausea. I was probably a fool to think the threat of moving on would bother him, but it wasn't fair I was the only one hurting.

Inside the house, I went straight for my bedroom. I grabbed my bag and flung it on the bed. My boobs protested the use of my pecs. They'd been deliciously sore and ready for his touch earlier. Now they were as cranky as me.

I started gathering my clothing and stuffing it inside the suitcase. Time to return to my family. They wouldn't turn on me like Evander.

"What are you doing?" he asked from the doorway.

I jumped and let out a yelp. He was wearing boots. How was he so quiet coming after me? He had to be seething with emotion, but he was stealthy as a...a trained soldier.

"Leaving."

I glanced over, and it was enough to send my pulse racing. I wasn't scared, but the sight of a grouchy man with his veiny arms crossed in front of his chest, blocking the doorway, unlocked fantasies I didn't think I had. He could pick me up and carry me wherever he wanted to, and I'd let him.

Pack more, lust less, Violet.

"We haven't gotten the results yet."

I pushed my hair off my face. "I know what they are. You're the one who wants proof."

He set his mouth in a flat line. His roiling energy filled the room, but he was a poster child for calm and collected. Dealing with me was apparently nothing like being in battle.

"So," I continued, "there's no reason for me to wait around. If you want to tamper with the results, go ahead. It doesn't matter to me if you want to claim your paternity or not. I'm ready to raise this baby on my own." I prodded my temples. "I think I'd prefer it. I'm sick of men taking their hang-ups out on me."

"You're lumping me in with him again."

"And you're lumping me in with her," I mocked. I never thought a guy as tough appearing as Evander could pout, but here he was. "You're a category all your own. You know why? Willis treated me like I was beneath him, but he still put me on a pedestal. He just made sure his was higher. You kicked that pedestal out from under me and made me feel worse than nothing."

His scowl deepened. "I'm the one who's been lied to."

"I wasn't transparent about the landlord business. I get that. So sue me." That was childish, but I could pout too. "I didn't tell you about the stupid trust my grandmother made for all her properties because it's none of your business. I couldn't stop you from renewing your lease, and I didn't want to. That's all I'm guilty of. This?" I waved my hand down my torso. "Was as unplanned for me as it was for you. A baby is going to disrupt my life more than yours, personally and professionally, no matter how much you decide you want to be involved."

I zipped up my suitcase. I'd gather my toiletries on the way out. I wasn't muscling past him more than once.

The wheels of the bag hit the floor, but he didn't move. "Where are you going?"

The only home I had at the moment. Billings. I'd figure out the rest there. "You have my number. You can call with the results. Or not."

The troubled line of his mouth deepened. "Are you leaving town?"

"Not your business."

"If you're the mother of my baby it is."

Mild surprise cooled some of my irritation. That was the closest I'd ever heard him accept he was the father. "The baby will be your concern. Not me. And since it's not born yet, I'll do what I damn well please."

"I'm not stopping you."

I dropped my gaze to the floor where his feet remained planted on the hardwood.

After a heartbeat, he moved out of the way. "Someone should know where you're going this late at night."

Eight o'clock was not that late. Yet I was tired, and a long drive while my stitched-together life fell apart again was not something I looked forward to.

"I'm going home." Home tasted sour. Billings was no longer my home, and it hadn't been for a while, but I had a rental that was sitting empty. Until I heard about a job, Billings was my base.

He followed me to the bathroom. "That's a six-hour drive."

"We've been over that before." I snatched my toothbrush and toothpaste. Juggling everything one-handed, I unzipped part of my suitcase and crushed them inside.

"Jesus, Violet. Just stay here until morning."

The urge to drop my suitcase and do as he said was strong. I wanted to be with him. But he wasn't the only one who had developed a trust issue. "No."

"You won't get to Billings until two in the morning or later."

I finished in the bathroom. He was blocking the doorway. I pointedly looked at his boots again, then up to his face.

His mouth made another line, and he stepped out of my way. "Then stay in town."

"I'm already paying rent. I can't add more motel rooms on top of it."

"Goddammit, Violet."

I ignored him and swung into the living room. Thankfully, I'd kept my crochet projects in a bag by the couch so it didn't scatter and make his meticulous decor look cluttered. I looped the bag over one arm. That was it. Time to go.

My heart wrenched, and I swallowed a sob. I had been really happy here. I got to know me again, and not the me that I was expected to be in California. The solitude of Coal Haven became an oasis for me.

"You're not listening," he said. "Just stay and leave in the morning."

"I heard every word."

I faced him. He was in the middle of the path to the front door. I wanted nothing more than to go to the bedroom and tuck in for the night. Replay our kiss and the things he said about my boobs. But madness waited down that road. It wouldn't change Evander, and I wasn't the one who needed to change him. He was who he was. If I stayed, if I tiptoed around him and his past trauma, he wouldn't take accountability. The stories he told me were heartbreaking, but they were his issues. I refused to let them become mine.

Evander had troubles with women who clung to him and wanted to use him. Now he could deal with a person who could walk away and be just fine.

"I'm a big girl. I'll let my brother know I'm traveling." I'd tell him why. It was time I built my support network. I'd done what I came to Coal Haven to do. "Otherwise, let me know what you decide when it comes to your parental rights."

This time, I didn't silently ask him to move. I charged toward him, the suitcase wheels rumbling loudly on the hardwood.

He jumped out of the way, and my heart hung heavier. He was more upset than any man I'd ever dealt with, and his anger was because of me. But he was still being more respectful than anyone. Willis had sobbed and unloaded my luggage as I packed it. I had threatened to call my dad and brothers if he didn't stop. Then he'd used manipulative tactics afterward. And I let him.

No longer.

I was done with men.

Chapter Twelve

Violet

My brother leaned against the island counter in my parents' house. I'd called him to come over, figuring I might as well rip the bandage off to as many people as possible. Mom and Dad were at the breakfast table with me. They each cupped their hands around a mug of coffee. Decaf. It was evening. I'd slept in and took another two hours to get out of bed. A phone call from the refinery about the interview had fully roused me. I had a future to figure out.

Ripping the bandage off was easier than a game of telephone. I'd had to wait for Alder to get off work. I invited him over and initiated a group call with my siblings. Either karma really wanted me to suffer, or luck was on my side. They all had answered.

I told the story of the last four months as emotionlessly as possible, leaving out the specifics of my falling out with Evander. I didn't want them to hate him.

Leaving out the fight about when he learned about the trust, I just said he'd had terrible experiences in the past with women trying to take advantage of him, and he's cautious and waiting for paternity.

My heart ached, but I'd had a six-hour drive to purge any tears that gathered. After a full night of sleep, the hurt lingered, heavy and smothering, but I could distance myself enough to tell them everything.

"So, yeah," I finished. "That's where I'm at."

Alder's scowl was deeper than normal, and it matched the one Dad wore. Mom hid her astonishment well. Only her eyes had widened, and in the depths, happiness mingled with the concern.

"Oh. My. God," Clover said, her voice soaked in disbelief.

"I can't believe it!" Poppy screeched. "Violet! You're closer to home, *and* I get to be an aunt again! This is amazing."

"And we don't have to deal with Vasectomy Willis," Jasper said.

I might regret telling them about Evander's name for my ex, but it wouldn't be today. Their support overwhelmed me. It was exactly what I needed after yesterday.

"Are you really moving to Coal Haven?" Excitement lined Lily's voice.

I nodded even though she couldn't see me. "I loved Coal Haven while I was staying there, and I wanted to work in the oil and gas industry when I went to college. Now I finally get to." The phone call had been to offer me the position.

"That'll be amazing!" she squealed. "I love my in-laws, but I miss all of you. The kids miss you, and with two of us here, the others are going to have to visit more."

Alder lifted a brow.

"You gonna be like Grandma and try to get us all to move there?" Jasper asked with a laugh.

"I don't have to be," Lily countered. "Grandma's still trying to work her miracles through her trust."

"It won't be through that stupid house." With the beautiful property, the acres of pumpkins, and the two barn cats who cuddled me every morning. "I'll find my own place to live."

"Eliot and I are here when you're ready to move. Just give me a call." My nephew Kellan cried in the background. "I gotta go. Keep me up to date."

She hung up, and one by one, all my other siblings disconnected. That wasn't so bad.

"How far along?" Alder asked.

"Three and a half months." My stomach twisted, but I didn't have any food to heave up. I had yet to find a more permanent place than a vacation rental.

"And you're moving to Coal Haven?" he asked woodenly.

Yep. "I'll be Daisy's coworker."

A muscle in his jaw popped, and he shifted his gaze to the floor.

"So it was fortuitous I came back. I can check out of the rental." I had so many things to do in two weeks, but the big move out of California was done. The rest would be shifting my items to another place. Finding furniture. Preparing a nursery.

My stomach acid churned.

"Are you really letting the property go?" Mom asked. Sadness touched the lines around her eyes. She liked having me in town. We had lunch. She'd come to visit.

Now I was leaving again. This time with a grandkid on the way.

"Yes. I don't care what Aunt Linda does with it. I'm tired of games." I was just tired. Already, I was ready for another nap. "I'm done playing by someone else's rules. I'm finding a house I like." If I could afford it. "And I'm doing a job I want. I'm raising this kid on my own terms."

"What about Evander?" Dad asked, his eyes flashing on Evander's name.

"I don't think he'll be involved that much." I clenched my stomach to fight the urge to cry.

"What if he accepts that he's a father and wants to be involved?" Mom asked gently.

I inhaled a shuddering breath. The longer the day went, the more I fought tears. Yesterday afternoon, I would've been thrilled if he were invested in our baby. I'd have filled my head with fantasies like I had for the last seven years. Today I knew better. If he wanted to be involved, it would be for the child. Not me. "Then I'll have a home base and he can decide what to do around that."

Mom took a long sip of her coffee. She exchanged a discreet glance with Dad.

"What?" I snapped.

"Nothing." Mom sighed and held her mug like it was the middle of winter and the power was out. "I just hope it's that simple. People can make trouble, and the Barrons have the money to do it."

"He's not Cameron's kid."

Dad snorted. "Thank goodness for that." He wiped a hand down his face. "Although I heard his own kids gave him plenty of trouble. But no, sweetheart, we're just worried. We don't know Evander. Is he volatile? Will he get obsessive? Would he use the kid as a way to control you?"

No, no, and no. For a man I'd known all of two weeks and that one night, I was stubbornly confident in my answers. "I think he's an honorable man who's afraid of getting hurt again."

Mom reclined in her chair and regarded me. "You don't think he'll cause drama?"

"I don't think he wants to deal with me that much."

Disappointment filled her eyes. Dad nodded. Yeah. My answer had been bleak.

"You should stay here," Alder said. "In Billings. You'll have more family, and you can get more help."

"She won't," Mom replied before I could tell him no. "She's made up her mind."

I nodded, grateful they weren't going to hound me about my decisions. "Billings doesn't feel right. I really liked Coal Haven, and it's small. Easier. Lily and Eliot are nearby. My son or daughter will have cousins almost next door."

"A baby," Mom said, delight in her voice. She gave Dad a fond look. "Our grandkid count is really starting to rise."

For the first time since the first pregnancy test, anticipation tingled in my belly. I was having a baby, and my parents were excited. I might be an adult, but I didn't want to travel this path alone.

"When are you moving?" Alder asked.

"I told them I could start in two weeks. I'll find a rental this week and hopefully move the weekend before I begin."

"I wish you would've told us earlier," Dad said, "but

hopefully this Evander will realize how considerate it was for you to make sure he was the first to know."

I nodded even though considerate was the last way Evander would describe me. At least he'd only have five and a half more months to endure running across me in town. Then I was sure he'd be gone and out of my life.

***

Evander

"...cannot be excluded as the biological father..."

I read the line for the hundredth time.

I was going to be a dad.

Violet was pregnant with my kid.

She'd vomited on my porch, but the pregnancy hadn't resonated as real to me. She wasn't obviously showing.

I brushed both hands over my scalp. Dammit.

I was going to be a dad.

I exhaled a heavy breath.

How badly did I fuck up?

She'd lied. Sort of.

She'd manipulated. Sort of.

Then she'd taken it back. Had that been a ruse? A way to win me over because she thought she had time to do just that?

Did she think I'd put on a ring on it and say I do before the lease was up?

I put my elbows on the table and buried my face in my hands. Confusion fogged my brain.

Was I wrong?

I had been before, only in the opposite way. Was Violet like Kandi?

I wasn't the same naive private I'd been when I was twenty.

What if I was wrong?

Except for when you make me feel like crap.

When did I become that guy?

I pressed both palms against my eyes. My head fucking hurt.

Now all I had was her number. She lived six hours away in some vacation rental. Her family was close, so there was that.

I closed the lid of my laptop with a snap and pushed it across the table. Meowing from outside caught my attention. I went out. Humidity and heat swarmed around me, along with a few mosquitoes. I batted a few off and found the problem. Flo had scaled up the post of the porch to the top. Her eyes were wide, and she looked side to side, her little tail whipping back and forth. Poly stared at her from the bottom.

"You stuck?" I had to rise to my toes to reach her, but I clamped my hand around her squirmy body and lifted her down.

She didn't fight to get away. The kittens were as tame as could be after getting cuddles from Violet for the last two weeks. Longing hit me hard as I held the kittens the way she used to.

I curled Flo into my chest and went to the steps. I sat on the top step and scratched Flo's ears. Little claws pricked into the side of my leg. Poly crawled onto my lap.

The pounding in my temples eased. I didn't know how long I stayed with the cats, but soon the sound of an engine cut through the day. Mom's beige SUV came into view. I hugged Flo to me harder. I hadn't heard from my parents since the failed meal. She still thought Violet and I were seeing each other. I thought I had time before I had to break the news to Mom that Violet and I had gone our separate ways.

Mom would likely think it was my fault. She'd be right.

Mom looped around by the garage and parked in the driveway, facing out. She got out and gave a tentative smile.

"Hey, Mom."

Relief filled her features. "Evander."

Had she been worried I'd tell her to fuck off? What a fucking son I was. No wonder Dad wished Derek was the one still around. He'd have made Mom happy. I started to rise, but she waved me to sit.

"I've been inside all day. I need some fresh air."

"It's muggy."

She smiled, the lines around her eyes deeper than ever, almost giving her a sad look. "I'm sure you've been through worse."

"Benning can get brutally humid." Fort Benning, or whatever its new name was, had been my home for six years total, three years each time.

She looked past me like she was trying to see into the house. "Is Violet around?"

"She returned to Billings." The words were thick.

Mom must've read something in my tone. Her face fell, and she nodded.

Fuck me. Was she blaming herself? About the argument or how she'd raised a son who drove every single woman away?

I could leave it at that. Mom wouldn't pry. But words clogged my throat. "There's more to our story—or lack of one."

Mom tipped her head. I caught the glint of surprise that I'd elaborated as much as I had.

"She's pregnant. It's mine."

Mom's mouth fell open. A choked sound came from her. She blinked, and I caught sheer happiness. She blinked again. Dismay. Another blink. Confusion. She oscillated through a series of emotions. I knew the feeling.

"I..." I put Flo down, but she climbed right back up my cargo pants and batted at her sister. "Remember Kandi?"

Her mouth tightened. "That girl. Yes."

"She fucked me up, Mom." She didn't flinch at my language, so I continued. Mom had always given me space when I least expected it. "I've made sure to protect myself. I was right to. Over and over. It was like I was a magnet for them."

Mom's gaze went soft. "You started to think all girls were like Kandi."

I ground my teeth together and nodded. What if they hadn't been? What if I had assumed the worst and chased good people away? "I'm not proud of it—and I don't know that Violet's not like Kandi." Comparing the two made me want to retch. Violet was nothing like her.

"But she could be?" At my lack of an answer, Mom nodded. "I see. You ran her off."

"After I made her stick around to take a paternity test that I oversaw." I could leave Coal Haven, but I was still a Barron.

"You got the results? It's yours?"

Hearing the words out loud didn't calm the turmoil inside me. "She lied."

"About the baby?"

"No. Maybe?" I explained what I'd pieced together from what Linda said about a trust and that Violet has to marry to get this property. And I had thought my grandpa had been manipulative. At least I had known. Violet and her siblings had been taken by surprise. "I guess she can't live here unless she's married."

"So you thought she was baiting you?"

"She might've been," I said stubbornly. I had no proof. Violet hadn't acted like a leech.

Mom's shrug was casual. "Possible."

"Why are you so quick to give her the benefit of the doubt?" I was her son, but she wasn't raging about Violet. She'd had choice words to say about Kandi. One of the few times I'd heard Mom call someone a name.

Mom pressed her palms together. "Well...I've known women who manipulate, and they usually have more edges than Violet."

I snorted. "And their last name is Barron?"

Her chuckle was soft. "That's not so much the case anymore, but yes. For much of my married life, it was. Likewise, I've known my fair share of Barron men who lash out because they've been deeply hurt. They aren't quick to forgive or forget."

Touché. "I've been right not to."

"Until you're wrong."

I dropped my chin. Mom wasn't this forward, but she was when it came to Violet. Discomfort scratched over my skin. I'd rather move on to a different topic. "Why'd you come? Is there something you need?"

"I wanted to see my son. Surprising you seems the best tactic."

I coughed out a laugh again. She wasn't giving up on me. That made her the only one. "You know how Dad and I are."

"I know." Poly hopped down the stairs and toddled to Mom's sandaled feet. Mom smiled and picked her up. "I guess I'm just tired of walking on eggshells because of how others in this family behave." She snuggled the kitten close to her face. "I miss my son. I only have one left, and I'd like to talk to him while we're in the same zip code."

My heartburn flared. "I don't have much to say. I never wanted to worry you."

"I'd be worried anyway." She set the kitten down, and Flo bounded toward her, nearly face-planting off the first stair. "I have a casserole in the car. Would you like it?"

She hadn't said much, but she'd said a lot. She wanted to see me while she could.

"Yeah," I said gruffly. "You eat yet?"

Her smile was pleased. "I have not. I wasn't looking forward to leftovers. I still make too much food for just the two of us. Then I make way too much when we have company, like the last time Liam and the kids were over..." Her smile flickered.

I didn't hate Liam. He'd been there when I hadn't. He'd been there for my sister-in-law who was now his wife. He'd been there for my parents when I'd gone farther away. He'd been hurt by a lot of people, and he was still a stand-up guy.

I hadn't been sure how I felt about him, but when I searched myself...I was curious. I was tired of being on the outside. "Why don't you tell me about it inside?"

I got up and went to the door.

"Evander." When I stopped, she hesitated. Was she afraid I wouldn't let her in after what she had to say? "What Kandi did to you was deplorable. But the real shame would be if it ruined something wonderful. You're going to be a dad." Hearing those words spoken by someone other than me or Violet was a slam to the chest. "I don't know Violet, but she really seemed...like the entire package. I hope you two can work something out. Not for me, an excited grandma, but for you."

Defeat swelled in my chest. I might have ruined that.

No. Not me. Violet was the one who hadn't been transparent. I was clear as fuck. The righteousness that had raged right before she left was gone. Diminished. "Yeah. We'll see about that."

Chapter Thirteen

Violet

Alder helped the delivery guy haul my new bed in. I'd bought a full-size one on sale that was half the size of the one I'd shared with Willis. But if it was just me, I didn't need a big bed.

I rubbed the center of my chest. Was my morning sickness acting up? Moving was stressful.

My phone buzzed with a message.

Poppy: Give me the address immediately. I'm putting in leave to come visit.

Another followed immediately after. Poppy had made a group text.

Clover: Let's get the sister band back together.
Poppy: I'm going to rub that baby belly all over.

No one wanted to hear us sing, but I'd take sister visits any day. I didn't have to clear it with anyone. **Here's the address. I have weekends and holidays off.**

Another buzz. My other brother this time.

Jasper: Ouch. Thanks for the invite.

The corner of my mouth kicked up. **You're always welcome when you can pry yourself away from your new cowboy life.**

He'd taken over managing Eliot's family ranch in eastern Montana.

Jasper: I'm not rubbing any of your bellies. Maybe Alder's.

Smiling, I tucked my phone away.

In only a week, I'd secured an open rental. The house was by the elementary school. My drive to work would take twenty minutes on a busy day. I didn't have much for furniture. I'd left California with the items I had purchased and only what had fit into my car. Basically, my clothing, a few end tables, and some kitchen items.

Everything was on track. My job. My living arrangement. Yet my optimism dimmed while I stood in the middle of the kitchen of my new home.

The musty smell wasn't as strong as when I first entered. I'd peeked into the basement once, and that was the end of that. If I had furnace or water heater problems, I might just move versus going down into that dank darkness.

Alder wandered in. "Delivery guy's gone." He glanced around the kitchen. "It's not bad," he said lightly, his expression carefully neutral.

"It's not good." I took in the thin cabinet doors. Old contact paper lined the insides, but spots were worn through to the wood. I wouldn't put any dishes inside until I scrubbed them well. Two doors hung crooked, and the one closest to the sink didn't close all the way.

The table Alder and I found at the secondhand store was as old as that house, but it was small enough to fit into what the landlord described as a dining room. My parents' breakfast nook was larger.

The place had been built in the sixties, but some of the decor had been updated twenty years ago. The kitchen didn't boast many of the updates.

Still, the carpet had been replaced after the last renter. I could handle old and worn-down woodwork. It might not be the cute little farmhouse I'd never get to own, but I could make it a home for the baby.

An old, weathered home with light fixtures and wallpaper older than me.

People raised kids in worse. This place wasn't what I envisioned, but neither was being a single mom.

Alder scratched the back of his head as he took in the kitchen. He was dressed down in khaki shorts and a polo. His casual style used to be jeans and a T-shirt, but for the last decade, he'd adopted the wardrobe of a golf-playing CEO. Maybe it was a *dress for the job you want* sort of thing. I hadn't asked about his wardrobe change, and if I had, he would've pretended not to understand what I meant. Just like he'd played obtuse when we'd asked about his divorce and he'd answered with *we grew apart.*

"You sure there's nothing better out there?" He opened the cabinet closest to the sink. The hinges squeaked.

"It was either dump money into a motel room or move in somewhere. I'd rather have a house than an apartment."

"I get that, but…" He turned on the sink. Water sputtered out, and the pipes thumped. He quickly shut the knob off.

"I'm sure it hasn't been used in a while."

He gave me a dubious look. "Did you test the shower and toilet? Is the rest of the plumbing shady?"

"It's not shady." My response lacked conviction.

He walked into the living area and flipped the switch for the small round light fixture in the middle of the ceiling. Nothing happened. He looked over his shoulder. The light above me hadn't turned on either. He flipped it again, and we both looked around.

"What's this for?" He circled the rest of the living room. Any switch he came to, he flipped. The hallway light turned on with the switch farthest away from it. Otherwise, nothing happened. "The electricity is shady."

"I can get a lamp." My stomach was slowly sinking. "Believe it or not, there was a worse house I looked at yesterday." It was why I had taken this one, knowing that it was move-in ready because there wasn't a line waiting to get in.

"Let me find something to check all the outlets." He grabbed a lamp and went through all the rooms, testing the switches. "I don't like this, Violet," he called from my bedroom.

"Doesn't matter, Alder. I'm living here until I can afford to buy a place."

He appeared in the hallway. "Mom and Dad will help you get into something new sooner."

Starting a new job after an almost four-month lapse wasn't the best time to get a loan. I'd only get more pregnant or have a baby when I closed and moved—if I could get that far.

I let my shoulders hang. "I'm not going to be in my midthirties and still need their help."

"Don't be too proud. That's how you ended up with that douche for so long."

"He really was a douche."

"*Is* a douche. He'll never change." He spun in a circle. I had a blue Rubbermaid tote and a coffee table in the living room with my crocheting, and that was it. Everything else he'd hauled from Billings for me was in the bedroom. I had little other furniture. "I'm going to buy you a chair."

"You don't need to."

"I'm not leaving my pregnant sister in a house with no chair."

I waved my hand at the small table he'd hauled from the thrift store. "I have two whole kitchen chairs." They were also older than me and made of metal. Someone had repaired the plastic seats at one point with brown, chevron-patterned vinyl. They were cute but dated.

"Load up," he said and went out the front door.

I could ignore him, but my butt liked the thought of the metal chairs less than he did. My tight sweats neared unpresentable, but it wasn't like I was trying to pick up a man. I followed him and locked up. The dead bolt took a few turns, and I had to push the door with my shoulder while turning the key before it thunked into place.

Alder waited at his black pickup, his flat expression saying a lot.

"It has character," I said as I crawled in.

He stayed true to his word, driving straight to Coal Haven's lone furniture store. He bought the clearance couch and recliner I picked out.

He was inspecting a dresser to buy me that I insisted I didn't need—I could really use it though—and I wandered to a nursery set. The heathered-gray wood finish on the crib and the changing table reminded me of Evander's house. This would've gone perfectly in the guest room; the space would've fit the three-drawer-wide dresser too. An extra plush glider rocker finished off the set.

Unexpected tears pricked the backs of my eyes. I spun on a heel to return to Alder's side.

"Can I add the dresser to the shipment too?" Alder asked the older woman who owned the shop.

Hattie grinned from behind the counter. "Add anything you like, and I'll make it happen. When would you like it? I've got a crew working Wednesday evenings and Saturdays if weekdays don't work for you."

I arranged the delivery time for Wednesday. Four days in a metal chair. I'd survive.

Okay. I was set. Alder wandered through a display of welded items, and I followed.

There was a firepit with an intricate grill that was nicer than it should be for something that would see nothing but flames, two horseshoe crosses, and a set of bar stools. But it was the cutest little end table that caught my eye. The lacquered wooden top was nice enough, but the supports underneath it called to my chemist's heart. Two metal connections hooked the tabletop on one end and connected to two half-circle points on the bottom. Three metal rungs stretched between the half circles.

Hattie appeared at my elbow. "A local artist makes those. I've sold his work for years."

"I wonder if he knows he made an acetylene structure with his weld."

Alder and Hattie both tilted their heads to inspect the end table.

I pointed to the three rungs. "Three bonds between the two carbons. The half circles." I indicated the metal bar attaching the half circles to the wooden top. "The hydrogen bonds. I mean, technically, there's only one wooden slab and not two things to mimic hydrogen, but...it's ironic, right? Acetylene structure. Welding." I waited for the scoffing. Irony had no place in science according to the stiffs I used to hang out with.

"Huh. That is cool," Hattie said. "I'll have to ask him. He'll be delighted at the coincidence if it isn't intentional."

"Oh. Cool." Pleased, I played with the collar of my shirt. "Tell him it's an amazing table."

"Are you interested in it?"

Yes. Absolutely.

I also didn't want this gorgeous piece of art in a house I could barely lock. "I was just admiring it. Thank you, though."

"Do you want it?" Alder asked.

The price glared at me in bold red numbers. Yes, I did want it, but the table cost more than the couch Alder had bought me. He could afford it and probably everything in this place, but my pride would not let him spend more money. He was already giving me his time, and that was more than I'd had with my oldest brother for years.

I smiled, hiding the yearning. The dark finish of the wood on the table would make all the wood in my house weep. "The less I move into that house, the less I have to move out. Should we go eat?"

"All right."

I waved goodbye to Hattie.

"I'm taking you out," I announced when we were in the pickup. "And I'm craving steak Alfredo." Mostly the pasta. And the escape from the house.

"Twist my arm. Let's try that new place."

"If you mean Rattler's, I think it's been open for years."

He smirked. "If it wasn't here when we lived here, then it's new."

We approached the restaurant. The outside looked like most newer bar and grills. Lots of wood architecture, a peaked gable over the entrance, and wide picture windows with decorative sections. Alder parked on the less crowded side of the parking lot. More cars pulled in behind us. When we got to the door, he opened it for me. I stepped in and was greeted by a broad back I knew all too well.

Evander was at the hostess station, and a paper bag with Rattler's logo of a rattlesnake around a mug of beer on the side was on the stand next to him. He was tucking his wallet into his back pocket.

I stopped, and Alder bumped into me. "Dang, Violet. You're blocking the way."

At my name, Evander whipped his head around.

It'd been two weeks since I'd seen him, but the time had stretched longer than the three months between our first and second meeting.

"Thank you," the young hostess said, her voice chipper. "Enjoy your food."

Evander grabbed the handles of the bag without looking, shock rippling through his gaze. "Violet?"

"Evander." Someday, I'd be able to say his name without sounding breathless.

Alder tensed next to me. "You're kidding."

"Small town," I muttered.

Evander's steely gaze landed on Alder. His hand squeezed tighter on his purchase until recognition flared in his eyes.

Did he think—of course he did. The last I'd told him I was going to find a man to marry. He didn't know I had no intention to. Thankfully, Alder and I looked like siblings. We both had dark hair, only Alder no longer kept his long enough to feature his natural curls. His eyes were a darker blue than mine, and he was nine inches taller than me, but the resemblance had been commented on all our lives.

People pushed through the door behind us. I stepped to the side. Did I give Evander a nod or breeze past him? The last time I saw him, he had my nipple in his mouth shortly before we fought.

I was not used to navigating waters like these.

Evander's gaze dropped to my stomach. I had on loose basketball shorts that fell to the tops of my knees and an old UCSD T-shirt I had never worn because it was too big. I had to shop for maternity clothes soon, but these had been fine for moving.

Had I known I'd run into the man who'd kicked my heart out the door and slammed the locks shut behind it, I might've chosen differently.

"Did you get the results?" I kept my tone light, but I really wanted to demand why he hadn't reached out. Of course he'd gotten the results. Someone could've walked from the testing lab to Coal Haven and hand-delivered them by now.

His nod was curt. "You know what they are."

"Without a doubt," I responded, and he winced.

I got a little satisfaction from his reaction. So why hadn't he messaged to tell me I was right and he wanted to move forward? It'd been a month since he learned I was expecting.

I hardly knew this man, yet I felt like I was begging

for scraps of his attention. "Okay. Well. See you around." I nudged my brother to keep going. He didn't move. Neither did Evander.

"Did you get that job?" Evander asked. "At the refinery?"

"Yep." I shoved Alder's shoulder. He was slightly more movable than a mountain, but he didn't budge.

More people flowed around us. All the tables would be full before this showdown was over.

"Where are you living?" Evander asked.

"In town" was all I gave him.

His eyes darkened. "We should talk."

My patience snapped. I'd been low-key spoiled by my parents since I told them I was pregnant. My siblings had all called to talk about the baby and my job, and Alder had taken the whole weekend to help me move. I'd gotten attention and affection from my loved ones. They reaffirmed why I left California. And why I'd left Evander's house. "You have my number. You've had my number for the last two weeks."

His cheek twitched. "Violet—"

"Enjoy your food." I hooked Alder's elbow and towed him around a stunned Evander.

"There are two of us," I said to the young hostess.

And when Alder was gone, there would only be me.

Evander

· · ·

I sat on the top step of my porch. The more I sat out here, the more the kittens wanted to play and cuddle. The more I remembered the tinkle of Violet's laughter when she'd do the same with them.

A week had passed since I'd run into Violet at the restaurant. My blood still boiled at the initial thought that she'd been on a date. I hadn't recognized Alder at first, but I'd seen his stubborn expression, the set of his mouth, the slope of his nose before. His sister had the same features.

Only her eyes picked up the violet hue. They flashed with more indignation. A sign with no words that said *I'm sick of your shit.*

Yeah. I might be sick of my shit too.

My ego pointed out that women usually put a lot more time in before they wrote me off, making Violet the smartest person I'd ever dated.

You didn't date, jackass. You fucked her and then treated her like shit.

My phone was on the railing above me. The damn thing had been quiet. I had no soldiers who needed to call me anymore. Mom had taken to just driving out when she wanted to visit. We'd had lunch once, and she'd brought a rhubarb pie as dessert.

There was no one else to call me.

You have my number. You've had my number for the last two weeks. So much of what Violet had said haunted me.

We really did have to talk. I didn't want to be an absentee dad, but I was also still wrapping my head around the idea of being a dad in the first place.

As if she wasn't doing the same being a mom. Fuck, I was a dick. I had to talk to her.

Before I could question myself, I grabbed my phone and tapped out a message. **Where are you living?**

There. I texted her.

Several minutes went by. I continued to stare at my screen.

Goddammit. I put the thing down and scratched around Flo's ears.

Was Violet going to ignore me? It was her right.

Should I drive around town looking for her car? Too stalkerish?

My phone buzzed. I snatched it up so fast I scared Flo off my lap. **I'm fine, thank you. How are you?**

My lips twitched. I started typing out **How are you feel—** I deleted it. She saw through my shit. **Puke on anyone's lawn lately?**

All my food has stayed down. Especially all the pasta I've been eating.

Was that a pregnancy thing? Was she getting enough to eat? Did she make it herself, or was she worn out after work? **Steak tortellini?**

Steak Alfredo.

I waited for more. Nothing. Damn. **Mind telling me where you live in case anything comes up?**

The blue house adjacent to the elementary school.

Good. She finally answered.

Yeah, when you don't act like a caveman. **Can we talk about how this is going to work?**

We can draft a custody agreement for after the birth.

No, goddammit. I just wanted to talk to her. I wanted to see her.

The desire went one way. **Fine, but can we talk in person about it first? Casually?** No fucking lawyers.

Too many minutes went by before she answered. **I'll be home by six the rest of the week.**

I'll be there tomorrow.

Was I rushing? Maybe. But I'd dragged my feet for weeks, so it was time to move forward and figure out where the fuck I was going.

Chapter Fourteen

Violet

Daisy walked me to the parking lot. I'd been through small towns that weren't as large as the refinery. Administration resided in a building closer to the entrance gate. Behind them was the square brick building with the lab I worked in. Behind those two plain office structures, the heart of the refinery sprawled along the countryside. Cylindrical structures of all widths and sizes dotted the view.

Another wider entrance in the chain-link fence surrounding the property was to the east. Tanker trucks entered and exited through there. A rail line bordered one side next to the large round crude tanks that stored the oil pumped off the wagon cars. Next to the tank were the taller, often cylindrical structures of the crude oil distillation unit. Some had smokestacks that pumped out white steam clouds. Thankfully, the wind was often from the north and kept the unique hot plastic smell away from the bulk of Coal Haven's population. Other stacks were surrounded by metal piping and platforms.

The products coming out of this particular refinery were gas, diesel, and kerosene. More giant, round, squat tanks lined the edge of the processing unit for the finished products. The bulk of the tanker traffic came and went from there.

The wind ruffled my hair. Not many cars were left in the lot, but I reached mine and stopped. Daisy's small, yellow pickup was a couple spots away. Ever since I'd known her, she'd driven a yellow vehicle. In high school, it'd been her parents' Bug.

"I'm looking forward to finally getting my hands dirty again," I said. It was Friday, and Monday I would be in the actual lab.

"The first week is always the roughest. Boring office stuff."

"It's a lot of sitting." I rubbed my hands down my jeans. No amount of adjusting would make them comfortable. The dress code was nothing nice that still looked presentable. Clothing that could get ruined. I found a loose top that hid my unbuttoned jeans. I had an order of maternity clothing on the way. Hopefully, it would arrive soon. My zipper dug into my belly.

Daisy smiled. "Once you're done with all the computer learning, then you can come do more computer training."

I laughed, hating how true that was. I had onboarding for the refinery itself, learning about the layout and process of refining crude oil, safety measures and drills that would take place each year, and security. Once I got into the lab, the learning would drill down to my job, the safety measures, and security.

Daisy clutched her sunflower lunch bag to her chest. "Um, can I ask you something?"

"Hmm?"

"In our meeting on Monday, Raj mentioned that we should keep the extra duties we had. I understand that you'll have train-up time, but he talked about it for if you're gone. It didn't sound hypothetical, if that makes sense."

It did. I didn't want to get hired and then walk on eggshells because I had to tell my boss I'd need maternity leave shortly after I started. I made it clear in the interview. Not recommended, but I also didn't want to work for a place that wouldn't hire a woman because she was having a baby. "I'll need to go on maternity leave in five months."

Her eyes flared. "Violet! That's awesome."

I grinned. "Yeah?"

"Yeah. I mean, it is, right?"

Now that I was going to a job every day and learning the quirks of my new place, excitement started spiking at the most random times. After I had ordered maternity clothes, ads for baby products started showing up when I was looking for new bras.

I had a nursery to decorate. Baby equipment to buy. I needed to get in with a doctor in Coal Haven. I'd had an appointment in Billings shortly after I realized I was pregnant, but I wasn't driving all the way back for another.

My new life finally hit the ground running. "Unexpected but awesome." And tonight, I would get to see Evander. I was nervous, but one of my pregnancy cravings was seeing him. The run-in at Rattler's had only made my need worse. I should be upset with him. Wary. And I was. But I'd also get to hear his voice tonight.

"I'm happy for you. I can't wait to run across Lily and see her kids."

"Why don't you come over sometime? I can see what works for Lily."

"That'd be fun." Her brow furrowed, but she squared her shoulders. "Anytime."

She'd braved a personal question. I'd do the same. "Are you afraid of running into Alder?"

She turned sheepish. "Maybe a little."

"He did help me move, but normally he doesn't just pop in. He's very structured, and work is his life."

A smile ghosted over her lips. "That's new."

"Not new, but it definitely happened after you."

Regret passed through her eyes. "Seems like a lifetime ago. But yes, let's get together. Have a good weekend."

We said our goodbyes, and I drove home. The closer I got to town, the more active the butterflies in my stomach got. How would it go with Evander? Our last couple of conversations didn't make tonight promising.

All I wanted was an amicable relationship. But this kid couldn't pay for all the betrayal Evander hadn't dealt with.

No one was parked outside of my house when I pulled in. I hit the button for the detached garage. Nothing. I punched it again. Nothing.

I parked and got out. I let myself into the garage. There wasn't room for much more than a car. I jumped to grab the release rope so I could open the door manually. Then I hefted the big, old door up. God, I needed to do some strength training.

With an oomph, I lifted the panels above my head. I let go and stepped outside. A slow creak started. By the time I spun around, the door was sinking down and slammed against the ground. I jumped at the crash it made.

Okay then.

It was summer. I'd prefer to have the car under a shelter in case it hailed, but I'd park outside for now and let the landlord know.

It'd been a week, and I hadn't heard back from him about the sputtering water pipes.

I dialed his number anyway. He didn't answer—again. I left another message and threw in the mention of the pipes. And the crooked cabinet doors. Damn, I should've added the living room light. I had gone back to Hattie's store and bought a standing lamp. My little one didn't have enough juice for me to crochet to.

I checked the time. It was a quarter until six. Should I wait for Evander before I made dinner?

My stomach growled. My hunger had returned in full force since my life got back on track. I went inside and started dinner. I tossed in more pasta than normal. Evander might arrive while I was eating. I also added more sausage and paid extra attention to my homemade parmesan cream sauce with sun-dried tomatoes.

I dug out two plates and looked at the time. Six thirty. I paused, tapping my fingers on the dishes.

Wasn't he coming? Should I call him?

Was everything okay?

I rolled my eyes. He was an adult, and he'd probably resent my worry. I shoved the second plate back in the cabinet and swatted the door shut. Wood creaked, and the edge of the door fell even farther down. The hinge that wasn't working properly was no longer attached.

I'm happy to have a place to live. One that's all my own. I'm happy to have a place to live.

My mantra staved off the panic. By the time I finished eating and packed the leftovers away for lunch tomorrow, it was after seven. My phone buzzed. I dove for the table where I had left it.

Evander: Sorry I can't make it tonight. I'll call you later.

Oh.

I stood in the middle of the kitchen. My disappointment was strong enough to make my stomach roil.

He wasn't coming.

At least he'd let me know. After an hour of waiting. I scratched my forehead. What had happened? Did he change his mind? What if he decided—

I let out a growl. I didn't know, and I wouldn't if he didn't want to share it with me. I sent a message back. **Ok.**

I was doing my own thing tonight. Evander was doing his. My life was going in a different direction, one I liked. Evander was on his journey. If they didn't intersect, so be it.

⁂

Evander

I knocked on Violet's front door a full fifteen hours after I said I'd be there. A large shipping box rested on her front step beside the door.

How bad did I fuck up? I hadn't forgotten her last night. In the rush and the wait, I wasn't sure what to tell her. At least I had sent her some sort of notice. Over an hour late.

"Who is it?" she yelled from inside.

"Evander."

The door jiggled and jerked on the hinges. The dead bolt squeaked as soon as it was loose. The door popped open. Her hair was in a clip on top of her head, and she was makeup-free. She wore red basketball shorts and a baggy Denver T-shirt. Fucking beautiful.

"What the hell is wrong with this door?" I ran my finger inside the notch for the dead bolt. Little more than a few millimeters of wood kept the metal in place, and that wood was weathered. A solid shoulder to the door and the whole thing would be worthless.

Violet blinked at the assault of sunlight streaming past me. "Good morning. I'm well. How about you?"

In the text, it'd been cute when she did that. She was still sexy, but today, I let out a heavy exhale. "I'm shit. Sorry about last night."

She tilted her head, her gaze narrowing. She took in my more rumpled than normal appearance. I wore the same clothing as yesterday. She wouldn't know. Nor would she know that I was on my way into town from Bismarck.

"What happened?" she finally asked.

"Dad." My throat grew thick, and speaking got hard. I coughed, but my chest only tightened. "He had a heart attack last night."

Her eyes flew wide, and she opened the door all the way. "I'm so sorry. Come in. Is he okay? Have you eaten?"

Hunger was nowhere to be seen. "No, but I haven't eaten since lunch yesterday." I grabbed the package and carried it in. The main area was small and old, except for the carpet. I could see into part of the kitchen and view the worn linoleum floor from decades ago. Violet was heading in there.

"Let me heat up some food and tell me what happened." She stalled right before the kitchen. "If you want to."

I did want to. I'd never talked to a woman about my family, but the first person I wanted to call last night was Violet. During the long wait outside of surgery, it was her voice I had wanted to hear, but I wasn't sure if she wanted to hear mine. Our meeting was to be about the baby, not us.

I walked through the sparse, small living room. Was this the best rental Coal Haven had to offer? The sofa and recliner looked new, and that was about all that did in the house. The dark wood grain of the trim and floral wallpaper made the whole space dim, but the beige carpet fought against the shadows. The walls were still bare, and that was for the best. I wasn't into fashion, but even my mom couldn't find something that'd match the pattern on the walls.

The kitchen was worse.

She put a plate into a big microwave that still had a turn dial and hit the massive start button. The hum of the machine started and stopped. She repeated her process before giving up and digging out a kettle.

"Is the microwave broken?" I asked.

"Must be." She dumped a pasta dish into a pot on the stove.

"You don't have to make anything."

"Sit."

I did as she asked, too tired to look into the warmth filling my gut. The metal bars of the chair cut into my hips, and the seat was hard as hell. "Mom called at about four yesterday from the hospital in town. They were getting ready to transfer Dad to Bismarck."

"How's he doing?"

"Recovering. They did a bypass right away. Mom's... she's worried."

"I imagine," Violet murmured. She left the stove to pull out one of the two chairs she had. "Have either of you gotten any rest?"

I shook my head. "Mom didn't want to leave the hospital. She was fretting about chores. Liam swung by earlier, and I'll do the water runs this afternoon and take care of everything now until Dad recovers."

"I was going to see if everything was all right when you didn't show, but..." She dropped her gaze. "I figured it wasn't my business."

I struggled to form a reply, but I didn't know what to say. My dad was the grandfather to the baby, but we'd barely messaged each other. I had accused her of trying to deceive me.

"Don't ever worry about it. Ask away."

The corner of her mouth tipped up. "Okay." She popped up and returned to the pot to stir the contents inside.

This moment struck me as so natural my heart started aching. Chatting in the kitchen. Cooking. I could've had this, and I'd fucked it up. So much so that when I was absent, she didn't bother to check on me. In such a small amount of time, I'd scared her away.

In the army, if I wasn't where I was supposed to be, someone came hunting for my ass. I'd taken that feeling for granted. Was it gone for good?

"Kennedy's going to Bismarck today to check on

Mom," I said to keep talking, the question of how badly I fucked up kept at bay.

"Do you need to go to Bismarck too?"

"No. I'll take care of the ranch. I'm just relieved I don't have to go to another funeral." My brother's had been the worst. My dad's wouldn't be far behind.

She tipped her head while she stirred the food. "You've been to a lot."

My big mouth. I wiped a hand down my face and leaned forward, propping my elbows on my knees. "Honestly, no. I quit going." She was quietly watching me. Waiting. She wasn't demanding access to what I was thinking. She'd already proven she'd walk away. I stared at the faded linoleum floor. Some of the brown squares were nearly transparent. "Too many. I just couldn't keep doing it."

She padded over to me and stopped when her bare feet were level with the tips of my boots. She squatted down, and I was pinned with those big blue eyes. "I'm sorry. It's okay if you quit going to funerals. My mom always said they were for the people left behind, so if it's harder for you to go, you need to take care of yourself."

Her words eased a rusted knot in my chest. Each time I skipped out, the sense of failure grew stronger. "I wouldn't miss my dad's."

Her gaze softened. "I know you wouldn't. But it's not the thought of a funeral that's bothering you, is it?"

No. It was how our relationship would've ended on a toxic argument. Every family member I'd run into told me Dad had changed. I hadn't believed it, and I didn't care.

But maybe I did believe it. Maybe I did care. Maybe I was tired of avoiding home.

My throat was having troubles again. No words were getting past. I inhaled, and the smell of burning food teased my nostrils. "The stove."

She gasped and popped up. My gaze followed her chest as I went from an emotional wreck to a creep in an instant.

"Shit." She yanked the pot off the stove. "I think if I take off the top, you won't get a burned flavor." With as much surgical precision as the doctors used with Dad last night, she removed a portion of the pasta dish and slid the plate in front of me.

"I made extra last night. Just in case."

Guilt twined around my esophagus, but I took a bite. Not bad, and there was no charred tang to it. I gobbled the rest down. She set a banana in front of me. I ate that too. Next was a glass of cold milk. I gratefully took everything she offered. Nothing about this was for her. She was taking care of me because she was a decent person.

She had one for herself. "Milk seems to be my craving. And orange juice."

She took a big chug and licked off the white mustache left behind.

Milk shouldn't be this sexy.

I picked up my dishes. I could wash them. It was the least I could do. When I turned the faucet on, water splattered out of the nozzle. "Jesus."

"Yeah, the house is old."

The front door. The microwave. The plumbing. What else was busted? "It's almost a dump. This was the best option?"

"The other house was worse, and I couldn't bring myself to live in an apartment. All the buildings were square brick ones that aren't much more than a hotel room, only I'm doing all the housekeeping."

She'd had a nice place. My house. Which was her house. *Should* be her house.

The tendril of guilt grew bigger, its hold tighter. "I can bring my tools tomorrow and fix the front door."

She frowned. "What's wrong with the front door?" When I cocked a brow, she shrugged. "I know it's sticky."

"It's not sticky. It's shitty installation. And it's not safe."

"You don't have to. I doubt the landlord will repay you."

From her tone, the landlord wouldn't do much of anything. She'd only been in the place for what? A week? I wasn't waiting to see if the landlord would act on anything. I was the one who'd run her off a perfectly good house. "I know. It'll keep my mind off Dad."

Low blow using my family emergency to get her to let me help her. Violet's independent streak was wider than I anticipated. I finished washing my dishes with only half the flow of water that should be coming out of the old pipes.

When I turned, she was standing behind me, twisting her hands together. "You said you wanted to talk about the baby and what our arrangement would be."

No, she'd put words into my mouth, and I let her so I had a reason to stop by. But I nodded. I wasn't ready to leave, and without the paternity talk or my tools, there was no reason for me to be here. "Sure."

Tension tightened her mouth. "Okay. Let me go to the bathroom and then we'll talk. You can, uh, have a seat in the living room. Might be more comfortable."

Anything was more comfortable than those kitchen chairs.

I went to the couch and sank into the corner. The damn thing was softer than it looked, instantly cocooning half my body. The hinges of the bathroom door squeaked, and the door shut with a thump. It must not be straight on its hinges either. Like half the cupboard doors.

The house might have good bones, but the skin was peeling everywhere.

If I had my tools with me, I could fix a few things. I yanked the throw pillow out from the corner and nestled in farther. Stuffing it behind my shoulder, I rested my head on the cushion. The fatigue from the last twenty-four hours surrounded me, and I closed my eyes. Just for a second.

❈

Violet

I stared at myself in the dingy bathroom mirror. Did I really spend the last hour with Evander looking like a frumpy poodle?

Basketball shorts? These were an old pair of Alder's that he'd left when he'd helped me move, and I wasn't giving them back until my belly could no longer fit into them. But my white legs sticking out from the bottom weren't going on any lingerie posters in the near or far future.

I patted my hair down, but the curls bounced right back up. Full frizz had taken effect since I hadn't put product in my hair. I had thought I'd be catching up on reading and fixing a few things around the house today. I stuffed it back into the clip. Now I looked half wild.

Sniffing an armpit, I frowned. Ugh. I swiped on more deodorant just in case.

For good measure, I brushed my teeth again. Quietly. I'd be mortified if Evander heard me prepping in the bathroom. He'd made it clear we weren't a thing, but I didn't need to look like a not-so-hot mess around him.

The bathroom sink coughed out water. Droplets splattered my shirt.

This fucking house.

Panic started to seep in. I was fine. I had a roof over my head. A good job. It'd take a little longer to get a place that wasn't an ever-growing to-do list.

I was fine.

So was the man in my house. Hot but worried. His weariness hung over him, softening his usually hard edges, but he'd had quite a shock that wasn't helped by the unresolved conflict between him and his dad.

Today wasn't about me. We would talk about the baby, but I wouldn't push him to make any decisions. He wasn't in the right frame of mind.

Time to face the ruggedly hot man in my living room.

"Sorry about that." I was rubbing lotion into my hands when I rounded the wall separating the hallway from the living room.

Evander was slumped to the side, his head resting on a throw pillow. His breathing was deep and even. Those long, dark lashes of his brushed over his cheek.

I'd never seen him sleep. I'd seen him naked. I'd seen

him in the shower. But we hadn't slept together in the same room.

His strong arms rested limply on his lap, and his lips puffed open with each breath.

He was out cold.

I scratched the side of my neck. Should I wake him? He mentioned having to do some things at his parents' ranch this afternoon.

I checked my phone. It was only noon. He should nap a little longer, but it wasn't my decision. I also didn't need him to think I was sabotaging his life for whatever selfish reason he'd come up with.

I squatted in front of him. "Hey," I said softly.

He didn't move.

"Evander."

His right arm twitched.

I put a hand on his knee, close to one of his hands, and gently wiggled him. "Evander," I sang, not wanting to shout and give him a rough wake-up.

His bleary eyes creaked open, and his lips curved up. "Hey, my beautiful wildflower."

My heart crawled right onto my sleeves. Fully awake Evander never called me that. Half asleep Evander didn't have his guard up. What'd it mean?

That he wasn't awake. It meant nothing. "You fell asleep."

He inched his fingers toward mine. "I miss waking up to you."

"Uh..." I needed to put a stop to this, but instead, I did nothing as he threaded his fingers with mine.

"I miss being inside you."

A strangled sound left me. "I enjoyed it too."

"The way your ass pushed against me with each thrust."

"Evander."

He tugged me toward him.

I fell forward, and both my hands were on him now. This was not waking him up. This was not putting a stop to anything. "Ev—"

"I wanted to stay that night." His eyes were barely open, but I was pinned under his gaze, our faces inches apart. He shifted on the couch, lay on his side, bringing his boots up to the cushions, and cupped my cheek with his other hand. "That mouth consumes my thoughts."

I was a responsible adult. I had handled dangerous chemicals and ran analyzers that cost a million dollars. But I was helpless against a sleepy Evander who let his walls down.

Our lips touched, and I groaned.

He brought our connected hands to his crotch and flattened my palm over his unmistakable erection. He ground his hips against my touch, his zipper hard underneath my skin.

"I need to be inside you again, Vi."

I usually hated being called Vi, but both times Evander had done it, I let it go. Vi, in his deep growl, was different from how everyone else said it.

He deepened the kiss, and maybe I wasn't such a dunce for brushing my teeth.

He pulsed his hips against my hand, but alarm bells went off in my head. This wasn't right. He was distraught and tired. He wasn't thinking straight.

He'd never forgive me if I let this go further.

"Evander." I tried to pull away, but he slipped his hand behind my neck and held me right where he wanted me. His tongue plunged into my mouth, and oh, god. If I let this kiss go on, my brains would get scrambled. I wanted this. He did too. The timing sucked.

I yanked my hands off him and reared back. "We can't do this."

He blinked, his eyes losing focus.

A sinking pit opened in my stomach. He wasn't sleepy. He had still been sleeping. It was a dream. My hopes plummeted.

He sucked in a breath and held his hands away from him, frowning at them. Then he blinked hard like he was afraid his eyelids would stick if he didn't open them right away. He lifted his gaze to mine, his brow furrowed.

"You fell asleep," I explained. My pulse continued to jackhammer, but my face grew hot. Hello, embarrassment.

"Shit." He sat up, his feet hitting the carpet next to me. He rubbed his eyes, then skimmed his hands over his head. "Shit. I'm sorry." He looked down at himself, then to me.

"I think you were dreaming." I stood. My body hummed, missing his touch, greedy for him. If I were a guy, I'd have an erection to hide.

Evander discreetly pressed against his cargo pants. "I didn't mean to, uh...did I..."

"You were dreaming," I said again and spun away. "We can talk another day. There's time. You should probably get a nap in before you do the water run."

"Right. The cattle." He stood and tugged at his pants again. His erection was obvious, but he didn't seem to be hiding it. More like he was ordering it to behave. "Thanks for waking me."

"Sure."

I stuffed a toe into the carpet. How red were my cheeks?

The man was fully awake, and his guards were back in place. I was good for a wet dream. That was it.

He gripped the back of his neck, making his biceps flex. God, that was hot.

He glared at the front door. "I'll stop by tomorrow and fix that door."

"It's fine. It still closes and locks." It wasn't that I didn't want him to come by and give me eye candy when he did repairs. It was that I would look forward to it for the rest of today and tomorrow until he arrived again.

"Not good enough."

"You have a lot going on."

"It's not safe, Violet." What happened to *my beautiful wildflower*? And *you're carrying our kid. It's the least I can do*.

The cold splash of reality was unwelcome but needed. I already knew he only let me in when he was dreaming, but to be relegated to nothing but the mother of his child carried its own type of hurt. A pain I didn't want to inspect. Otherwise, I might admit how deep my feelings for Evander really went.

Chapter Fifteen

Evander

I was on the phone in Violet's front yard. I'd been at her house for two hours. The front door repair was taking longer than expected. I had to replace part of the frame to get a decent latch for the bolt. After two trips to the lumber yard and hardware store, I was finally ready to finish when Mom had called.

"You know I have it taken care of." I adjusted the cap on my head. The sun was beating down on me, but I didn't want to disturb Violet's day more than I had.

She was subdued when she'd answered the door and overall had been quiet. Not like before when she'd been staying with me. Was she feeling okay? Had my dream kiss upset her?

It'd been a good fucking dream, but I'd go back and kick myself awake if I had messed up things between us.

"I know," Mom said. "But I hate to put it all on you."

Whatever Dad had done on the ranch, he'd taught me to do. "I don't have kids."

"Yet," she said softly.

Yet. My lungs constricted. "So let me do it. Liam's got enough on his plate. I know he doesn't mind, but I'd be home picking my ass otherwise."

Her soft chuckle gusted over the line. "Don't let your dad overhear you swearing. It'll give him another coronary."

That was enough to get me to smile. Dad had always treated Mom with velvet gloves. They were very traditional, and growing up, that had chafed. I wanted to just be me with my mom, but my brother and I had to treat her like a matriarch. "I won't tell if you won't tell."

"The list is going to get long."

I grinned. She used to say that to me and Derek all the time when she busted us doing some crazy shit like racing —bareback, the four-wheelers, snowmobiles, pretty much anything that could be ridden. Or the time when she busted us thinking up new and unique ways to swear.

The pressure around my lungs grew, but I didn't shut the memories out this time. "Dad's doing okay?"

"Yes," she said, the tiredness returning to her voice. "His doctor said he might be here until the end of the week."

"He's going to bust out long before that." Dad had never sat still. The fact that he was scared the hell out of me. We had shit to settle between us, and I didn't want to do it with a gravestone.

"Not if I can help it," she said firmly.

"Tell him not to worry. I got everything covered. Unless that'll drive him battier. Then tell him Liam is doing everything."

"You know, I think he'll be more relaxed knowing it's you."

Nothing about me put Dad at ease. "Really?"

"He won't owe you. He likes having the boys help. Stetson and Holden are always happy to lend a hand. But it also makes him feel, oh, like he's failing. Aftereffects of growing up under Cameron. With you, it's just natural. You're his son."

I hadn't been around to help very much since I'd turned eighteen. When I had come home, I'd jump right back into chores. Some years, I had taken leave in July to help hay. Then, after Derek died, things changed. Home was quieter. Harder. Dad and I fought more. I had less tolerance for my aunt and uncle.

"I got it," I said. "If I need anything, I'll buy Liam a beer."

"Thank you, Evander." A long pause went by. "It's nice having you home."

Maybe I'll stay ran through my head. I didn't shove the idea away. My lease might be up in five months, but I'd take this junky rental so Violet could have the house.

Only she'd have to get married to move in.

Goddammit.

I didn't want my baby behind a flimsy lock. I didn't want anyone to have access to Violet. *I* didn't have access to Violet.

Mom disconnected the call, but I barely noticed.

Violet wasn't mine, but that dream yesterday had felt really fucking real. Her soft lips. Her hand in mine, pressing against—

I blew out a breath. I'd stroked off twice in the shower since then.

"Hey," Violet said through the screen door. "I'm going to make some tacos for supper. Want a couple?"

Since I hadn't eaten more than some toast since her pasta dish yesterday, fuck yes, I wanted tacos. "I don't want to put you out."

"You should've thought of that before you got me pregnant."

A smile tickled my lips. "I'll consider that next time." *Shit.*

If she read more into my comment, she didn't show it. "Super sperm," she muttered. "I'm having a craving for a shit ton of black olives, but I have to run to the store. Want anything else?"

You? "No, I'm good."

She pushed out the door. Today, she was back in her loose linen shorts. The basketball shorts were cute on her, but the ones she wore showed off more of her legs. Always appreciated. And her shirt was tighter.

Her boobs were bigger too.

"Be back in a few," she said and hopped into her car.

I was almost finished when she returned. She parked in front of the garage again.

A tiny niggle at the back of my brain fired up. I jogged to grab the groceries. "Why aren't you parking in the garage?"

"The opener doesn't work, and the door slams down. I think the whole contraption's busted."

It should stay up. I studied the old, heavy panels. The door wasn't safe. I put that on my list.

I brought the groceries inside and went back to my project. By the time my stomach was going to gnaw itself out of my body from the delicious smell, I had wrapped up my repairs.

Violet came out of the kitchen and inspected my handiwork. "That looks a lot sturdier."

My damn chest puffed out.

"You can grow pumpkins and fix doorframes." She smiled. "Dinner's ready."

I followed her like a puppy to the kitchen.

After we were seated at the table, our plates piled with food, I dug in. I had inhaled two soft-shelled tacos before she finished her first. Old army habits died hard.

"How are Flo and Poly?" she asked.

"Getting big. They like their morning scratches."

Her eyes danced. "You give them attention?"

"You set a precedent."

She laughed, and I soaked this moment in. I'd like more. We continued eating.

"How's the job?" I asked when I forced myself to quit at four tacos before I ate her out of house and home.

She finished chewing, her gaze thoughtful. "Nice. I work with Daisy. Remember I told you about her? Alder's ex-wife. She's fun. My boss is down to earth, and my coworkers..." Her lips curved. "They're quirky. It's awesome."

"How so?"

She built herself another taco. "One was talking about playing her didgeridoo. It's that long horn that goes to the ground."

"Like the cough drop commercial?"

"That's the one. She will also talk the entire lunch period about her roses. Then there's the one who makes his own wine. I've heard a lot about winemaking over the last two days when I was finally in the lab. It's not stuffy. I like it."

"Good."

"How's your dad?"

She'd asked when I first arrived, but she must've figured I'd been on the phone with my mom. "He'll be in the hospital for a few more days. Maybe until the end of the week. I told Mom not to worry. I'm here, so it doesn't matter how long he needs."

She considered me, then went back to her taco.

We hadn't discussed the baby yet. Nor had I mentioned how long I planned to stay in Coal Haven. The last she heard, I was leaving as soon as the pumpkins found a home. I needed to find out what she thought about it all. "About the baby...I want to be involved."

She nodded and continued to chew. Her expression remained impassive, but her shoulders were stiff. "Okay."

"I want..." A family. My heart seized. I had not thought those words since I'd been a young soldier who trusted the wrong person. "I want to be a good dad."

Her smile was encouraging. "You will be." She put her half-eaten taco down. "Where will you live?"

"Here." I wasn't leaving. The decision was easy. My family was in Coal Haven. All of them. "But I'll move out of the house."

"No." She shook her head. "Don't. Like I said, I'm not dancing to anyone else's tune. I'm not finding a guy to marry me for some stupid trust. I like the place, but this house is just fine."

I slid my gaze to the cupboard door hanging by a hinge.

A flush crept up her neck. "It's well-used, but it's safe."

The garage door said otherwise. Winter would be here soon enough, and I hadn't been away that long to forget how bitterly cold it got for a lot of months. Or how much snow we could get.

"Anyway," she rushed on, "it's good enough. I can look for a decent place, and after a few paychecks, I can talk with the bank about buying a new house."

The taco meat spoiled in my belly.

I wanted her in a better home. My stomach twisted even more at the thought of her buying her own place.

She pushed her plate away. "I should also mention that I have an ultrasound appointment in a month. Do you...want to come with?"

"Yes." I'd be there. She had asked, and that thought burrowed in right next to my heart. Her pleased expression cuddled in right next to it. "Don't you want the rest of that taco?"

She waved her hand. "My full switch turns on in an instant. I'm ravenous, and then there's no room."

I stored away the detail, hungry for any information she gave me about her and the baby. I snatched up the rest of her taco and shoved it in my mouth. There were no other leftovers. I owed her a meal. Two meals.

Would she let me repay her?

What if I didn't give her an option?

I'd figure it out. I pushed away from the table. "Let me go clean up. Then I'll fix that damn cupboard."

Violet

. . .

I waved bye to Daisy and pulled out of the parking lot at work.

On Monday, I had texted Evander to check on his dad. The updates were good, but his dad would still be in the hospital for at least a few more days. On Tuesday, Evander was the one who messaged me to ask if I was feeling okay. I told him I was. Even better since my maternity clothing had arrived. I didn't tell him that part.

Today, he didn't message. During each break and on every lunch break, I had tapped out a few different messages and deleted them all. I didn't want him to think I was after him and make things uncomfortable. I also didn't want to feel like I was chatting up a future love interest. I'd been there and had the impromptu shitty rental to show for it.

No. I'd been the one to chase Willis, thinking he was the ideal partner and that it was me who didn't measure up. If only I could be better. If only I was more worldly. If only my interests weren't so pedantic. Then I'd clung to Evander, convinced we had something. I was having his baby. It was predestined.

No more foolishness. I was an independent woman.

I had the door I didn't fix and the cabinet door I didn't repair to show for it. "Real independent, Violet."

My impatience to get home didn't rise the closer I got. Once the baby came, life would be lively. Right now, I was a little bored, not gonna lie. I was used to living with someone.

I might not be as lonely if there wasn't one specific man I wanted to be with. A man who seemed worried about the quality of the place I lived in and didn't wait around for the landlord. A guy who was handy with tools.

"Stay strong." My pep talks couldn't become a nightly thing. I couldn't talk myself off the ledge of wanting a man, needing him, after a couple of interactions where he showed no interest. Not when he was conscious, anyway.

I sighed and turned down the street that'd pass the elementary school before my house.

A large silver pickup sat in the front of my place. The garage door was open, and metal parts were scattered inside. Next to them was a ladder. All I could see were cowboy boots and cargo pants.

Evander was fixing my garage door opener?

He only needed to be strong enough to lift the door to get inside. The thing was probably light as a feather for him.

My conviction to stay strong, single, and abstinent wavered.

When had the abstinent trait snuck in?

My hormones were alive and well, and they were thrilled to see Evander.

I parked in the driveway. "What are you doing?"

He looked away from the motor of the opener long enough to sweep his hot gaze up and down my body. I was wearing my new maternity jeans and an empire waist top. Everyone at work probably guessed I was pregnant after Monday if word hadn't gotten to them otherwise.

I'd earned curious looks. Nothing like the heat in Evander's gaze. A primal possessiveness had flashed for a second and then was quashed. Did I imagine it?

He continued screwing something in. "It's a patch. The whole door needs to be replaced, but you can at least park inside now."

"Thank you."

His ball cap was on backward while he worked. The warmth from his perusal sank lower, stopping between my thighs.

Damn hormones. I was never this horny. At this rate, I'd take morning sickness all over again. I kept wanting to feel comforted, treasured, because he was here for me, but I was carrying his baby. Now that there were no doubts about paternity, he wanted to do the right thing. That was all.

"No problem." He grunted and shut the light cover. "I just have to program the remote, and then it'll be good to go."

He climbed down the ladder, and my ovaries quivered. I was already pregnant!

"I have something for you." He beckoned me after him.

I followed him to his pickup, curious at his neutral tone.

"I also owe you a couple of meals, so I've got one of Mom's casseroles to throw in the oven."

"You don't owe me—"

He pulled a cat carrier out of the bed of his pickup.

"Are those the cats?" I yelled as I practically elbowed him out of the way.

"They missed you."

I glanced up. His words while he was sleeping drifted through my head. *I miss waking up to you.* I ignored my sudden yearning. "I missed them."

I carried them to the stairs in front of the house and took them out. They'd grown since I'd last seen them. He'd been feeding them well. Both were purring before they were on my lap. I laughed, nuzzling into their warm bodies. When I glanced up at Evander, he wore a strained expression. His gaze jumped from me to the cats.

"Thank you," I said, struck by sudden shyness. He did this for me? The kittens had nothing to do with the house.

"I thought since I was coming..." He cleared his throat. "They sleep all afternoon anyway, so I figured they could nap while I worked."

Their little bodies were warm and fuzzy, and I couldn't get enough of them. "They're getting so big." I couldn't hold them curled in my palm anymore.

He held a hand out. "Wanna give me the house key, and I'll throw the food in the oven?"

That'd mean he was staying for dinner. He wasn't rushing off, knowing the baby was cared for. He could just be hungry.

He must've read something in my expression. He dropped his hand. "I can just leave the food too. You've probably had a long day."

I clutched Flo to me. If he left, he'd take the kittens. Yet it wasn't only the cats I'd miss once I was alone in the house again. "No." I dug through my purse. "No, you need to eat, and I'm sure it's a ton of food." I handed my keys over. "It's not an elk-based casserole, is it?"

Relief passed over his expression, and he smirked. "Plain old hamburger."

"I have lettuce and tomatoes left over from taco night. I can mix up a salad."

"If you insist on a well-rounded meal."

"It makes up for the bag of chips I had last night for dinner."

"Mom puts vegetables in her casseroles. Fair warning."

"Duly noted."

His grin was a quick flash but also a major triumph. And dangerous. The chemistry I felt around Evander was a fluke. An oddity. I'd never been so blatantly attracted to someone. I could write it off as my imagination. My hormones. Joking around with him? Liking him inside and out?

I should be grateful we were getting along. We were having a kid together. Instead, a small pool of worry trickled into my stomach. Would I spend our kid's life wishing I could have more than an amicable relationship with their dad?

Evander

Dad was supposed to be discharged yesterday, but his doctors had kept him another day. Almost a week and a half from when he'd had his heart attack, he was finally coming home.

I had arrived this morning and fed the dogs and cats, filled all the water tanks, and moved some hay bales in from the pastures where Dad preferred to store them until he needed them.

Liam had stopped in to see if I needed anything. My cousin was older, mellower, but I saw the wild kid he used to be when he grinned, and he seemed to do that a lot lately. He'd never been a messy guy, but his brown hair was neatly trimmed, and he was no longer a lanky teen. Just an inch or two shorter than me, his shoulders were just as wide. The contented gleam in his eyes was different too. Not only was he quick to grin, but he seemed to be all-around happy.

The pressure was back in my chest. Did I need a checkup? Was what happened to Dad hereditary?

Good thing Mom and Violet were feeding me more vegetables.

Liam put a hand on the bed of his pickup. "Let me know if you need anything. I have three twelves at the mine starting on Monday, but Stetson or Holden would be happy to swing by. Even Archer or Colt."

I was surrounded by family, but I'd hardly seen them. "Will do."

Liam took his ball cap off and pushed a hand through his hair. "I mean it. I know Bruce might need more time to heal. We're around."

I nodded. I didn't anticipate needing them for much. Dad had slowed down over the years. The work he did all day I could get done in half a day. "I didn't realize how much Stetson had taken over."

Liam's smile dimmed. "He could tell Bruce was moving slower and slower, but you know how your dad is. Wouldn't ask for help."

"I'm glad he had you. After Derek." The confession surprised me. It had been one of those observations I had never said out loud.

Liam shrugged and hooked a thumb in his pants pocket. "It was years after Derek, and I was the last one to see it coming." He grinned. "Except for maybe your dad and every other Barron in the county."

"In the world." I'd been in Iraq when Mom had casually mentioned Liam, Kennedy, and the kids had been over. It was like I'd been gone for generations.

He ran his lower lip through his teeth. "I always wondered how you took the news."

I mirrored the motion he'd made with his ball cap, only I had no hair to run my hand through. "I'll be honest, I'm still not sure how to take it."

"I'll be honest, me too." He squinted at the house. "He was never Uncle Bruce to me, but now he's like a father figure. Stetson's kids and my kids play together. I talk to Isla regularly. All of a sudden, I have siblings. Fuck, man. It's been a trip, but I guess we've all had our journey." He lifted his chin. "I, uh, hear you might be on one."

"What do you mean?" Small goddamn towns.

"I've pieced together some comments. Isla said Violet Duke was at your place last month, and now I see your truck outside of a house with one Violet Duke when I'm taking the kids to the park to play."

"We're..." Friends? After a couple more nights of fixing her cupboards and doors and eating dinner together, I'd say we were that. We weren't dating. Word would get out. Those maternity clothes looked cute as fuck on her, and since I was the only guy hanging around her, people would piece together the clues.

"I dropped off some lawn ornaments with Hattie," Liam continued, "and she told me the Dukes were back in town, and one really liked one of my end tables."

He might be fishing for information, but that wasn't a surprise. What got to me was that I wanted to tell him.

"We had a thing, and she's pregnant."

He whistled. "Whoa. Wasn't expecting that."

Mom hadn't told him either. She'd respected my

privacy. My appreciation for her grew. I'd taken her for granted my entire life, and I needed to stop.

"Congrats." He peered at me when I only nodded. "It's congrats, right?"

Liam had been like an annoying little brother when he hung out with Derek. No wonder the truth pushed to spill out. "Yeah, I think so. It's one of those things. She just got out of a long relationship and isn't interested in —that's a lie." I came from a family that put the blame on others. I wouldn't do it with Violet. "I'm an asshole, and I didn't trust that the baby was mine or that if it was, she wasn't trying to use me."

Liam's brows rose higher and higher until I finished talking. Then he chuckled. "You can take the Barron out of Coal Haven, but he's still a fucking Barron."

His hard dose of clarity was hard to swallow. "I got used before." I had faulted my family for how they behaved. There had always been justification. Then I'd done the same thing.

"I remember when Derek told me about that. It was fucked up. But I have to say, I'm glad I didn't inherit that gene or whatever the fuck it is to carry long-ass grudges. I'd think you were Cameron's son instead of Bruce's."

I coughed out my shock. "Shit, Liam. Tell me what you really think."

He grinned. "I think I had fun watching Stetson trip over himself trying to win Lyric over after he acted a lot like you."

"Stetson?" He'd been the grandkid who'd never done wrong.

Stetson was a big, jovial guy around others, but he'd been used to them doing everything he asked. Just because he was nicer about it than his dad didn't matter.

Liam nodded, still grinning. Was this all fucking funny to him? "He stepped in it so bad. Lyric still gives him shit. She moved out, and he scrambled after her. Finally cut his parents off. That's the main reason why Cameron's not such an asshole. Besides getting leukemia and having to rely on family to test themselves for bone marrow matches."

"He's doing a bone marrow transplant?" I hadn't kept up on Uncle Cameron. My parents had quit mentioning him the rare times we had talked.

He shook his head. "Not until he has to, but he can afford excellent treatment. My point is...a lot of your family has gotten over themselves. So if you really like this girl, it's not too late."

Violet was more than a girl. She was smart, caring, and funny. She acted like she didn't want a thing from me, and even more shocking, I believed her. It made the way I treated her even worse. "I don't know about that. Derek wouldn't have fucked up like I did."

I didn't know what made me say that. My brother was gone. I hardly talked to my dad. I was having a kid, and I didn't know the first thing about being present in a kid's life.

Liam gave another casual shrug. "Maybe, maybe not. He was just a guy too."

"He's the guy who would've been a better dad. Better partner. Better son."

"He was or would've been all that, no doubt. But part of the reason would've been because of you."

"How?"

He puffed out his chest like he was mimicking me. "'Get back inside and help Mom clean up dinner.'" He kept his voice at a low growl and adopted a mock glare.

"'Quit fucking around on that four-wheeler and change the oil in Mom's car.'"

Amusement danced around the grief that welled up when I thought of Derek. "That's not what I looked like or sounded like." It was spot-on.

Liam laughed. "You were his role model more than Bruce, but he was a whole lot more conflict-averse than you. In fact, this family didn't start to repair itself until our generation got a lot more comfortable with conflict."

"I got too comfortable with it."

"Can't be that bad if you're always at her place."

"It's a shithole, and I wish she was in something better." She had been in something better. With me. "I'm repairing everything I can."

He was quiet for a moment, his boot tapping in the gravel. "You like her, don't you?"

"Obviously. We're having a kid."

"No, I mean, she's the one."

Fire burned up my throat. I swallowed, but my trachea burned. *The one*. Had I protected myself from all the wrong women only to ruin things with the right one?

⁂

Evander

I sat on the edge of the couch. Dad was in his recliner, a blanket over his lap. His face was full of white scruff that got lost in the pale pallor of his skin.

He hugged a pillow to him, and when he coughed, his embrace tightened, and he winced.

"Goddammit." His voice was sandpaper rough. "I hate that."

"Mom said it should get better."

He smacked his lips. "As long as I'm sitting around, it won't."

"If you don't sit around like you're supposed to, you're going to be lying in the ground."

He chuckled and then grimaced. "I forget how blunt you are. I should be used to it after forty-some years."

"I got it from somewhere."

His eyelids drifted shut. The water upstairs was running. Mom was taking a long bath. I told her I'd stay with Dad while she got some rest.

"I didn't mean it," he said on a sigh.

"Mean what?"

"About Derek."

I scrubbed my hand over my scalp. First, the raw conversation with Liam this morning, and now this? I hadn't dwelled on feelings this much in years. If ever. "We don't need to talk about it." Dad didn't need to be stressed right now.

"We do. I almost..." He took a long, shallow breath. "Didn't have a chance to. I lived a long time fearing I'd hear the worst about you. I thought when I got the call... it'd be you. I didn't want it. Don't *ever* think that—and I know you do. It's just the shock. I had years to come to terms with the fact that you picked a career that could cost you your life. Derek sold fertilizer."

I pinched the bridge of my nose. I wasn't ready for this conversation, but I couldn't bite Dad's head off and storm out without taxing him. "Yeah. I get it."

"You don't. I was hurting. I was still trying to process the shock. It drove you away, and I turned everything on Liam. I'm not proud." He let his eyelids fall shut. "I'm not proud of me. But I'm proud of you. Always will be. And I'm pretty damn excited to be a grandpa to your kid. Be a shame if our stubbornness got in the way."

"I can't just forget everything else." I wanted to. I didn't want the hurt son inside me to affect my kid. My family was blunt to the point of being hurtful, but I wouldn't mend this fence with Dad by lying to him.

"I'm not asking you to." He tucked the blanket tighter around him. "I'll apologize until I'm blue in the face, but I know that won't move you. Just maybe don't expect the worst when I put my foot in my mouth."

This was the most open I'd ever seen Dad. He'd have never brought up conversations he'd regretted before. I was the one who'd thrown them in his face, then he'd get upset, we'd argue, and I'd leave. He really had changed. I could too. "Deal."

He cracked an eye open. "Yeah?"

"Yeah," I said gruffly. I crossed my arms and kicked my ankles out. Dad was tired, but I wasn't leaving the house until Mom had her bath and a nap.

He closed his eyes again. "Care to tell me what's really going on between you and Violet?"

Mom had probably caught him up, but since he'd extended an olive branch, I'd accept it. "We're fine. Friendly." I wanted to spit on that word.

"That it?"

"Yep."

He peeled another eye open. "You want more."

Didn't matter. "I ruined it."

"You're still here talking to me, and I wrecked a lot of the years."

"Violet has choices. She doesn't need me."

I had fucked up my chance. I could've offered to marry her to get her the house, and then I'd have a whole year to work on convincing her to stay married.

Would that still be an option?

"Even better," Dad said, gripping his pillow. "She might be more forgiving."

"I don't know about that, Dad. She's intent on doing this her own way. I'm not the only one with a bad relationship that changed me."

"Mm." His breathing was growing deeper. "Maybe tell her what you want instead of everything you don't. Just talk to her." His volume got lower with each word. A long exhale eked out of him, and a small snore escaped. "Or you might need more actions and fewer words. Isn't there a song about that? 'A Little Less Talk and A Lot More Action'?"

Could it be that simple? More importantly, was I willing to find out?

Chapter Sixteen

Violet

I paced in front of my house. A few weeks had passed since Evander had fixed the garage door. Since then, we've seen each other a couple of times a week. Since his dad was home and recovering, Evander had been spending more time at his parents' place, making sure his dad wasn't stressed or attempting to get back out to work when he should be recovering.

He'd text me pictures of the barn cats around his parents' place. More pictures of the kittens.

I had nothing to share with him. I worked and came home. Once, I had shot him a screenshot of a crocheted cat sweater, joking about how I was working on them next. He'd returned my message with a screenshot of a cat sweater with drumsticks. A chicken costume for a cat. I'd giggled all through work the next day.

Today was the ultrasound. My belly was a habitat for butterflies, acting like I was going on a hot date.

I had worked during the morning, trying to spare the paltry leave I had earned. My boss had let me adjust my hours. Moving had been the right decision. All my decisions had been good. They'd been mine.

Evander pulled up, a light dust coat on his pickup from all the gravel roads he'd been navigating back and forth from his place, his parents', and town. He hadn't complained. In fact, he seemed lighter, happier each time I saw him.

He got out and jogged around to the passenger door. He was in his normal cowboy boots, but he wore jeans today that molded over his thighs and pooled around the ankle. His green polo was new, too, and the sleeves were short enough that the dark tattoos around his biceps peeked out.

My belly quivered, and I pressed a hand to my stomach. I was used to the rumpled retired veteran. Evander was embracing his farming and ranching background. I was not prepared for the effect he had on me.

"Ready?" He opened the passenger door, giving me that heated up-and-down look I was starting to thrive on. My stomach was getting bigger and my shirt puffed out more, but when Evander turned that gaze on me, I felt like I was a lingerie model.

"Yes. Thanks for picking me up." I climbed in, and he shut the door, closing me in with his fresh linen scent. I inhaled deeply before he got in and caught me sniffing his pickup.

At the clinic, we were directed to the radiology waiting room right away. I pressed my palm to my abdomen, growing more nervous with each step. Evander put his hand on the small of my back as we maneuvered into the waiting room.

We sat next to each other. I grabbed a magazine from the end table. It had a grinning mom and baby on the front. I paged through it with Evander looking on.

I stopped at a staged nursery. "That window is bigger than any in my place."

"That crib is almost bigger than my bed."

I chuckled. My name was called, and I tossed the magazine down.

I was directed to lie on a small bed. The glow from the way he'd looked at me earlier dissipated when my pants were tugged down, my shirt pushed up, and my rounded belly was sticking up in the air.

Evander was in a chair beside me. Curiosity filled his face, but I caught his gaze, the corners of his eyes creasing, and he gave me a small smile. I returned it. This was it. When the tech squirted the warmed gel on me and then rested the wand on my belly, I held my breath.

"Did you want to find out the gender?" she asked.

"No." Wait. I'd asked Evander here, and he was the dad. I looked at him. "I guess we never talked about it." I had been juggling my work schedule and the butterflies I got when I thought of Evander.

"If you don't want to know, I don't want to know."

I studied him. If he had a preference, I couldn't tell. "All right. Let's get started." She clicked on the keyboard.

A squeak left me when the little image appeared on the screen mounted in front of us.

Evander's hand found mine, and I squeezed his fingers.

The room was silent except for the clicks the tech made as she took her measurements. I only peeled my eyes off the baby to peer at Evander. Wonder shimmered in his eyes, along with a stark yearning. A healthy dose of terror was also in his gaze. He'd almost had this once before, and it'd been taken away from him.

His fear scared me. Would he push me away again? He didn't look at me like I might steal the silver anymore, but we weren't under the same roof. Was he better at hiding it to keep the peace?

He met my gaze. The tenderness that formed in those amber eyes choked me up. "It's a baby," I said.

His eyes were full of awe. "It's a baby."

I inhaled a shaky breath. "I've been through morning sickness and tight clothes. I've had cravings and mood swings. But now it seems really real. I don't even have a crib," I whispered. "The spare room is empty, and it's the *worst* color of yellow."

"Just so happens, I can paint." He grinned.

"So can I," I said playfully.

He tipped his head toward the screen. "Not with that thing in your belly."

His protectiveness was in the same category as his handiness. Hot.

But also for the baby. I had to check myself. This appointment was about our child, not for me to fall for its father.

* * *

Evander

Violet studied the images as we walked out of the clinic. "A January baby. I guess it'll miss Christmas."

"Good timing." Damn. That didn't sound the best, but she didn't flinch.

My mind was whirling from today. Even when Kandi had been stringing me along, I hadn't been able to accompany her to appointments. She'd wanted money for clothing and baby supplies, but my presence hadn't been as critical.

The baby in these images was real. I was the dad. Violet had invited me along. I hadn't fucked up everything.

I opened the passenger door of my pickup for her. She crawled in, giving me an almost shy little smile. I jogged around the hood and loaded up.

Dr. Abdallah had been warm and welcoming, but we'd pretended we were a pair the entire time. Violet spoke in "we," and the doc had assumed we were a couple. Not two strangers having a baby together.

Only Violet didn't feel like a stranger. And I didn't want to drop her off and head home to process this afternoon all by myself. "Wanna grab a bite to eat?"

She glanced up and carefully folded the images into one neat bundle. "Oh, I don't have much at home, but I could—"

"My treat. Let's go to Rattler's."

"It's a Friday."

"Yeah." I pulled out of the parking lot. The restaurant was only a half mile away.

"You don't mind if the whole town thinks we're a thing?"

I didn't give a fuck if every single person in Coal Haven thought Violet was mine. "A lot of them have figured out we're having a baby together."

A slow smile spread across her face. "In that case, sure. I'd like that."

Then I could overwrite the fleeting moment when I saw Violet and before I recognized her brother. I'd wanted to smash the man's face in. The panic that she had intended to find a husband stayed with me.

Within minutes, we were seated in a booth at Rattler's. The place was still quiet, but more people continued to filter in. Violet took a sip of her water, and her gaze stroked over the wooden beams and exposed pipes arching above us.

She let out a small sigh.

Was she...nervous? Uncomfortable? We'd eaten together several times since she'd moved into the rental. Our chats usually revolved around work and family. Pumpkins. We'd just come from a major appointment about the baby, and the awkward silence was louder than the dishes getting cleared two booths down.

I filed through my memories. What kind of shit did parents talk about when they were expecting? I was in my forties. The last time I thought I was expecting, I was barely more than a dumb kid.

"What do you think of names?" I asked.

She worried that plump lower lip between her teeth. "Um...I haven't."

"Not at all?"

"It seemed so far away. I guess it's not." She wiped her hands on her thighs. Goddammit, she was nervous.

"Am I making you uncomfortable?"

"No?"

"Are you asking me?"

She let out a soft laugh. "It's not you. It's..." She gestured toward her stomach. "A baby. I don't even have a crib. The nursery should get a fresh coat of paint and have time to air out before the baby arrives. Then there's...god, I don't even know. Changing tables. Swings. I haven't had time to read or research. But I've crocheted two little cat sofas for Flo and Poly."

"They're done?"

She nodded, her shy smile almost embarrassed. "I can give them to you when you drop me off."

"The cats will love them." I leaned forward. "You don't need the whole nine months to learn everything. You're smart."

"Maybe I need to talk to Lily. None of my friends in California had kids." She wrinkled her nose. "That should've been a sign. Willis wouldn't even socialize with people who had a family."

I hated hearing his name, but that asshole had left her with a lot of things to work through. I'd be the guy she could do it with. "Not enough focus on him."

"How can you see that so fast? I lived with him and was clueless to how selfish he was."

"People like him know exactly how to string along someone to feed off their ego."

Sympathy welled in her blue eyes. "Kandi."

I waited for the hit of resentment at her name, but it was barely a ghost. "They sound a lot alike."

Her gaze softened. "And here we are."

"Here we are." I didn't care to be anywhere else.

For once, I didn't have to think about leaving in a year, two years, or three. I told her I'd be gone as soon as my lease was up, but I didn't see myself anywhere but with her.

"Names." She got a thoughtful look. "I don't know. I

guess since we didn't find out, we'll need both a boy and girl name."

"Is there anyone you want to name a girl after?"

"I'm relieved you don't have a plant name, and I won't feel pressured to continue the trend. Um..." She chewed the inside of her cheek and peered out the window. "It's not going to be Annie after my grandma. Not after that stupid trust."

"Fair enough. No naming the kid after grandparents who made trusts. Liam's got a son named Derek. I'm not interested in starting a new generation of beefs."

She laughed. "Also fair. Any other family?"

"Aunts and uncles, all out."

"Willow's a pretty name."

"I talked to my dad." Shit. That came out of nowhere. She mentioned my mom and the floodgates opened.

"How'd it go?" she asked softly.

"Good. He doesn't get a free pass, but I'm tired of fighting with him. When Mom called me from the hospital, all I could think about was our last conversation." Understanding filled her eyes, giving me courage to continue. "Maybe I can give him a break. For both of us."

"I noticed a change. In you. I thought it was the ranching. You went back to your roots and realized the goddamn pumpkins were fun to grow."

"Fuck, Violet. I do like growing them. Goddamn pumpkins. Can you believe it?"

She laughed, and I soaked it in.

There was something there. Between us. I wasn't giving up. The more I was around Violet, the more I was realizing that not only might she be worth the risk, but she might just be everything.

Chapter Seventeen

Violet

I pressed my hands against my stomach. Evander was painting the nursery. He'd asked me last night if he could paint today after he did chores. Then tomorrow, we'd go to Bismarck with his pickup and buy baby equipment.

I couldn't say no to this man. It was a miracle I wasn't wearing his ring in his house and counting down the days until I reached three hundred and sixty-five.

Why wasn't I?

I walked past the bedroom for the millionth time. He had the window wide open. All the windows in the house were, while the AC was pumping at full force. He'd tried to get me to spend the day at his house, where it was paint-fume-free.

Paint these days didn't smell that bad. And his house didn't have an Evander with a backward-facing baseball hat, paint-splattered cargo pants, and tattered boots. His shirt hung loose off his wide shoulders and pooled around his waist. Many times, I was close to seeing a glimpse of his rippled stomach with the dark ink trailing down his torso, but that damn shirt was too long.

I liked the look of him. I liked him. But I wasn't rushing into a relationship. He'd run me off barely over a month ago.

I also wasn't getting into a relationship with anyone until I knew I wasn't doing it for validation. Or because I was scared. Which I was. Each day, I worried my decrepit rental would burn down from the shady outlets and light fixtures that were wired who knew where. What if I woke up one day to no water? Every sputter sounded like the last. What if the water went out and I had a newborn?

I could call Evander.

There was the rub. I appreciated Evander. He was trying to undo his attitude from when he didn't trust me. That didn't mean he was sure about me. Getting together with him didn't mean I wasn't searching for someone to supply my dreams for me. I wasn't going to fall into that trap again. I'd get the life I wanted on my own terms.

Was I sure those terms didn't include a hot guy doing repairs around the house?

I backed into the doorway again, crossed my arms, and leaned against the frame. "I gave the landlord a list of all the repairs you've done. He gave me a hundred off rent this month. I can cut you a check."

Evander glanced over his shoulder before reaching high with the roller. My breath suspended. Would this be when I got to see more than abs?

"Keep it." He painted a strip from the border line he'd painted from the ceiling to the floor. His biceps mesmerized me. "Nothing more than a few screws."

Except for the garage door opener and the supplies

for the new dead bolt and doorframe repair. Evander wouldn't budge. He didn't like to feel like he owed anyone. After living with a guy who made sure I knew how much I owed him, I could respect that.

I lingered in the doorway. The way his ass filled out his pants should be a sin. A butt should not look that good going from jeans to cargo pants to nothing at all.

He turned and bent to dip his roller full of paint. More biceps flexing. The roll of the veins in his forearms under his skin. The man was restrained power. No wonder he was a machine in bed.

I feathered my fingers around my collarbone and lifted my gaze to his strong chin, admiring the way his lips made a manly pink bow. The wicked things he could do with that mouth. It'd been so long—

I caught him watching me, the paint roller hovering in the air, and his eyes narrowed on me.

Oops. I was lusting after my baby's daddy. Miss Independent, my ass.

"I need some water." I backed up so fast I smacked into the far wall. Damn these hormones. I scurried to the kitchen.

I found my water bottle on the counter where I left it and chugged it. Water sputtered from the bathroom. Did I make him uncomfortable? Was I left to paint the rest of the room?

I didn't think he'd leave me, but just in case, I scanned what I was wearing. I had on a loose blue maternity skirt with an equally loose blouse. I would have to change.

Evander stalked into the kitchen and pinned me against the counter. A thrill zinged through me, heading right between my legs. He planted a hand on either side of me. "Do you realize how you were looking at me?"

Like I wanted to strip him down again? "No?"

"Like I look at you."

"Oh."

He spoke his words plainly, but questions muddled my brain. Did he want me? He'd seen me in basketball shorts and an old T-shirt with my hair wild. He'd seen me vomit over the side of a railing.

Yet he'd kissed me since then. He'd dreamed about me.

I was having his baby. We'd already done the deed.

Still, I had to know for sure. "And how is that?"

He crowded closer, his pupils going wide. "Like I remember how you looked with your legs spread wide open."

A little whimper left me.

His head was next to mine, his nose buried in my hair. "Those needy little noises."

"It's been a long time."

"Just as long as me," he murmured.

Startling and acute relief washed through me, heightening the thrum in my veins and between my legs. I had never asked him, but I'd hoped I'd been the only one since that night.

He put his hands on my stomach. His long fingers were splayed over my belly. My body lit from head to toe, but a warm, fuzzy sensation also set in. He was closer to the baby than he'd ever been. I met his gaze, and he was watching me like he was waiting for my approval.

I gave him a little nod, and he flattened his hands. I knew what he felt. I did the same move at least twice a day. Firm. Sloping.

My chest rose and fell. Awe filled his face.

A line formed between his brows. "I want nothing

more right now than to take each piece of clothing off you and devour you on that old fucking table."

Oh. Wow. "The table is old."

His brow arched ever so slightly. "I won't if you don't want it."

I licked my lips, and he tracked the movement. I wanted him to do exactly as he said. My body was different, but just like that night at the motel, I didn't care how I looked. He was primed, ready to pounce at my word. Just like before.

It was intoxicating.

What happened to Miss Independent?

Couldn't she get laid? He hadn't been with anyone. I hadn't either. We each knew where we stood and our addresses were different. He wanted to have sex, and so did I. Did it have to be more complicated than that? "I mean, we've already done it."

He skimmed his hands over my shirt like he was mesmerized. A shiver traced over my skin. "It doesn't have to change anything. We're two adults. Fucking."

Fucking. Great minds think alike. Still, a small tendril of disappointment cooled my arousal. I was in the right place at the right time. Just like at the brewery. "Yes. Nothing needs to change."

He put his mouth close to my ear. "Except for the orgasms."

"It's not like I'm going to accidentally get pregnant."

"No." He tucked his hands under my shirt. Once he hit the material of the skirt, he tugged it down. "What about a condom?"

Oh. My pulse kicked up. No barriers. I'd be closer to him than ever while trying to maintain my emotional distance. I could do it. I'd make sure of it. The only other option would be for him to stop. "I've been tested."

"So have I. Before you."

"Then..." I gripped the hem of his shirt and lifted it over his head. A hard exhale left me. "Finally." I pawed at him. Unashamedly, I stroked my palms over the eagle, spanning from a hard pec down his side, then over his stomach. His abs clenched. I followed the trail of dark hair down to his waistband, then back up. His shoulders. His biceps. If part of his torso was in his reach, my hands were on his fevered skin.

"You're a greedy one, Vi."

"I usually hate when people call me Vi." I bit my lower lip. "I like it when you do."

Can you say "my beautiful wildflower" again?

He lifted my shirt over my head and set it on the counter next to his shirt. A groan left him when he cupped my breasts. Those had definitely changed since he'd last seen them. Instead of being a handful, they overflowed in his hands.

"Your tits are fucking amazing." He claimed my mouth as he reached around me and unhooked my bra. I didn't care where he put it.

Our tongues tangled, and I tried to twine myself around him. My body was different. I couldn't get close like before. As if sensing my struggle, he carefully lifted me by hooking my thighs from behind. Then we were moving. Where to, I also didn't care.

My ass hit the edge of something. The table. He leaned me back until I caught myself by bracing my hands behind me. My breasts hung free, and my maternity skirt was wedged below the swell of my belly.

His greedy gaze ate me up. "Fuck me." He buried his

head in my chest. Hands, his tongue, the scruff on his chin were everywhere. Squirming, I couldn't get enough.

Was this an impulsive thing like before? Would he realize that I was a better one-night stand, that I wasn't worth more than that?

He licked across my nipple, then lifted his head. "You're getting in that beautiful head of yours."

He'd been able to sense that before. We'd been just like this at the motel, and I had been stricken by a thought that I should be self-conscious. That I was taking too much for myself. He'd put me at ease then, one orgasm at a time.

"Is this a one-time thing?"

He traced a finger down my chest and over my stomach, his pupils wide. "It's however many times you want."

"In one night?"

His chuckle rumbled deep between us. "One night. Every night." He lifted his head, certainty in his eyes. "I'm not seeing anyone. Neither are you. You're having my baby."

"Might as well?" More disappointment sprinkled over my arousal. I'd known I was convenient, but having confirmation left the loneliness I'd been experiencing just a little bit emptier. My body was still lit up like a Christmas tree, so I'd shut that part of my brain off to get another night with him.

His jaw was clenched, but he nodded.

I nodded. More questions piled into my brain. And after the baby? How long do we keep doing this? What if he found someone else?

He worked his way down my neck, kissing and licking, and my head tipped back.

What was the question?

I no longer cared about the answer. The last time I lived in the moment, it cemented my decision to be on my own. And that was exactly what I needed now.

⁂

Evander

Violet went pliant in my hands. I knew the moment she shut that clever mind of hers off and gave in. She arched into me, heedless of the new curves on her body. Thank fuck.

Desire pounded through my veins, behind my temples, and in the erection that was finally free to rage around her. I'd show her how much she turned me on. I didn't drag her skirt off. Instead, I pushed the material up to reveal her creamy thighs and the soft pink fabric of her full-coverage panties.

Okay. So the underwear was a little more to fend with than the last time we were together. They'd gotten rolled down with the waistband of the skirt and all the material bunched under her stomach like a modern-day chastity belt.

Challenge accepted.

I slid the material down, careful not to tug or rip them. "The more you cover yourself, the more I want to unwrap you."

"I'm wearing normal clothes."

"Nothing looks normal on you." I slid her underwear

off and shoved it in a pocket to keep from dropping the garment on the floor. "You make it better."

Her lips parted, and her eyes took on an even more glazed effect. "How are you real?"

I wasn't the one haunting dreams. "I just tell it like it is." I hooked a chair with my foot and slid it behind me. My dick got pinched by my zipper, but I ignored the shot of pain. It only amped up my lust. "Now spread those pretty thighs and show me what I've been dreaming about for months."

Her eyes flared like she couldn't decide if I was serious. So I put a hand on each knee and gently shoved her legs apart.

"Evander."

I growled. "Say it again." Hearing her call me Evan had bothered me more than I thought. A girl like Violet wouldn't go home with the real me. She wouldn't move in. She wouldn't meet my parents.

But she had. Until I chased her away.

"Evander," she said, her gaze direct. Unflinching.

This woman had seen the worst in me. She witnessed the guy who didn't trust. The nearly estranged son. The asshole who didn't want to like living the life he'd been raised in as much as he did. Yet she was spread out on the table in her home. For me.

I took my time. We weren't limited to one night. I had all fucking day.

I kissed along her thigh, loving the way a shiver racked her body. Finally, I was at her sweet center, licking and sucking and wringing all those needy little noises from her. My body was tight, nearly painful with the arousal pumping through my veins, but my pleasure was happening right here. Seeing her. Hearing her. This was all mine.

She arched her back off the table and tipped her head back. I got an eyeful of baby belly, and something about that stroked the primal bastard inside me. That was my kid in her. *Mine.*

She was mine.

I just had to convince her. I'd start with the first orgasm.

She was growing taut, nearing her peak. I pushed a finger inside of her, and she hitched her knees higher. I could come from the fucking sight.

"Oh my god, Evander."

"You need this, don't you?"

"Yes." She was on her elbows, riding my hand. Her feet were on my shoulders, and her heels dug into my clavicle. There was nowhere else I wanted to be.

I circled her clit with my tongue. "How bad do you need it?"

"I need it," she panted.

Fuck. So did I. I was ready to explode, and so was she. The only problem was that I knew how tight that sweet pussy of her gripped me when she climaxed. I had to be a little fucking selfish, or I'd nut in my pants.

I rose, my finger still pumping in and out of her. She wriggled against me, seeking her finale.

"Soon, wildflower. I'm going to make you come long and hard."

I yanked my zipper down and wrestled my demanding cock free. There was no waiting. I pushed right into her, slowly to keep her from feeling any discomfort, filling her with everything I had. Her walls convulsed around me, hugging my dick so damn tight.

Every sensation was heightened. I'd fucked without protection once, and since then, I'd been covered each and every time. The squeeze of Violet on my bare skin was worth the wait.

I grunted, kicking my hips back and then forward. The slickness of her coated me even more. "Christ, Vi. You're fucking perfect."

She might think I was talking about her pussy, but I wasn't. Even her flaws were as adorable as those cat sofas she crocheted. When she allowed me into the house, into her, it was because she wanted me here. I just had to keep giving her reasons to want me around.

"Evander, I need you..." She rolled her hips. I hung off a precipice, waiting for her to finish. "I need you to make me come."

I'd do anything she wanted. She hooked her feet behind me and took everything I gave her. She was careening toward her peak, and I gritted my teeth, holding my orgasm back until she toppled off the edge.

"Oh my—" She stiffened, and her mouth dropped open. "Evander!"

There it was. I'd never tire of her calling my name like I meant everything to her. I dropped the gate damming my release, and I came. Hard. "Fuck. Violet."

A drop of fear trickled into my blood as that first jet of release shot into her. I bent over her until her stomach pushed into my abdomen. There was nothing to worry about. She was already pregnant. It was mine. And that was no longer terrifying.

Her walls rippled and milked my cock as we climaxed together.

She ran her hands over my head and down my shoulders. My pants had fallen to my ankles during all the thrusting. Good thing the house was old and the kitchen window was small and faced the garage.

I pulled out, missing her heat immediately. Then I helped her climb off the table and handed her underwear back. I yanked my pants up while she tugged her underwear in place and smoothed her skirt down.

She glanced behind her, her cheeks flushed, then she met my gaze and smiled sheepishly. "I guess I should clean the table off and make us some dinner."

Dinner could wait. I was still a starving man. "Grab a snack, wildflower. Because I'm not done with you."

Chapter Eighteen

Violet

Last night, Evander had taken me on my kitchen table. Then in my bed. And in the shower. He might've stayed over and done more, but my eyelids had been drooping when bedtime rolled around. So he'd tucked me in, finished painting, and this morning, he arrived with ham-and-cheese breakfast sandwiches from the gas station.

Now we were in a Bismarck department store, staring at baby items. My mind insisted on returning to the sexcapades. He was right here, and my pheromones were going wild. I was already pregnant, dammit. They could cool down enough to let me shop without distraction.

There was so much stuff. So many items I needed.

I propped my hands behind my hips. "Why is everything in such a big box?" My back was aching just looking at the size of the crib container. I skated my gaze to the stroller. Not as large. And it all had to be put together.

Acute gratitude cooled the hot panic rising. The

nursery had been painted within a day of mentioning it to Evander. Two days later, he'd probably have the crib put together. Weren't those notoriously hard?

Lily had done all this. Mostly by herself too. Sure, she'd lived with Mom and Dad when her son had been born after her divorce, but she'd been largely on her own.

In a way, her ex-husband and Willis weren't that different. They'd both isolated us. Her ex had shamed her into it, convincing her an adult woman shouldn't rely on her family. Willis had kept me isolated by being a pain in the ass about everything and making me think it was my fault.

Except for Evander's initial doubt, which had been valid, he didn't make me feel that way. I'd never had so much support. A girl could get used to that. A girl could also get hurt if that support was ever yanked away.

Evander studied the cribs, checking the details on the tag. "Which one do you want?"

The nursery was going in the rental, but he didn't want a say? This was his kid too. "I'm partial to white, but Lily says that with kids, she'd never buy anything white now."

"A baby can't make that much of a mess."

We both looked at each other with an unspoken, *can they?*

I giggled. "I'm as lost as you are. I was halfway across the country for most of my niece and nephew's lives."

"You like white? We'll get white."

My heart constricted on *we*. "What if—"

"Then I'll buy the walnut one." He tapped the crib next to the wooden one he stood in front of. "Or the mahogany."

Two cribs? Wasn't that—Oh. He'd need one if we

were shuttling our kid back and forth. "Okay. White. It'll lighten up that dark room."

He grunted as he toed the box. "The builder of that place spared every expense on windows. We'll come back for the crib after I find a flat cart."

That place. Not *my* place. I missed the natural light. And the neutral tones punctuated with pleasing grays, like how he'd decorated his house. Of the two of us, his rental was superior. "Okay, a stroller next. I think."

He took out his phone and tapped at the screen. "Did you want a changing table?" He spun around. The display was behind us.

I eyed his phone. Was that the Notes app? "Did you make a list?"

He flashed the screen toward me. "Made my own op orders."

Op orders? "Is this a mission?"

"An important one." He tucked his phone away. "Want the matching white changing table?"

I really did. And the glider rocker I saw at Hattie's that was plush with a footrest that looked softer than a bed. I wanted that end table with the acetylene molecule in the weld for the nursery too, even if it didn't match the white aesthetic. It had rounded edges. Good enough. Then there was the double dresser combo in Hattie's place, finished in the heathered tones. It'd balance the rest nicely and light up the room.

Even if I had some spare money and wasn't saving for a maternity leave when I didn't have enough leave to cover the wage gap, I wouldn't buy the quality pieces from Hattie's place. Department store furnishings in the old house didn't break my heart quite as much.

By the time we were done, Evander had tracked down an employee and secured a flat cart to haul the boxes on.

I mentally tallied everything as he'd stacked each piece. I pushed the cart with the smaller items—a diaper bag, starter packs of clothing, blankets, and onesies. All in neutral tones.

My limbs grew sluggish as we reached the counter. The rest of the retirement I'd been living on would take a hit. But I needed everything.

The cashier gushed about each item as she rang it up. She chattered to me and Evander. He didn't do more than nod once in a while. I fought my blood pressure as everything crept closer to four digits. Ouch. I should've stayed living with my parents after I left California.

Just as she took the portable scanner to the flat cart, Evander dug his wallet out.

I put a hand on his elbow. "Oh. No. You can't pay."

He arched a brow. "Why?"

"It's...not fair." He'd paid for the rental repairs he was not getting reimbursed for. He'd painted. He got the tab at Rattler's after our appointment. I rifled through my purse.

"Violet. I got it."

The cashier rambled off an absurd number. The same digits taunted me from the pay pad. A brick formed in my belly. So much money.

I was a big girl. I had a good job.

I had a few months of leave that I wouldn't get paid for.

Weakly, I retrieved my card.

Evander snaked a hand around my waist and put his mouth to my ear. My skin tingled, and a shiver traced down my spine.

"Put that card away," he said in a low growl, "or when we get home, I'm going to bend you over until your ass is nice and high in the air and spank it—with my dick."

A strangled sound left me, and my gaze flew to the aloof cashier. My cheeks grew hot. Did she hear? She smiled at us like she hadn't.

"Is that supposed to be a threat?" I whispered.

He banded his arm harder around me, and he tapped his card to the reader. "It's a promise, wildflower."

The relief was swift, but shame washed right behind it. I was a lot further ahead than a lot of single moms, but I shouldn't be nearing a panic attack about supplying my baby's needs. I'd had a good job for years.

I'd also had a shitty partner who liked to live extravagantly and insinuated that if I didn't keep up, it must be my hang-up and not his.

Evander placed a kiss at my hairline, then accepted the receipt from the cashier. The quick show of affection satisfied the longing of a young Violet in me. Evander was matter-of-fact, and he hadn't been putting on a show. He'd only meant to offer comfort and affection, and I soaked it up like a long, dry sponge.

God, I could get in so much trouble with this man.

I pushed the regular cart to his pickup. He loaded the big items like the boxes were full of feathers. I put the rest in the back seat of his truck and got in, blowing out a weary breath. So much stuff. I hadn't been ready for the final total, and it hadn't been like we were shopping at a luxury baby boutique. The furniture Evander had bought was nowhere near the quality Hattie sold in her store.

He remote started his pickup, so the air kicked on, then returned the flat cart.

After he got behind the wheel, he leaned on the

console. "Care to share why the thought of letting me buy everything made you look ready to run?"

No. I swallowed the sudden lump in my throat. I owed him something. His purchases surrounded me. "I'm taking the full three months of maternity leave. My boss encouraged me to, but the pay…"

Understanding filled his eyes. He worked his jaw as his gaze aimed out the window. "After the birth, you'll get child support, right? If it's not official by then, I'll still pay it. We'll start the paperwork."

Child support. Custody. Topics I didn't think I'd have to maneuver as a mom. Tears burned the backs of my eyes. I was living off him. I'd moved out so he didn't have the upper hand, so no one could make me feel small again. Only I needed him.

Did he see how pathetic I was?

"I'm an adult, Evander." My anger flared, quick and hot. He recoiled. None of this was his fault. It was all mine. "I have a graduate degree. My career is decent…and I almost died when I heard the amount I owed. I'm going to have a good job—that I'm not getting paid for—while I have a newborn. No leave. I'm using all my sick days. I'm in my thirties. Do you know how hard it's been not to move in with my parents?"

"It's not a sign of failure."

By every standard I'd been told all my adult life, it was. "You're already retired. I'm just starting. It's embarrassing. I'm the oldest sister, and I'm barely more than homeless with a baby on the way. In high school, I used to babysit people who now have investment portfolios worth more than I've made in my entire career. But no, I let Willis insist that we go to Bali after I paid off my loans." A trip I financed. Because he was in the prestigious field of academia that paid pennies while I worked for a private lab.

"You have me, Violet."

"I can't—"

"You can. I acted like a dick when you showed up, and I regret that. I had no idea what I almost lost by being a cranky bastard. But I'm here now. I'm by your side. We're partners." I didn't know what flickered across his expression, but he clenched his jaw. "In this. We're partners in parenthood. I like being able to care for you."

"That was your worst fear two months ago."

"And that changed. *You* changed it. I'm here, Violet. You're having my kid. I'm going to pay for everything. You need rent covered? I've got that too."

He was being generous because I was having his baby. There was the emptiness again. "I'm not using you."

"Maybe I want to be used."

Silence fell between us. My heart pounded hard enough that it might echo through the cab.

Maybe I want to be used.

What would that make me? Dependent. I was better than Evander's ex but it wasn't feeling like by much. I hadn't lied to him about being the father, and he had proof, but I was squeezing his hard-won retirement out of him. It wasn't supposed to be like this. I should've built myself a stronger foundation.

Stress clogged my vocal cords. "I'm just stressed. It's the hormones."

If he only knew those hormones were why he'd had me spread out on the table yesterday. They weren't why I couldn't be his charity case.

I had to stand on my own. His motivations were baby-related. One of us had to be clear-headed enough to see that our only connection was the kid. His feelings weren't about me but his obligation to his child.

His phone started vibrating, but he didn't move to answer it.

"You can get that."

His soft exhale was barely audible. He tore his gaze off me, and I was left with the heaviness that I'd disappointed him.

He dug his phone out. "Hey, Mom."

Her high voice came over the line, but I couldn't make out the words.

"I have some things to finish up, but I'll swing by later." Pause. "No, Mom. You can't let him. No, Liam doesn't need to either. I'm here. I can make sure the combine is ready to go. Tell Dad to sit his ass down, or I'll play hide the combine in all the Barron shops."

Her soft laugh was clear.

"All right? Good. I'll see you in a few hours." He hung up and kicked the pickup in gear. "I'll need to cut tonight short. Dad's getting anxious about harvest."

"Goddamn wheat?" I asked, grateful we could move on from the earlier conversation and the worries it magnified.

He chuckled. "More like corn, and there's plenty of time."

"He's feeling better then?"

"A lot. We don't argue when we're talking logistics."

"Good."

"I'll be back later this week to put the equipment together," he assured me.

"I can do some of it."

He shot me a warning glare. "That wasn't an empty threat in the checkout."

Heat spiked in my blood, and I gave him a sly grin. "We never established if it was a threat or a promise."

He wove through Bismarck and hit the interstate in the direction of Coal Haven. "I clearly stated it was a promise."

Evander

I finished up at my place and Mom and Dad's. It'd been two weeks since Violet and I started having sex. I'd never looked forward to seeing a woman before. Violet wasn't my girlfriend, but she had become an important part of my life. She always would have a pivotal role. She was on her own, and the need to contribute rode me hard when I was away from her. A few equipment breakdowns around my parents' place kept me from being able to assemble all the baby equipment we'd bought, but I had told Violet I would come over this weekend.

I pulled up in front of her house. A black pickup was in my usual spot. Did she have company? A work friend? She didn't want to be dependent on me, and I didn't want her to be. But seeing her move on, relegating me to nothing but the role of baby daddy, left an emptiness inside of me I didn't want to peer too hard at.

Violet flung the door open before I knocked. Her smile was falsely bright. "My parents are here."

The announcement was a direct hit to my gut. Wasn't I too old to meet the parents? Violet had talked about her family, but I'd kept them in a separate category. A "not in Coal Haven" classification that was out of sight and out of mind. I had my own family issues to worry about.

I scanned the living room behind her, ready for them to jump out and demand to know why I didn't treat their daughter better, but my gaze landed on the stroller. It was out of the box and assembled already. Damn.

Violet chewed her bottom lip. "And Dad's putting the crib together."

She said it as if she knew it was something I wanted to do. I'd ordered her not to touch it, citing that she didn't need to worry about it after a long day of work. But I'd been looking forward to it. My kid would sleep in something I sort of built, not just paid for.

A woman walked from the kitchen and headed toward the hallway, but she glanced over and veered toward us. "Violet. You have a visitor." Her smile was wide and familiar, like she already knew who I was and was grateful to see me. Her expression was matronly, a lot like my mom's, and just like when Mom greeted me so warmly, there was a beat of guilt. Would I let her down too?

Violet flashed me a smile full of apology. "Mom, this is Evander. Evander, this is my mom, Magnolia."

I was still on the stoop, but I extended my hand. I'd make damn sure I lived up to Magnolia Duke's—and my mother's—expectations of treating Violet well. "Nice to meet you, ma'am."

Magnolia chortled. "Oh my goodness. Don't ma'am me, please." She pumped my hand with the strength of a college linebacker. "We surprised Violet with a visit." She released me and leaned closer. "Gives my kids less of a chance to claim they're busy."

Pink dusted the tops of Violet's cheeks. "That won't be the case anymore."

Ah. The ex. He must've always had an excuse why the Dukes couldn't visit Violet.

Magnolia nudged her daughter and winked at me. "Maybe I'm warning Evander."

Violet choked. "Mom."

"Warning heeded, Mrs. Duke."

Magnolia rolled her eyes. "Mrs. Duke is Weston's mom, and she left behind a trust that's messing with my kids. Call me Magnolia, please." She waved her hands. "Come in, come in. It's not my house, but Violet's still obligated to listen to her mother."

Violet stepped out of the way, smiling fondly at her mom.

I adjusted the brim of my baseball hat. Violet was in a loose dress that summoned all kinds of memories of how easy it was to get to her when she wore that.

Thinking about flipping up that skirt would embarrass me in front of her mother, not to mention it was wildly inappropriate. Still, I couldn't help but put my hand on the small of Violet's back when I asked, "Does your dad need any help?"

Violet relaxed into my touch for a moment before she started toward the hallway. "I'm sure he wouldn't mind."

Magnolia stayed beside me. She was an inch or so shorter than her daughter, with the same wild curls, only hers were laced with gray. She wore some sort of sport sandals with her short pants, where Violet always wore dainty sandals. Violet claimed it was because she couldn't wear fun footwear in the lab, but now they were easier to put on around her growing belly.

"He does need help," Magnolia muttered. "Don't let

him tell you otherwise. He struggled to put the kids' cribs together all those years ago. We had three different cribs through all the kids. It got to where when Lily was born, I was tempted to go from a bassinet right to a twin bed just to avoid the headache."

Metal clattered from the bedroom. "Goddammit. Why aren't these instructions clear?" A deep voice raged.

Humor traced through me. Now that reminded me of my dad.

"Hey, Dad." Violet rounded the doorway. "Evander's here. Need a hand? He was planning to put the crib together today anyway."

I lingered behind Violet, awkward as fuck in the tiny hallway with a smirking Magnolia. She might seem aloof, but the woman's eyes were as sharp as her daughter's. She didn't miss a thing. I was being studied. My actions, my behavior, everything from how I dressed to how I spoke, especially in relation to her daughter.

Good thing this was the exact environment I'd had a career in for so long. Inspections had been a part of life.

Weston looked up from where he was crouched on the small nursery floor, surrounded by loose screws and the wide, rectangular sides of the crib. The small amount of light didn't lend much aid to the dim light fixture in the room, but the print on the instructions appeared to be a two-point font size from where I was standing.

He peered at me over a pair of reading glasses. "Evander Barron?" He rose, wincing as his knees popped. "Bruce's boy?"

He hobbled over, straightening further as he went. His shake was almost as hearty as his wife's.

"Yes, Bruce is my dad," I answered. He knew exactly who I was, could probably tell me when I was born, and had likely heard a few stories during his time working for my uncle Cameron about the trouble Stetson and I would get into. But I went along with it. "Nice to meet you."

He nodded like I'd passed some secret test just by introducing myself. Was Vasectomy Willis really that big of a douche? "You know what? I'm going to take the help. I can read contracts all day long, but apparently, I can't figure out the drop side of this damn crib."

Violet moved out of the way. I put a hand on her waist as I scooted past her, using any excuse to touch her. She exchanged another apologetic look, but I gave my head a slight shake. If I learned anything in my time in the army, it was to expect the unexpected and pivot.

"Are you hungry, Evander?" Magnolia asked. "West and I brought sandwiches, fruit, and cookies to make up for our intrusion."

My stomach threatened to growl, but I clenched it. "I'll eat whatever, whenever." Another benefit—consequence?—of my career. "Thank you."

A pleased smile graced Magnolia's face. She hooked an elbow through Violet's. "Come on, hon. You can put those feet up, and we'll let the guys work for a bit before I get the sandwiches ready. Tell me about work. How's Daisy doing?"

They disappeared, and I took a spot next to where Weston had been working. "Where we at?"

He sank to the floor and huffed his way through an explanation. I organized the hardware he'd scattered and started from the beginning. A half hour later, the crib was together and placed against the wall. In a handful of months, a baby would be sleeping in there. My baby.

I'd make sure it had everything, including family.

Putting the crib together with a grandpa was the first step.

Weston faced the crib and rimmed his hands around the waistband of his khaki shorts. I was in my usual cargo pants and boots. He looked ready for the golf course, and I looked ready to saw more lumber for another crib.

"We'll tackle the changing table after lunch," he said.

"Should go faster."

"I don't know. Have you seen how many drawers are on that thing?" He shook his head and scowled at the box with the image of a white, fully assembled changing table on it. "I wish she would've let Alder buy the set she admired in the furniture store."

"She had something else in mind?"

He nodded. "Yes, but you know Violet. She's going to do her own thing, and that doesn't include letting her brother buy her baby supplies."

She'd let me, but I hadn't given her much of a choice.

He faced me, and I stiffened, like I'd been called to attention for an officer. "I like how you're taking care of my daughter."

Humbled, I glanced from him and the door. "With respect, sir, I'm not doing much."

"You're letting her do her own thing. That says a lot."

"We're not..." He knew my role in Violet's life was limited, right? "We're not together."

A knowing gleam lit his eyes. "I understand. I don't know what you've heard about her ex—"

"Nothing good." I didn't mean to interrupt, but the urge to tear shit apart when that fucker was mentioned roared strong in my head. "He was a manipulative asshole."

Approval filled his expression. "You're making her life easier. I respect that."

"I didn't at first." I didn't know what he knew about me, but I wouldn't hide behind how I had acted to Violet. He was her father. I'd face his wrath.

"You mean when you let her stay with you until the paternity results came through?"

The back of my neck heated. Shit. He'd heard about that. "Yeah. She didn't have a choice."

"West?" Magnolia called from the kitchen. "Evander? Lunch is ready."

He clapped me on the shoulder. "We always have a choice." He waved his hand around the small, dim room. "Just like this house is a choice. Let's get some food before we tackle that changing table. I want to talk to you about meeting your parents."

Chapter Nineteen

Evander

It was a shitty thing to say that I should be grateful for Dad's heart attack. If we hadn't taken the first step of our reconciliation, I wouldn't be at their kitchen with Violet next to me and Weston and Magnolia across from us, witnessing the toxic way Dad and I interacted. Instead, Dad and I might be a little tentative around each other, but without the constant defensiveness rising like a tidal wave, we'd had some good chats. When he asked questions about the pumpkins, I'd just answer them instead of assuming he was being critical. Turned out Dad no longer brimmed with criticism. He'd changed in the last several years, and since his medical scare, I could finally accept it.

Though I might not have had to worry either way. Dad and Weston had been chatting nonstop since Violet's parents had walked through the door.

As soon as I called Mom and told her Weston's

request, she'd been thrilled, gushing about hosting and mulling over what she'd make.

I requested a simple beef dish. No elk.

Last night, I'd dug out my nicest pair of jeans to show I made a little effort. Violet was in another sundress, a cream one covered in wildflowers that made me want to run my hands up her legs all through the meal.

Dinner was over now. I listened to Dad tell Weston everything I was doing around the ranch and how I was getting ready for harvest, and *by the way, have you seen his pumpkin patch?*

Dad was bragging about me. Shock tried to convince me I'd entered a different timeline. How else would I be growing pumpkins that Dad gushed about?

We were going to look at the pumpkin patch after dinner. As if I didn't stare at them in wonder each morning. Ten acres of orange fucking dots, sitting in the field, waiting to be plucked. All because I didn't know what to do after retirement, and I didn't like hearing about my youngest cousin getting screwed over.

"Isla and Stetson have a big pumpkin-picking day planned," Dad said.

When had he heard that? I had discussed time frames and harvesting tactics earlier this week with Isla, but Dad hadn't ventured far into pumpkin territory since I'd started helping on the ranch. He'd had opinions, I chafed over them, and we fought. But he seemed invested, and pride rang from his voice.

"That sounds fun," Violet said with a smile, then she bit back her grin. "I'm sure you have such a good crop."

She hadn't seen it since she'd left. Since her parents had been at her place, I didn't have a chance to tell her either. "I talked with Isla this week," I said to her, uncaring of who heard. "She's lined up some giant crates and a few wagons."

"Will that be enough?" Dad asked. He folded his white napkin in half, then folded it again, like he was nervous.

"Probably not. I planted too many goddamn pumpkins."

Weston snorted, and Dad snickered. I chuckled with them, not at all self-conscious about my new endeavor. It gave me something to do, and I suspected Dad knew that.

"Evander always put a hundred and ten percent into a challenge," Mom said fondly, and I preened like I was goddamn fourteen.

My chest grew tight. "All I'm concerned about is getting Isla what she needs. The pumpkin patch will take as many as I want to donate, but they're not the big carving pumpkins." I glanced at Violet. "Want to come watch us pick some pumpkins?"

The corner of her mouth hitched up. "Can't I help harvest?"

"Not if you want my blood pressure to stay normal." She laughed, but her dad's words from yesterday ran through my head. "I'll give you ten minutes with no equipment moving to pick to your heart's desire."

Her blue eyes danced. "So generous. I can be the lemonade runner. September's aiming to be a hot month this year."

"Deal."

We exchanged a smile, and the silence sunk in. Violet cleared her throat and tucked her chin down.

"Anyway, we're loosely planning for two weeks from today." I took a huge pull of the glass of milk Mom poured me. I had asked her to have some for Violet. She didn't tell me she was still craving milk and orange juice, but her fridge was stocked with plenty.

"I'll pencil it into my busy schedule."

"Is anyone hungry for dessert?" Mom rose. "I made chocolate silk pie."

Violet let out a little groan next to me. "That's my favorite."

"Is it?" I avoided Weston's gaze. I'd asked him yesterday. Just in case the main meal reignited Violet's morning sickness.

Her hot gaze brushed the side of my face, but I started to clear plates. Mom would want fresh ones for the pie.

After dessert, Dad wanted to take Weston for a tour. Magnolia stayed inside with Mom after Mom had asked what kind of books she wrote. I had a feeling that before Magnolia and Weston left, Liam and Kennedy's kids would have lots of books ordered for them.

Violet and I lingered behind, letting our dads geek out about everything farming and ranching, which had turned into reminiscing about what had changed in Coal Haven since the Dukes had lived there.

"Was the meal okay?" I asked Violet. I clenched my right hand. Otherwise, I'd twine my fingers through hers. This was just a mutual meeting of the parents to make things easier and open communication after the baby was born.

Just because it felt like a significant step in a real relationship was only in my imagination.

She rubbed her belly. "It was really good." She narrowed her eyes at me. "How did Willow know chocolate silk pie was my favorite?"

I shrugged. "I have my sources."

She slid her gaze toward her dad. "You two chatted a bit while putting baby furniture together."

"It was mostly about which screw went with which hole, according to the directions."

She giggled. "I thought you had that part figured out." She spread her hands over her stomach.

I laughed, but I caught the hint of tension around her eyes. "You feeling okay?"

"Sometimes my skin feels too small. I'll probably need to order a few more maternity clothes. My pants are already getting tight for work." She bent to look at her knees. "And my belly is starting to hitch these dresses up pretty far."

"I'm not complaining."

She rolled her eyes, but the grin was a personal reward.

I called to Dad. "I'm going to show her the old car in the shop." There would be somewhere for her to sit inside. We could go in the house, but I hadn't had her to myself yet this weekend.

Our footsteps crunched as we walked across the drive. The shop door was half open from when I mowed the lawn this morning.

When we entered the shop, the air grew cooler. Violet rolled her neck. "I can't believe that my back is already bugging me from standing. I have three and a half months left."

"I'm not sure if I should tell you that Mom always said I was a big baby."

She groaned. "It might've been best not to know that. I shouldn't be surprised. Everything about you is big."

I coughed out a laugh.

"I didn't mean—" She shrugged. "It's true."

I took her hand. Any excuse to touch her. "Come on, wildflower. Let's find you somewhere to sit."

"You didn't want to go inside?" She walked toward the zero-turn mower. "I could sit here."

"It's dirty. We could've gone inside, but we haven't had a chance to talk all week. Over here." I led her to the back of the shop. The other side had a smaller door that was rarely opened. Dad would use it for his dad's old Cadillac. The Eldorado was a polished brown with chrome accents. The outside matched the inside. I pulled open the passenger door. "This is the cleanest spot in the shop. Dad keeps her running and mouse-free."

"I'll trust you on the mouse-free." She sat on the edge of the seat, smoothing her dress under her and scanning the brown leather and chrome interior. "Grandma Duke used to have a car like this. She was so proud of it. Grandpa bought it for her." A nostalgic smile tilted her lips.

I propped my hands on the open door, which opened the opposite direction than most modern cars, and the top of the frame. "Liam said Dad takes Mom for a spin. He drives ten miles an hour until he leaves the gravel."

She laughed and ran a hand over the wide dashboard. "He probably uses at least one gallon of gas to get to town."

"One gallon just to start the damn thing."

Her laugh chimed through the inside of the shop. "It was really nice seeing you and your dad so relaxed around each other. He's really proud of you."

"Yeah, I think he is."

She tilted her face up, her gaze expectant. "What did you want to talk about?"

I frowned, trying to think of what she meant. Right.

I'd used that as the excuse to squirrel her away. "Nothing. Thought a little one-on-one would be nice."

"Sorry about my parents—"

I leaned down and pressed my lips to hers. "Don't be. I'm glad I could meet them." I stayed bent over, our faces inches apart.

She feathered a hand across my shoulder. "I didn't think putting together a crib could be a bonding experience, but my dad seems to like you."

"He's just relieved I'm not that other asshole."

"You say it like you're also an asshole."

"I am."

She patted my cheek. "Not to me, soldier."

"I learned my lesson." I'd almost lost her, and I wasn't sure I'd get her back. Things between us were good. We had time, and I'd give her all she needed.

Her blue irises went liquid. "You can be really sweet when you want to be."

I crowded between her thighs, gently tipping her back. "What else can I be?" I smoothed my hands up her legs. Soft, warm skin slid underneath my palms.

"Bossy."

"Not bossy enough." Otherwise, she'd be in my bed every night. I pressed a kiss to her hairline and worked my way toward her mouth.

"Contemplative." Her lips moved against mine when she spoke.

"I have a lot to think about." She consumed my thoughts. I licked into her mouth and stole a long, greedy kiss.

She clutched my shirt, whether she wanted to or needed to in order to keep from tipping backward, I didn't know. I reached her underwear, and nothing else went through my head other than elation.

Finally. I had her to myself.

She tipped her head away to break the kiss and peered around me. "Can they see?"

"Even if they come inside, the loader's in the way." Part of what had kept me from Violet all week were the damn hydraulics on that thing.

She dropped her gaze to my crotch. The jeans I wore secured my erection a lot better than cargo pants, but also outlined the damn thing a whole lot clearer. "Can you make it fast?"

"Honey, it'll only take me a minute," I drawled.

She clawed at my fly. Taking her cue, I yanked down her underwear. I could put them anywhere in the car, but I shoved them in my back pocket. Within seconds, my erection was free.

As much as I wanted to shove into her and thrust away, I waited. I circled her clit with my thumb and pushed two fingers inside. Her moan was swallowed by the interior of the car.

"You're already fucking wet." I pumped in and out.

"I was hoping you'd do this."

Fuck. I wasn't going to keep her waiting. I withdrew my hand and notched myself at her entrance. She hitched her legs up, her sandals digging into my hips, but I didn't let that stop me.

Bracing my knees at the base of the seat, I thrust, coating myself. Once I was ready to pound into her, I held her steady with one arm and rubbed her swollen little clit with the other.

"You know how much I wanted this pussy all week?"

Her groan was my only answer.

My thrusts were too powerful. I'd lose my hold and face-plant right into the baby. I gripped the front seat, the concentration helping me last until she came. Her walls gripped me hard, and my thumb was fucking soaked. She was coming already, and wasn't that an ego stroke.

"Come hard, Violet. But don't let them hear you." She'd be mortified, and nothing could ruin this experience for her.

"I'm almost—" She gasped. "I can't believe how fast this—" She stiffened, and her legs were a few pounds of pressure away from splitting me in two. "Evander." Breathy pants filled the air as she tried to hold in the noise.

She was coming. Hot energy shot down my spine and through my cock. My hips kicked and bucked. She took it, holding on to my shoulder and the front seat, her hand next to mine.

"Fuck, Violet," I growled as quietly as I could. "Fuck."

I finally came to a stop. Our breaths mingled in the air.

A rock skittered outside.

Shit. I pulled out. Before I shoved my dick back in its cage, I gave her the underwear and helped her get them over her sandals.

A flush filled her cheeks and crept up her neck.

I couldn't stop my grin. I tipped her chin up. "You look freshly fucked, wildflower."

She playfully scowled at me as I tucked myself into my pants. "We can't go inside now," she whisper-yelled. "Thanks to you."

"I'd say sorry, but I enjoyed that too much." This evening had been damn near perfect. I had a good meal with my parents. Violet was there to see me act like a damn adult instead of a moody kid. And I got to have her in my arms, no matter how brief.

An almost shy smile graced her face. "It was fun, wasn't it? How many generations of Barrons have had sex in this back seat?"

I froze midzip. "Damn, I do not want to think about that."

She giggled and pushed me back. When she stood up, she straightened her dress and touched her cheeks. "We need to walk around. If they ask why I'm so red, I can say it's from the exercise and not be lying."

"Only if you promise to wear this dress to the pumpkin harvest. Remember, I have a shop too."

Chapter Twenty

Violet

Happiest day of our lives.

I had gotten another group text from Lacey. This one also included a picture of her and a beaming Willis on a beach. She wore a wispy wedding dress and was holding out a bouquet of white roses and lilies in one hand. Her other arm was curled around Willis. He was grinning and looking off to the side.

"Seeing if your friends approve, jackass." I deleted the message. The most recent one beyond that was from Evander. I pulled up the image he'd sent. A gorgeous pink-and-purple sunset. The sun hung close to the horizon, crowded by puffy clouds. Rays shot up through the clouds, making the pinks brighter.

The only thing better would have been to see it in person—with Evander.

I glanced out the window to the trees that blocked the sun when it was that low. One more strike against this house. A pickup pulled into the driveway. Lily and Eliot were picking me up.

I stepped outside and shut the door behind me. Lacey and Willis could do what they wanted. I no longer wanted to be a part of that life, and I was grateful I didn't marry him. It would've been the worst mistake of mine I'd ever made.

Lily bounded out of Eliot's pickup parked by the curb in front of my house and flew toward me.

"Oh my god, you're even more adorable than last time." She slowed right before she reached me and threw her arms around my neck.

Touched, I hugged her hard. "I never got to compliment you on how cute you looked pregnant."

She pulled back, a twinkle in her blue eyes. "You might have the chance to soon."

Excitement had me jumping up and down, but I had to stop and support my belly. "Oof. That's no longer a thing."

She laughed. "Not for your bladder. Come on." She grabbed my hand and towed me toward the truck. "No one knows yet. Just between us?"

Fuck Lacey's message. She could deal with the whining and the microcontrol tactics. I'd rather spend my time with a man who built me up instead of tore me down. A guy who gave the best orgasms and listened to me talk about work without the snide "in academia" comments. A baby daddy who sent me a gorgeous picture of the sunset.

Besides, if I had stayed in California, I would've missed out on times like this. "My lips are sealed."

"That's what he said." She snickered.

My niece, Cali, hung out the window. "Hey, Auntie

Violet."

"There's my favorite girl. You ready to pick some pumpkins?" I had cleared the extra guests with Evander. Since I wouldn't be an active part of the harvest, I could watch the kids. Eliot and Lily had been happy to help and probably more than a little curious about Evander.

"Yes!" Cali cheered.

Lily could show Eliot and the kids the property our grandparents used to own. Evander would only be in the house for another three months, and the new renter may not want us on the land.

A heaviness at the thought of Evander moving off the property lingered on my shoulders as I climbed into the back seat. Cali's booster was behind the driver's seat, and my nephew Kellan faced the rear of the back seat. He gave me a toothy smile and wave, kicking the little athletic shoes on his feet. His chubby cheeks lightened my mood.

Evander said he was staying in Coal Haven. His budget was likely better than mine. He'd find another spot. Would there be land for pumpkins? Maybe he didn't want to grow them again.

He didn't talk to me about his future, and I was afraid to ask. He'd said he was staying in Coal Haven, and he wanted to be a good dad. Did he know what he'd do, or was I just not a part of his future beyond the baby?

I was settling into a nice routine. My own routine that didn't revolve around meals at just the right place and saying the right thing around people I didn't care for. I could hang up my lab coat and come home. Work stayed at work. I didn't have to talk about the newest, most complicated fluorescent marker to impress Willis's PhD colleagues.

I had crocheted a throw blanket each for Cali and

Kellan. The current one I worked on was a corner-to-corner blanket for Alder for helping me move. All my siblings would eventually have their own.

First, I was working on one for Evander. A gunmetal-gray blanket that would match the furniture he had in his living room. Each time he came over, I hid it from him. I didn't know why. He'd set up the cat couches in the shed for Flo and Poly. He'd sent me a picture of them lying in one. A few skeins of yarn knotted together wasn't a promise ring, but making a blanket for a guy said more than we're just fuck buddies who happen to be having a baby.

I'd give Evander the blanket when I was done. What if it was too close to Christmas? What if he thought I was taking us too seriously and backed off?

Shouldn't I be relieved? Evander was becoming my co-parent. Nothing more. Eventually, he'd find someone he wanted a life with. Someone he trusted from the start. Someone he trusted with *our* kid. And he'd marry her so quickly it would make my head spin. She'd send pictures to everyone she knew to celebrate, even me.

Lily craned her head around. "How are you feeling?"

"A lot better than when I moved here."

"The house looks nice," Eliot said, his eyes on the road. "Well cared for."

Until you had to use the faucet. Two more cupboard hinges had popped out. "It's something. I think well loved is the term for something that's ready to fall apart."

"You'll find a better place when you're ready," Lily reassured me.

"Don't hesitate to give us a call," Eliot said, turning onto the highway. "Baby or not, you don't need to be moving by yourself."

"Also, don't hesitate to drag Alder away from the office," Lily said. "Especially if it's back to Coal Haven."

"He hasn't run across Daisy yet." If that happened, I didn't know if I'd ever get my brother to return. He never spoke about her, but the rest of us thought that was a sign in and of itself that he wasn't over the end of his marriage.

She'd moved on after him, and that had hurt. Seeing happy pictures of an ex, one that I was over, still burned. To know I wasn't worth the effort by myself...

I wasn't thinking about Alder's situation anymore.

When we arrived at Evander's, pickups lined the driveway. Some were parked in the grass alongside the gravel. The spot I used to park at in front of the garage was open.

I pointed. "You can just park there."

Adults and kids roamed by the fence line. Evander was jogging in from the field by the time I got out. His easy gait belied the power in his body. I knew firsthand how well he moved, how he used his strength for the utmost pleasure. A quiver traveled over my skin, but I ripped my attention off him before I started licking my lips.

Two tall, dark-haired men trotted behind Evander.

"Hey, hey," Eliot called to them as he swung Cali out of the pickup, and she giggled. "Did you bring Aggie out?"

One of the guy's grin was wide, as if the mere mention of Aggie was enough to brighten his entire day. He must be Aggie's husband, Ansen. "She might stop out later, but she got a call on a couple of donkeys for the rescue."

Evander introduced us. The two guys were his cousins Ansen and Archer.

Archer smiled at Cali. "Emmaline's here if you want to go play. Evander's letting all the kids pick as much as they want before we get started."

Cali looked at Lily first before she ran toward the fence where the adults watched or helped the kids pick pumpkins.

"It's a real family reunion," Ansen said. "At least for us cousins. First time we've all been together." He chuckled. "Archer and I only just met you this year."

Evander stuffed his hands in his pockets. No emotion showed on his face. "Better late than never."

"Good thing you didn't know what you were missing with our company." Archer flashed a grin.

"Dad!" a kid called from the field. All the guys but Evander turned their heads as if they'd been summoned. A young boy waved, and Archer trotted away.

Evander's attention was on me. I gave him a little smile, but I silently asked if he was okay. Wasn't this outside of his comfort zone? A yard full of family, and he was the host after he'd been away from them for decades? Would we ever be like this? Milling around a yard, laughing and talking. Would I be the single mom of the group?

"Glad you found your open parking spot," he said. "You wanna come see the harvest for a bit?"

"Sure." I had worn jeans today just in case. A dress had been tempting after the back seat of the Cadillac, but Evander's priority was the harvest. Then his relatives. I was last on his list. Besides, there'd be a lot more people milling around today. The old T-shirt I wore covered the maternity panel and made me look really pregnant.

His gaze brushed over my belly, affection filling his

eyes, then he tilted his head for me to follow. "I'll introduce you to everyone. Brace yourself."

"How many more relatives do I have to meet?" I had almost as many siblings as he had cousins, but with their spouses and kids, they far outnumbered the Dukes.

I had already met Isla and Stetson, but I was introduced to them again. Isla's husband, McCoy, was easy to pick out because he didn't look like a Barron in the face. Lyric waved from where she was helping a young girl juggle pumpkins. Neither Isla nor Stetson made mention of how I'd been in Evander's house claiming to be his landlord when I was really his baby mama.

Next, I met Evander's cousins from his aunt Kira, Holden, and his wife Emery. They pointed out all their kids, mentioned one, or was it two, was in college. Holden's sister, Nora, was there with her husband, who had the same welcoming personality as Evander. Where Nora was bright and bubbly, Colt dipped his head in greeting, and that was it. Evander and Colt probably got along quite well.

I officially met Liam and Kennedy. Teen boys who were twins and spitting images of Liam were helping the younger kids in the field.

"Wow. That's a lot of people," I said to Evander.

"Overwhelmed?"

I shook my head, watching Lily and Eliot follow Cali into the field. Eliot had Kellan on his shoulders. My nephew wore a small cowboy hat that was so fucking adorable, I could probably get baby fever again. "No. It's nice to see." I rested my arms on my stomach. "After my family and I learned about Lily and Eliot, we all gathered at her place for a picnic. She asked why we didn't do more of this. We're all so spread out. I realized that part of the reason was me. I rarely came home. It wasn't worth the fight." I inhaled and wiped those thoughts from my head. They were the beginning of the end of my relationship. "Maybe when I get a decent place, I can have everyone over."

Evander's expression flickered, but I couldn't catch the emotion in his eye. "Your plumbing would never survive all the guests."

I laughed, hating that it was true. "It's survived this long. I don't want to see what'll finally break it."

His eyes crinkled, and with the way the brim of his cap shaded his eyes, the twinkle felt like it was just for me. Butterflies took flight in my gut.

I had to be careful. Evander was in a new stage in his life. He had a renewed relationship with his family, a possible business, a kid on the way—all priorities that wouldn't be me.

Evander

I wielded my clippers with ruthless precision. Clip. Toss. Repeat. Stetson drove the tractor hooked to the wagon, but he only moved when everyone had cleared out of the way and did a head count. There was no room for error when it came to all the kids roaming around.

Kids. My place was filled with kids. Boys and girls wandered through the patch, reminding me of my cousins when they were younger. Mine would join them one day. If I kept growing goddamn pumpkins.

Liam picked next to me. Kennedy had taken their kids to the shop to see my mom and dad.

Isla blew a whistle. It was time to move the wagon. We'd just swapped out the buckets she'd procured. McCoy switched with Stetson behind the wheel, and we waited for everyone to drift away before we moved the tractor up.

Liam straightened and groaned. "Good god. A guy might think he's getting old doing this work all day."

"A guy might be right." I rolled my shoulders and stretched my arms over my head. Despite part of the summer being dry, I had a good crop. Next year, I'd have to implement an irrigation system.

Next year? I was getting ahead of myself.

"That same guy might be sucking on an ibuprofen bottle tonight. What are you going to do next year? Get a pumpkin picker but still throw a party?"

I'd fielded several of those questions but hadn't been able to give more than a noncommittal response. Isla had approached me about propagating the raspberries at the edge of the garden. Nora had approached me about a few acres to grow some potatoes. She had a large garden on her land—she'd shown me pictures—but she didn't have room to get a nice crop of potatoes. Stetson and Holden had asked how long I planned to rent or if Violet would allow me to buy the house. I didn't bother to consider purchasing the property. The opportunity wouldn't happen for years yet, and I'd deal with that when or if the time came.

I didn't tell them about the marriage trust. It wasn't

my family business. I mentioned her aunt Linda and how she had the ultimate say.

I took my gloves off and slapped them against my jeans. "Know any rentals with some land that'll let me plant?"

Liam rubbed his chin. "Bruce told me. About the trust. None for you, one for Derek. He let the others know too."

Surprise hit me hard. Dad kept my business more private than his. It was an unspoken appreciation I had for him. "Dad did?"

Liam nodded. "Stetson asked him one time why you didn't retire earlier and buy a beach house or something instead of getting sent to the desert."

I snorted. "I would've been too pigheaded to take the money anyway."

"It would've waited for you." He shook his head, his jaw hard. "Shit thing to do, but I know a guy who has land who won't require you to rent from him."

Dad. "I didn't think about asking him."

Liam gave me a questioning look. "You're actually considering making all this yours?"

I stuffed my hands back into my gloves, my gaze landing on the house. Violet was walking from the porch toward the shop with a bowl in her hands.

Liam let out a low whistle. "So it's like that. Everything working out? You talked to her?"

Violet and I were definitely in the more action stage. Not as much talking. She was here, so maybe we'd get to that point. "We're in a good place."

"That's all?"

"Nosy fucker."

His grin was shameless, and I laughed, relieved he

wasn't prodding deeper. Also happy just to be able to easily talk with him. Being with Liam was like having a small piece of my brother back.

"I'm just saying," he said. "You were pretty protective over that parking spot."

"We're having a baby together."

"That all?"

I wouldn't tell him we were doing more. Other than sex, was there more? "She's just..." The mom of my baby. The person I look forward to seeing the most. The woman I can't quit thinking about.

"That's what I thought. Maybe you need to tell her what 'she's just.'"

The tractor fired up. Any more talking would get swallowed by the rumble of the engine.

Violet was starting to mean a lot to me. I thought I'd ruined everything. She was still gun-shy of relationships. But adults talked, and she was always open to a discussion. Maybe it was time to figure out if I was "just" anything to her.

Chapter Twenty-One

Violet

"We're making good time," Lily said as I finished washing off the fruit. "And it helps that Evander gives zero fucks about whether we save every pumpkin. I think we could leave five acres and he wouldn't care."

I smiled as I cut cantaloupe away from the rind. "All the kids want to be outside. I'm almost obsolete. But at least I can help Willow get the food ready."

Willow and Bruce had arrived with a ton of food. Bruce wasn't allowed to canvass the field in the heat, so he'd brought his grill and found an old one in the shop. After some tinkering, he'd gotten it working.

Willow had set up tables and chairs. Happiness radiated from her like today was what she'd been dreaming of for years—a giant Barron family event.

"She looks like she's in her element. I can't believe she didn't ask anyone to contribute. I could've made Mom's cookie salad."

I groaned and dumped several chunks of melon into the bowl with the strawberries I'd already sliced. "Now you're going to have to make it. You incited a craving."

"What else have you been dying for?"

"Orange juice." Evander. "Milk."

She laughed and leaned against the back of the counter. "I heard Isla ask him about growing raspberries next year, and he said he didn't know where he'd be living. His lease is up soon."

A tendril of hurt wound around my heart. I cut more cantaloupe. "I told him he could stay. I don't care about the trust."

"Can I ask..." She tilted her head. We were the only ones in the house, but she was branching into a topic I didn't want anyone overhearing. "Why aren't you marrying him to get the land? He seems to like you."

"It's the baby." I thunked my knife steadily through the melon's flesh. My stomach twisted at the thought of Evander moving. "He would do it—he offered." Her gaze bored into me, but I couldn't look at her. It was never fun admitting that you weren't enough. "He's a good guy, and once he came around to the baby being his, he's been amazing. But in the end, it's for me because it's for the baby." I ducked my head down, wishing I could hide behind my hair, but I'd put it up in a claw clip.

She was frowning at me. "Do you really think that?"

"He has trust issues when it comes to women. I can't believe that he pivoted just like that for me."

"Why not?"

The two pictures appeared in my mind like they'd been summoned. The photos might be deleted off my phone, but they were clear as a bell. People changed their minds. Men who dragged their feet about marriage suddenly said *I do*. Evander could decide I was using him after all—for baby supplies or for handiwork. I wasn't, but I also wasn't in his head. "I just can't, Lily. First, he thought I baby-trapped him. Then he thought I was using him for...I don't know...healthcare? After that, Linda stopped over when I was staying with him, and she spilled the beans about the trust."

She gasped. "He didn't know before that? Oh no."

"Yep. He feels bad, but still. It's for the baby, and I'm grateful, but I can't fool myself."

She chewed the inside of her cheek. "I don't know, Violet. That man doesn't look at you like you're nothing but a baby factory. I mean, you two clearly had something, otherwise, there wouldn't be..." She fluttered her hands at my stomach.

I wanted to think we had something more than shared parenthood, but my practicality won. As much as it hurt, I'd tried to delude myself once before, and I'd wasted years of my life. "It was sex then, and it's sex now."

Her eyes flared wide, and her jaw dropped.

Oops. I hadn't meant to spill that detail.

"You two are sleeping together." Her voice pitched up like she heard the juiciest, most scandalous secret.

"Shh." I frantically looked around. Everyone knew that obviously Evander and I had sex five and a half months ago. I didn't need them to know we were still fucking. "I'm an easy option." My throat clenched around those words.

"Oh, Violet. You're more than that."

"I know. I just don't know if I am to Evander." I blinked back the heat of tears. "He only changed when he got the results."

Heavy footsteps sounded on the porch. I picked up my knife to continue cutting.

Lily squeezed my elbow. "I know you're just protecting yourself," she said softly. "But I wonder how you'd view this situation if it wasn't for that boring twat Willis."

Laughter sputtered out of me. "Lily!"

She shrugged, unrepentant. "I held back for years." When her gaze lit up, I knew exactly who had walked in. "How are my boys?"

"I think one of us is ready for a nap."

"Just one?" Lily joked.

Gah. They were too cute. Longing tugged hard at my soul. She never had to question him. Eliot's world revolved around my sister.

"I can lay him down for a nap," Lily said. "Unless Aunt Violet wants a little break?"

I took my chance to get away, to tuck my thoughts into the recesses of my mind.

As I carried Kellan to the extra bedroom where I had stayed when I was here, I could breathe easier. The heaviness of Lily's questions was left behind. I didn't have to make her understand. I knew where I stood. As long as I was true to myself, I'd be okay.

Chapter Twenty-Two

Evander

Everyone had left for the day. This morning, I would've never guessed how pleasant the bustle of activity was. All my cousins. Everyone got along. Hard work. Seeing my parents laugh with people they used to only fight with. And through it all, Violet had been here. I'd worried about how she was feeling and whether she'd been enjoying herself, but having her in my house assuaged many of those concerns.

Violet sat on the top step with Flo and Poly. Her serene expression knit itself in my chest. The woman drove me wild until I wanted to do nothing more than drive into her all day and night. Then she calmed me, filled me with a peace I had no clue existed. She smiled as she petted each cat.

They had gone into hiding for most of the day. They'd been frolicking in the pumpkin patch until more and more kids had arrived and taken an interest in the kittens. Eventually, the environment grew too unpredictable for the cats and they'd vanished, only to reappear again when the last pickup had driven away. I used to be like that when I'd been home on leave.

Violet had stayed behind, agreeing to let me drive her home. She came today, hung out with my family, and it seemed she wanted a little more time with me. All good signs. But were they enough? Did she feel enough for me to give me another chance?

Those crystal-blue eyes met mine as she petted the snoozing kitten in her arms. "You replaced the steps."

"I needed to make sure they were safe for pregnant ladies."

She smiled, but not all of it reached her eyes. Was she tired? "Did you have fun today?"

Yes. A ton. I'd felt like a kid again. Cousins everywhere. Laughter. The adults only stopping in to check on us. Aunt Kira had been by, and as soon as her eyes misted over when she took in the crowd, she'd left. The odd smile Uncle Cameron had worn the whole time, along with the wonder on Aunt Naomi's face, was nothing like my childhood. They hadn't stayed any longer than Aunt Kira. Then there was Uncle Allen, Archer and Ansen's dad. He'd been having as much fun as my dad. I'd never seen Dad grill for so long—or smile so wide.

Today was humbling. "It was a good day." I dropped to sit next to her. Poly ditched her lap for mine. "Weird though. There were so many people." Old pain turned fresh in my chest, if only for a heartbeat. "I kept thinking Derek would've had a blast, but I kind of feel like we only had today because of him. His death set off a chain of events."

She gripped my hand. Flo protested that the petting

stopped. "Things would've worked out somehow, when they were meant to. They're just different now."

"Yeah." If Violet wasn't here, I would've sat on that thought. I would've wondered how it would've been different if I had been home. It just was. "What about you?"

"I got to nap with my nephew and stay in the AC all day. Plus, I reaped the food rewards. I'm not complaining."

"Glad the guest room worked out again." I rubbed my hands together. I'd never been a chickenshit, but I was tempted to ditch the topic ramming around in my brain. If I didn't talk to her, then my stomach acid would eat me from the inside out. "Listen, uh, what do you think if I stay in this house?"

She blinked at me, then her gaze shuttered. "It's up to you."

"Not really. I'm asking for you."

"What about me?"

Was I mistaken? Or was I fooling myself that she could sleep with me for the last month yet want nothing to do with me beyond the role of baby daddy? "Us."

Her eyelids fluttered, and she clutched the cat closer. "Us?"

"Yeah. I mean, we've been doing okay together, right? And this place is supposed to be yours. So why not live here?" Breathing turned strained as I studied her bemused reaction.

"I need to be married."

I scratched at the back of my neck as discomfort writhed under my skin. This was what I got for avoiding relationships since my twenties. I was saying something wrong, but I didn't know what. I didn't know how to tell

Violet she meant a lot to me. "That would be a logical next step."

She drew back slightly, and Flo mewed at the disturbance. "In a lot of cases, but I told you that trust means nothing to me. This house means nothing."

A flicker of hesitation in the ocean depths of her eyes said differently. She was fond of this place. I was more than fond of her, and it was time to let her know. "It's not about the house."

Now she leaned closer. "It's not?"

I was on a precipice. Something whispered in my mind, *Don't fuck this up*. What I said next would be critical. "It's about us. And the baby. I have the guest room, and we could turn that into the nursery."

"Oh." She pursed her lips. "You're worried about the baby in my house."

"Not just that. I think we're good together."

"For the baby."

This conversation was going sideways, and I couldn't pinpoint why. She was smart, and I wasn't speaking in riddles. But I also wasn't being blunt enough. The one time I wasn't, and it was kicking me in the ass. "I like being with you."

The rigidity that had developed in the last few minutes softened. "Thank you. I'm glad we can get along, but I don't think we can make the decision about an 'us' when we're expecting a baby."

Betrayal swirled in my mind. Was she being purposely naive, or didn't she want a relationship? Violet was too smart not to know what I meant, but I kept trying. "There wouldn't be an us if there wasn't a baby."

Her sharp inhale didn't bode well. Fuck. What could I say? I told her I liked her. Hell, I thought about her all the time. I wanted to do up the nursery. I wanted her in bed with me. I wanted to wake up to her for once and not have to rush out of her bedroom because we weren't serious.

We couldn't get more serious than a fucking baby.

She hung out with my family all day. I hadn't even done that in my entire adult life.

"But I think you should stay in the house," she said. "I'm sure you'll want to own your place someday and not wait around for this property to be put up for sale. You should stay here until then or until this goes up for sale."

How the fuck did I respond to that? How the hell did I tell her that waiting around to see which came first, a "for sale" sign or her finding a fiancé, was a level of hell I didn't want to experience. After the last few minutes, she'd probably walk to town if I told her that.

"I guess we'll see," I said gruffly. "Wherever I'm at, the kid needs a room."

"Yeah," she said softly. "It'll need a room."

It. We'd barely talked about names. This unidentified baby was my only tether to a woman I could never forget. "How 'bout we call it Bud? Weird to keep calling it It."

"It is." She set the kitten down. "I should get back home. I had a nap earlier, but I'm tired."

She was avoiding eye contact, and her jaw was tight.

The foreboding in my gut grew.

She swallowed and studied her sandals. Her toes were painted a happy yellow. "I don't think it's a good idea for us to keep having sex. We should concentrate on parenting. Bud's coming soon."

Each word tore me apart. Talking. Actions. Nothing helped. In the end, the way I'd protected myself from repeating the past resulted in being alone.

Chapter Twenty-Three

Violet

I stared at the water heater that had to be from a different century. "Why did you have to start giving up now?"

A pipe creaked, and I jumped. I hated the basement. The musty smell was overpowering, and the lone light bulb in each room flickered. If a ghost appeared behind me, I'd apologize it was stuck in such a dank afterlife.

I scurried back upstairs before I could freak out more. At the top, I scrolled through my contacts and dialed my landlord. "Hi, Chad. It's Violet Duke. Hate to add to your list, but the water heater is dying. Can you take care of that before it's officially done for? Thanks. Bye."

After I hung up, I sighed. His list would be smaller if he actually fixed anything. In the two weeks since I'd last talked to Evander, the oven fan had gone out, and my bedroom window leaked during a rainstorm.

If the stovetop went, all I'd be left with was the new microwave I'd bought.

This was what I got for avoiding Evander. For texting him he didn't need to stop by last weekend. For replying to his message that no, I didn't need anything from Rattler's when he picked up his food.

I'd craved Rattler's Alfredo for six damn days because of that text.

I pushed a hand through my hair. I had meant to protect myself, but this felt a lot like punishment. One call. That was all it would take. One call and Evander would be over to fix everything. He'd probably arrive with a brand-new water heater in the back of his pickup.

There wouldn't be an us without a baby.

Why did that one line hurt so bad?

I didn't intend to baby-trap Evander, and I would not babytrap him.

I could also make it longer than two weeks without him before having a breakdown.

God, I missed him. I missed talking to him. I missed having sex.

I ran a hand over my stomach. The few moments after we came together when he held me were my favorite. Those windows of time where it was just us. In those minutes, I could delude myself that it could stretch on forever.

My phone rang, and I rushed to answer, hoping it was the landlord to tell me this was the weekend he was fixing all the shit breaking down in this money pit.

It was my sister Poppy. "Hi," I answered as if everything were rosy.

I'm fine. The baby's fine. The house was...shelter. My basic needs were met. But I'd look for another rental soon. Hopefully nothing more expensive. And better quality. My hopes dipped.

"Violet!" Poppy's excited voice came through the line. "Clover and I are coming up for the weekend. We're almost to town and want to kidnap you and Lily. Are you free?"

When wasn't I? "I'll have to clear my entirely packed schedule."

"You're being sarcastic," she chided, "but there was a time you would be so busy you could barely talk."

Thanks for the kick to the ego. "And you'll forever ask if I'm free to remind me of when I was needy and compliant."

"Yup." She had no shame.

"You'll thank us." Clover's tinny voice came over the line. "If another Willis pops into your life, we'll keep your memory fresh."

"We'll just run him off," Poppy added. "We're no longer scared of you."

I laughed. "You should be."

"You'd have to catch me, and I bet you can't right now."

I rested my arm on my growing stomach. "I'm not one of those moms doing marathons up until I give birth. When are you getting to town?" I grimaced and pressed my hand to my eye. "Um, the landlord is fixing a water heater issue. I'd love to entertain, but…"

"We'll come pick you up," Poppy said. "Then we'll go to Lily's. Eliot's taking the kids to the ranch today to give her some me time."

Gah. He was sweet. Evander would do something like that—

I could not romanticize the man. He was a good guy, and he cared deeply. He did the right thing. He'd keep doing the right thing for the baby. He might think he feels something for me, but he was confusing the sex for a real connection. I'd spent *years* with someone and fooled myself that it was real love. I wasn't letting someone else do it.

"But first, we're taking you out to eat."

"Sounds good." I hung up, but the smile on my face faded. The sister time would be nice, but it was also fleeting. When Poppy and Clover left town, I'd return home to my lukewarm water alone.

Each day, it got harder to stick to my convictions. I missed Evander. I missed his updates about his parents and how each time he spoke about them, he was lighter and happier. I missed sitting at that table with him. Casual. He didn't need to put on appearances or use me to boost his self-importance.

I hated this, but I'd thank myself in the end. When we were co-parenting and I was being a good example to my kid. I rubbed a hand over my stomach. *Don't let anyone diminish you, Bud. Don't let anyone decide your path because it suits them. Don't settle for less than real love.*

Too bad—that was what I wanted the most with Evander Barron.

***

Evander

"When is the next appointment?" Mom neatly folded her napkin. Her plate was empty, and the dinner crowd was starting to filter in at Rattler's.

"Couple weeks," I said. I finished my burger and fries, but my appetite had been shit since I dropped Violet off at home for the last time.

"And you're going?"

I nodded and folded my elbows on the table. She'd at least agreed to that. She hadn't been letting me do anything else for her. I had fucked up. I'd moved too fast. It'd taken me over two decades to get over the betrayal in my past, and I had thought my dick had cured her.

Still, I missed her and couldn't wait to see her again.

Dad was next to me in the booth, still eating because he'd chatted with at least three buddies since we'd entered. We'd had to wait twenty minutes to order because he'd been in the entry with another rancher from Crocus Valley. The side salad Mom had made him order instead of his usual smothered baked potato sat untouched beside his plate.

He tucked a cleaned rib bone next to the others and picked up the last one. "You still not seeing much of Violet these days?"

Thankfully, the growing crowd was getting louder. Dad's rough voice got lost in the din.

"No. She hasn't needed me." The sour taste of that statement chased away the savory flavor of the burger lingering on my tongue.

He gave me a sidelong look. "You can still...talk."

"She doesn't want me to get the wrong idea." Look at me telling my parents the truth about my lack of a love life instead of evading it. "She even wants me to keep renting the house until it goes for sale."

Confusion lined Mom's brow. "I'm trying to remember...when would that be?"

"If she doesn't marry, I don't know, six years?"

Dad paused from chewing on his bone and swallowed. "That's a lot of rent money. But it's your decision," he rushed to tack on.

I couldn't even chuckle at the way he tried to make sure he was doing nothing more than making idle conversation. Six damn years. I had no idea what things would be like between me and Violet by then. Six years of this would be...fuck. "Yep."

"But you don't want to?" Mom asked.

I didn't want the house. I wanted her. I'd give her more time, but what did I do until then? "I dunno. Kinda seems like kismet for Bud to have some connection to one of the houses in a town its mom grew up in."

Both of my parents nodded. If I wasn't miserable over Violet's rejection, I'd appreciate how far I'd come with Mom and Dad in the last few months.

"Well," Mom said, running her hands over her already folded and flat napkin, "you can stay in the house and keep trying to win her over."

"Who says I want to—" Yeah, I couldn't even pretend. "I really like her, but she doesn't feel the same." I clenched my teeth together. Fucking hurt to say.

Mom considered me. "Did you tell her that?"

"I told her I liked being with her."

Dad lifted a shoulder but kept polishing off his last rib. "Was that it?"

"What else should I say? If she's not into me, she's not into me."

"The baby suggests otherwise," Dad muttered.

"That was the one time." Except for all those other times she shuddered underneath me, calling my name. I couldn't win her with sex if she didn't invite me over.

"She was hurt before? Like you?" Mom asked.

"A little different, but yeah," I answered.

"Then give her time. Be there for her. Show her that you aren't that guy, just like she showed you that she's not those other women."

Hopelessness churned inside of me. It'd been months. I was being me. She didn't want me. When did I push the line of being creepy versus persistent? When did I move on?

The young hostess walked past us, her hands full of the large, laminated Rattler's menus. Two giggly women followed her, pointing at the fake snake curled in a corner of the beams. Dad said it'd been there for years. The kids loved it.

Lily was behind them, and next to her was Violet. Dark circles ringed under her eyes. Hadn't she been sleeping well? Was she feeling okay? Otherwise, she was still the most beautiful damn woman I'd ever seen. Something about her drew me into her orbit, just like that first night I met her.

Her eyes flared, and she slowed. "Evander."

Lily stopped and smiled. "Oh, hey."

The lightness to her expression must mean Violet didn't tell her sister she'd cut me off. Lily probably didn't know just how close we'd gotten. Violet might not talk about me. My heart twisted.

"Thanks again for letting us come over." Lily switched her attention to Dad. "Eliot's still gushing about your food. He's usually in charge of the grill, and I spent half the day afraid he'd push you out of the way."

Dad wiped his fingers, delighted to have found another person to chat with. "Any time he wants to jump in. An old dog can always learn new tricks."

Lily chuckled. "His tricks are pretty old dog too."

The other two women circled back, looking from us to Lily and Violet. I kept my attention on Violet. It felt like months since I'd seen her. My fingers itched to twine with hers.

"It's so nice to see you again, Violet," Mom said warmly, buying me more time.

"Nice to see you." Violet smiled at her. She adopted a neutral expression when she switched her gaze to me. "Evander, you get to meet more of my family. This is Poppy." She gestured to one of the women. They looked really similar. Both brunettes with light hazel eyes. She switched to the other woman. "And Clover. My other two sisters."

"Evander?" Poppy said, pushing closer and inspecting me.

I was crowded against the window, but I extended my hand, giving them each a brief shake. When the introductions with my parents were done, the sisters scrutinized me. I might be sitting, but they sized me up from head to toe.

"Nice to meet you," Clover said in a tone that meant it remained to be seen.

I dipped my head and shifted my attention to Violet. "How's it going?"

"Good," she said in a falsely light voice.

I narrowed my gaze. Did her sisters buy that? Or did they know what was wrong and it was none of my business? Unless I was what was wrong.

"Poppy and Clover took a week of vacation to visit all their siblings," Violet explained. "Lily and I get to hang with them for the weekend."

"Then we're going to Buffalo Gully to nag Jasper—have you met him yet?" Poppy asked.

"No. Not yet."

"Probably for the best," Clover said. "He'll put you to work. He takes his ranch manager job seriously."

"If he ever needs a hand, I'm sure I can be spared around here," I said.

Poppy and Clover blinked at me. Didn't they believe me? Shouldn't I have offered?

Lily grinned like she was in on some secret.

Poppy glanced behind her. "The poor girl is just waiting for us like she's stranded on an island."

The hostess with a deer-in-the-headlights expression lingered by a booth.

Clover waved. "I'll go save her. Nice to meet you."

Poppy faced me squarely. "Nice to meet you. It answered a lot of questions."

What'd that mean?

"Nice to see you guys again." Lily touched Violet's elbow. "Take your time." And she was off.

Violet adopted a look similar to the hostess.

"Must be so nice to have them in town." Mom saved us from an awkward silence.

This time, Violet's smile was genuine. "Yes. It really is. We never got to do this much."

"Because you lived in California?" Mom asked.

Violet's features grew pinched. "Yes. Because I lived so far away." She pointed behind her. "I really should—"

"Don't worry about it." I meant it. She needed time with her family, and I would not be the jackass holding it up, as much as I wanted to keep her talking. "I'll see you in a couple of weeks."

Her shoulders fell. "The appointment, yes. I'll let you know if it changes." With that awkward smile, she hesitated, then joined her sisters.

Dad pushed his plate to the edge. "Welp. That's going to be a tough wall to climb. Good thing you've spent over twenty years learning how to get past defenses."

⁂

Violet

"Quit staring at him," I hissed to my sisters as they kept glancing in the direction of Evander's booth.

Poppy craned her neck to see better. "They're walking out. His back is to us." She twisted back to face me. "That ass alone makes him a far better specimen than Willis."

I gave her a flat stare, but I one-hundred-percent agreed. Lily snickered.

Clover grinned. "Come on. That's the same upgrade Lily made going from Carter to Eliot."

"Carter and Willis were a lot alike," Lily agreed. "And Eliot and Evander have that swagger."

Evander stalked, he didn't swagger. "I'm not denying that Evander is hotter in every way."

"I figured he had to be," Poppy said. "I thought he must be smokin' to get Violet to have a one-night stand."

My jaw dropped, but indignation had nowhere to go. She was correct. "He's also really considerate. He helped Dad put the nursery together." And he'd fixed so many things in the house. He'd held a pumpkin-picking party.

Clover looked up from her menu. "So why weren't you in that booth on his lap?"

As much as I hated reliving the last real conversation

between me and Evander, I was grateful to unload on my sisters. I started at the beginning in the brewery and ended that day on the porch steps with kittens as witnesses. They listened, concern and confusion filling their gaze. Once the whole story was spilled, there was no confidence. No reassurance I was doing the right thing after hearing it all out loud.

"But you don't know that he's in it only for...Bud," Clover said. "Bud's not really a neutral name."

"Better than It. Bud isn't a psycho clown." I shrugged. "You weren't there after he learned he was going to be a dad. You didn't see how militant he was about the paternity test. He didn't trust me, and he's only different because of the baby."

"It sounds like he had a reason to be, but that doesn't mean he's not into you," Poppy protested.

Lily scooted her menu to the side. She'd probably been to Rattler's enough to know what she wanted. "I've tried to tell her, guys, but the tragedy of Vasectomy Willis continues."

I scowled at my youngest sister, who used to be so afraid to upset me. Ever since her divorce, she'd been frank when it came to my relationships, or lack thereof. "There's nothing wrong with being careful. I fooled myself about Willis for so long. Evander's just doing the same. He's seeing what he wants."

"He looked exactly like he was seeing what he wanted when he spotted you earlier," Poppy said.

I shook my head. "I don't know what you mean. He isn't looking at me any differently than normal."

Poppy leveled me with a flat stare. "Your stubbornness is keeping you from what could be a great relationship."

My resolution wavered. What if they were right? What if he liked me for me and not because he was making the best out of his situation, trying to make me better than I was?

"Evander could be everything you were looking for in Willis," Clover added. She held up her hands as if she expected me to argue. "Look, I know I don't know him. I only shook his hand, which, by the way, was not a limp noodle like your ex's. But Dad gushes about him—as much as he does about Eliot! And then there's what she said." She tipped her head at a beaming Lily. My youngest sister was probably thrilled about hearing Dad compliment her husband.

I know I liked hearing that about Evander.

"The pumpkin harvest." Lily nodded as if that was all the explanation needed. "I'm telling you—the way he looked at her was the same." Lily cast a smug glance my way. "He's a man obsessed, and you're convincing yourself it's just about the baby."

"It is," I insisted, with less heat than before. "What if it's a biological drive? Hormones. He doesn't know he's being influenced, and neither do I." I couldn't afford to uproot myself and move. There would be a baby involved. If he decided his feelings weren't real, the broken heart I'd be left with would be like a nuclear explosion compared to the fizzling of my feelings for Willis.

"You're a chemist, not a biologist, Violet," Poppy said pointedly. "And she's right. The longing in that poor man's eyes. He could be in the middle of a single ladies' cruise, and he'd never give another woman a second glance."

I flicked my menu up, glad it was high enough to

cover my stricken expression. It was like they thought this was easy. "None of you understand."

"We do," Clover said in the most serious voice she'd used all day. "That's why we're teaming up on you."

"You didn't team up on Lily," I snapped, "when she was going to divorce Eliot before she got the house."

"She didn't tell us. Just Mom and Dad." Hurt rang in her tone.

My irritation at their interference lessened, but it didn't evaporate.

"Eliot had his own emotions to work out from his past," Lily said gently. "And he did it and came back to me."

"I'll be waiting a while." The devastation in his eyes when I told him no. It had upset him, saddened him. I told myself it was because he couldn't be as close to the pregnancy or birth, but my sister's words wormed their way into my head.

"He's respecting your boundaries," Clover said. "There's a difference."

Poppy nodded. "If you want something to change between you two, but you were the one who put the limits in place, then you're going to have to be the one to break through the barrier first."

Poppy's insight hit like a brick but sank in slowly. I did set a limit. He obliged. But I didn't see what they did. He looked at me the way he had always looked at me.

Chapter Twenty-Four

Violet

I clutched my phone as I left a message. "Hey. It's Violet Duke again. The hot water heater officially died yesterday, and I'm still cooking with only the stovetop. Can you let me know when the repairs are getting done? Thanks, byeee."

I hung up and let out a disgruntled huff. Asshat.

My landlord had said he'd get a new water heater installed when I'd called him two weeks ago. Nothing.

I drove away from my work's parking lot. I had another checkup—as late as I could get on a Friday afternoon—and Evander was meeting me there.

I had left the dinner with my sisters wondering...what if. What if I was wrong? What if Evander had real feelings for me? What if... But our texts since that night had been about the upcoming doctor appointment and the cats. He sent me pictures of them snuggled on the porch by the door. Another of them perched on two wide wooden fence posts, side by side. And he'd asked how I was feeling.

Nothing that indicated I consumed his thoughts like he dominated mine.

Still, I'd get to see him today. A small surge of excitement trickled into my veins. I needed to settle down. It'd been bad enough that the week had gone by so slowly. For one, the pelvic pain was getting uncomfortable. The high stools at the lab benches were not pregnant-woman friendly, but I'd gotten hired into the best environment. I wouldn't complain about a seat I needed a running jump to get into.

I tapped my fingers against the steering wheel and hummed along to the radio. My gaze darted over the landscape. Old, dried corn lined a few of the fields. The pastures were full of round bales. And the surrounding hills and low buttes were already more brown than green.

When I reached the clinic, I spotted Evander pacing out front, his phone to his ear. My heartbeat kicked up. Watching him move was like admiring a caged panther. Nothing but contained power. He held so much inside.

He saw me and lowered his chin to speak into the phone as if he was afraid I could read lips. I kept sight of him from the corner of my eye. He tucked his phone into one of his cargo pockets and continued pacing.

Was he talking to another girl?

Would I get a picture of them in a couple of months?

I peeled my fingers off the steering wheel. I was being too paranoid. He wasn't talking to some other woman.

But he could be. There was nothing stopping him. I told him there couldn't be anything between us.

By the time I gathered my purse and phone and got out of the car, tears were stinging the backs of my eyes. I blinked any hint of moisture away. By the time I reached Evander, he'd quit pacing.

Lord, help me. I had noticed he wore a snug, long-sleeved shirt, but this close, I *noticed*. Pecs. Biceps. Shoulders. I couldn't pick my favorite body part. "Hey." I sounded breathless and not despondent.

"Hey. How you been feeling?"

His concern for me warmed at the same time it depressed me. I was selfish and wanted his focus on me and not just me in the role of being the mom of his baby. "Things are getting uncomfortable."

Thankfully, with no water heater, I didn't have to test how hard it was to get out of the bathtub.

Concern filled his eyes. "Anything you can do about it?"

"Other than go into labor and it's way too early, so no." Get a foot rub each night from him? Use his bathroom and take an actual hot shower?

I might have to phone in an SOS to Lily and swear her to secrecy. She might send Eliot to my place, but it'd be better than my parents. Mom and Dad would rush to Coal Haven, purchase a new water heater, chew out my landlord, then insist I find a new place. All valid. But they'd want to know why Evander was no longer helping me.

How did I say, *Well, guys, I thought I should quit having sex with him before he decides I'm not the one he wants and breaks my heart. I didn't want to find out if he moved on when I got too pregnant for intercourse, if that happened, or afterward when I've got a baby attached to the outside of me instead of the inside.*

No. I did not want to have that talk.

He opened the door for me, and I went to the desk.

The receptionist greeted us. "I'll let them know you're here. Have a seat."

When I turned to see where Evander had chosen to sit, he was in the corner, tapping away at his phone. As I approached, he tucked it away again.

My stomach started filling with dread. I had to be imagining it. The guy had a lot of family. Old army buddies even. Why wouldn't he be on the phone?

Because he hadn't fielded calls or texts when I'd been with him before. Nor had he acted like he was hiding the correspondence.

His brow furrowed as I sat next to him. The waiting room was empty, I could've sat one seat over or an entire row away, but then I wouldn't be by his warmth. I wouldn't be able to catch a whiff of his fresh linen scent. I wouldn't be able to torture myself by being so close to those muscles, yet too far away to touch.

"Something wrong?" he asked, giving me a once-over. No heat entered his gaze.

My stomach sank lower. This sucked.

You did it to yourself.

Was this self-preservation? Should I have taken whatever semblance of a relationship he wanted to give me until the baby was born and he realized there was no appeal?

"No, I'm fine. Heartburn." I did get bouts of heartburn more often these days, but not now. "You seem to be a busy guy." *Subtle, Violet. Subtle.*

He cocked his head like he was trying to figure out what I meant. "No more than usual, but harvest is always a busy time."

His phone buzzed, but he didn't take his attention off me.

I waited. He lifted his brows like he wondered if I had more questions.

I had to put this behind me. I had to move on, just like he might be doing. "How's harvest been going?"

The corner of his mouth tipped up. "Dad hasn't yelled at me once. I accidentally started driving away before he shut off the auger. A bunch of corn dumped on the ground, and he only laughed. When I was a kid, he would've chewed my ass and threatened to take it out of my paycheck."

"He's mellowed out."

"To put it lightly. Then when the grain truck busted an axle, he shrugged it off. Said it was looking like rain anyway, and if it was going to break, now was a good time." He shook his head. "I was ready to rage, and he just asked if I wanted to help him haul the new smoker he brought home. Next week, we're working cattle, and it's turned into a big family event, and he's now the meat guy."

Another big Barron family event. I wasn't invited this time. I would've heard by now. "I'm sure it is weird but nice."

"Hey, uh, Mom wants to sew a quilt for Bud. She wants to know if you're partial to a color scheme. I told her she could wait until after the birth, but I think she's bored. All her grandnieces and nephews have quilts, and Dad's gone all day this time of year."

His family was sweet. If I had Willis's baby, I would've been told what the color scheme was and that I had to buy only certain brands. "Anything she wants to sew will be amazing. I'm not picky, and Bud won't be either."

"Bud won't be demanding Gucci?"

I grinned. "Maybe, but I won't be buying Gucci on a chemist's wages."

He chuckled, then fell serious. "I hope it's okay that I have to run right after the appointment."

"Oh. Yeah. No problem." I crushed my disappointment. It wasn't like we'd go out to eat together again. "I'm sure your parents need you."

"No. I have an errand to run. That's why I had to meet you today instead of picking you up."

I had wondered if he didn't want to be with me any longer than he had to, and I didn't blame him. But the mysterious errand didn't make me feel better. Was it an excuse to get away from me as fast as possible? "Sure. No problem."

My throat grew thick. I'd been missing him and second-guessing myself. When I was in college, I thrived on getting questions right. I had that ego that Willis had preyed on. I wasn't sure I'd been right about Evander and how he felt about me, but the evidence was weighing in. It was the one time I wished I was wrong.

***

Evander

I had my pickup backed into the alley by the furniture store. The owner, Hattie, opened the loading dock door. "I have it all right here. I got it wrapped up too. Can't have these flurries seeping into the cracks and damaging anything." She blinked up at the sky, and snowflakes hit us both in the face. "Go on through the side door. Shouldn't take you but a minute to load everything. The smallest item is the heaviest."

"Sorry I'm a little late," I said after I entered the storage area. I had a stop to make first, and my hands were still freezing. My breath puffed in front of my face. An early winter storm had blanketed the region in a few inches of snow. "You got dug out all right?"

"Oh, yes. The city does a good job at keeping the roads open. And ever since your aunt retired, this is no longer the last block plowed."

I chuckled. Hattie told it like it was, and it was no secret my aunt Naomi had a vindictive streak. She probably still did but was more judicious about when she used it.

"I could've had this all delivered," Hattie said. "Still can. It's on the house. You aren't that far out of town."

"Nah. I got it." I was at a stopping point in the house. It was either sit around and wait for the delivery truck or do it myself. "I was in town anyway."

Hattie directed me, and I loaded everything into the box of the pickup, arranging the various pieces of furniture like a living Tetris game. Hattie's meticulous wrapping had saved the items from more than a few bumps and nicks.

After everything was loaded, I tossed straps over the load and tightened them. The snow was coming down heavier by the time I was done.

"Thanks, Hattie," I said as I climbed into the pickup. The snow was sticky. I rolled down my window and flipped the windshield wipers on.

"No, thank you. Anytime. I mean it." She peered

down into the window, snow dotting her dark hair. "Pleasure doing business with you."

I pulled away and crept down the alley, keeping my window open so I could see if the sidewalk was clear.

Violet was about to scurry across the opening of the alleyway when she spotted me. Her black parka covered her belly, which extended farther out than when I'd seen her at last week's appointment. Her bump was shifting, sloping downward more than out.

I clocked it all. I had missed so much. The distance between us was difficult, but I was trying to accommodate her needs.

A white stocking hat kept her hair out of her face. Those surprised blue eyes were on me.

"Evander. Hi."

Hearing her say my name would never get old, but I was tempted to speed off and hope she forgot about seeing me. She didn't need to find out what I was hauling, but her gaze slid to the bulky items.

Too late to hide anything. Hattie's wrapping was doing double duty. Protection and concealment.

"I was picking up some things from Hattie."

Her curious expression fell. "Oh. I suppose the lease is up soon." She shook herself, and hunks of snow cascaded off her hat. "Did you shovel out my place?"

My errand before Hattie's. "Didn't think your landlord would get to it in a timely manner."

She pulled at her coat collar with mittens that matched her hat. "You would be right, but he's there now fixing the water heater."

The water heater this time? "Good."

"Yeah, finally." Before I could ask more about what

she meant, she gave me that fake smile. "I should let you go. You're busy."

"Hop in. I'll give you a ride to your car." I put my truck into park. My ride was warm, and her cheeks were pink from the wind and cold.

"I'm just down in front of the bank."

The bank was on the other side of me, and there was a spot open by her car. "Get in. I need to talk to you anyway." That should get her to acquiesce. I wasn't lying, but my conversation could wait.

She paused for a moment, holding my gaze, before carefully maneuvering around my hood. I hopped out of the door for her, easily rounding the truck to reach the passenger door before her. She struggled to climb inside. When I got back in, I repressed a groan when the cab filled with her wildflower scent.

I kicked the pickup into gear. "Do you have more errands to run?"

"No. I'm just killing time. I don't like to be in the house with strangers." She rested her hands on her belly.

She could've asked me to be there. "They must've come right after I left."

She nodded. A droplet of melted snow trickled from her hat to her hair. "Raj let me come to work early so I could leave an hour early and meet them."

I could've done that for her, but she'd never ask. This woman and her stubbornness.

"Everything's okay? With the house?" I asked as I parked.

"It'll be better with hot water." She was looking out her passenger window. "What did you need to talk to me about?" Her voice was light. Professional. Infuriating.

"We need to get together to discuss more things

about the baby." What I had to say could wait. She was on edge, and she'd never admit it, but that damn water heater business had her stressed. "At the house."

"Why not at my place?"

Her place didn't have Flo or Poly. I checked on them before I came to town. Two furry bundles on their couches.

I had a plan, and I couldn't toss it out the window just because a pretty little wildflower was in my truck, refusing to be plucked. "All my appliances work."

Her lips thinned, then she chuckled. "You got me there."

There was more wrong in the house, and she wasn't telling me. "Do you want me to sit with you until the guys are gone?"

"You don't need to. Lily, Eliot, and the kids are meeting me at Rattler's soon. I'm taking the kids out for an early Christmas gift. In case, you know"—she pointed the tips of her mittens at her stomach—"Bud wants to arrive a little early. And now that it's snowing and the roads are slick, I don't know how much I'll get to Bismarck or Dickinson to shop."

"A meal out makes memories."

"That's what I'm hoping. Getting some time back with them that I missed." She gave me a tender smile. The conversation I wanted to have with her ran through my head.

How would it go? Hurting her wasn't an option, but if we were both hurting, then what was the point?

"Thanks for the ride, Evander," she said softly.

"Anytime. I'll be by tomorrow and hit your driveway again. You don't need to be shoveling."

Her smile was tight. "Thanks. Maybe I should just pay you the rent."

"Nah, go enjoy that hot bath."

A dry laugh left her. "I'll enjoy the hot water, but the bathtub is not baby-belly friendly."

Noted. "How about next weekend?" I had a few more things to piece together and finish up before I told her what I'd been up to.

A deep sadness I couldn't place dimmed the blue of her eyes. "Yeah. Next weekend. We'll talk."

Then she got out. I had no idea if I was on the right path, but I had a mission plan, and I was executing it. Next weekend, I'd know the result.

Chapter Twenty-Five

Violet

The pipes still sputtered and the oven hadn't been fixed, but I had hot water. I spent Friday night enjoying a warm shower after a week of heating water on the stove like it was 1889 and blizzarding out.

I tried reading a book in the living room, but my thoughts kept dipping to the conversation with Evander last Friday. What did he have to talk to me about? And why did he have a pickup bed full of what must be furniture? I couldn't think of anything else that came in boxes that size.

He was moving. He had to be. The talk would be about how he was moving.

Was he moving in with someone else? Once he'd put his heart out there and I gave it right back, he decided life was short and met someone else. They moved at warp speed, and how convenient, his lease was almost done.

I prodded at my temples. I would love to take a bath right now.

My hair was still a little damp, but after a week of snow and heating all my water on the stove, fatigue chased me to the bedroom. I put on my cozy pajama bottoms and a loose top with long sleeves. The heat in the house was as weak as everything else, and the temperature was well below zero. Had been since the day after I saw Evander earlier this week.

Under the covers, I sighed and attempted to put out of my mind what Evander needed to tell me.

I had fallen asleep but was woken up again. My bladder protested. Dripping water in my dream made me feel like I had to pee. But I always had to pee, so which had come first? The dream or the baby bouncing on my bladder?

Frowning, I held my breath and listened. No. The dripping was coming from somewhere in the house, and now that I was fully awake, the sound was more like running water.

I swung my legs down. As soon as my bare feet touched the carpet, I yelped. My toes were damp and cold.

"What the..." I went to turn on the lamp and froze. Was the carpet really wet?

I slowly lowered my foot. The temperature grew colder the closer I got to the floor. I slapped the carpet with my toes and was rewarded with a wet, smacking sound.

"Shit." I reached for the lamp again and clenched my fist. If everything's wet, then I shouldn't use the electricity. Right?

Dammit. I was a chemist, not an electrician.

I snagged my phone off the nightstand and scooted farther back on the bed. My little island.

What should I do? How did I fix this while I was almost seven months pregnant? I didn't know anything about plumbing, and I'd be stupidly optimistic to think I could figure it out in the middle of the night.

Miss Independent couldn't figure this out. I gripped my phone tighter. I needed help.

Who should I call?

Evander.

No. It wasn't fair to him that I told him there would be nothing between us, but he was the first one I ran to.

Lily and Eliot?

I let out a frustrated grunt. Everyone would be asleep. Lily and Eliot had kids sleeping. My mess might wake them all up. But I'd need somewhere to go. I drew in a shaky breath. The steady trickle of water taunted me.

The source of the leak had to be the bathroom.

Daisy? I had her number, and she'd come. Maybe her fiancé would help. Still, I didn't make a move to call them. It felt...intrusive.

I drew in a shaky breath. My heart pounded.

Mom and Dad? Alder? No. They were too far away.

Lily was the best option. Which meant Eliot would have to rescue my ass.

My vision went cloudy, and I blinked to clear it. I swiped at my cheeks. They were wet too.

I had to get out of the house. I had no idea what damage would be done or how bad the leak would get.

I closed my eyes and took a deep breath. Then I dialed the first person who came to mind.

Evander

I hip-checked the door and rebounded off the still-closed wooden slab. My jacket crackled like it was made of paper, but it was just that fucking cold out.

"Goddammit." Why the hell did I fix that dead bolt notch?

Holding the screen door, I stepped back, aimed, and kicked just above the doorknob. One more kick, and the door splintered open.

I entered and aimed the flashlight across the living room. The carpet didn't look wet, but closer to the hallway, it grew distinctively darker.

"Violet, don't move. I'm coming to you." My boots squelched a few steps into the room.

I swept the beam of light through the house as I went. Liquid shimmered on the bathroom's linoleum floor, and the sound of running water came from inside. Either a pipe had burst from the cold temperatures, which didn't make sense in a house that was inhabited, or all the futzing around with the knobs when the people were in to replace the water heater and look at the water pressure issue did the old valves in. Could've been both. The house was chilly.

Either way, I didn't fucking care. This house was a piece of shit, and Violet shouldn't be here.

I swung the flashlight into her room. The carpet was

nothing but inky darkness. The house was so small that the water didn't need to creep far to invade everything.

Violet huddled in the middle of her bed wearing nothing but pajamas. Her curls went everywhere like she'd been stuffing her hands into them. As much as I wanted to soothe her, I had to get her out of here.

"I-I'm sorry to bother you. I know it's the middle of the night—"

"If you keep apologizing, I might actually get upset." I shrugged out of my winter coat and handed it to her. "Put that on. None of this is your fault, and I'm glad you called me."

She put my coat on like I asked. "Thank you." Her voice was small, and it gutted me.

I'd have been beside myself if she'd chosen to call someone else. I'd have been relieved that she hadn't tried to tackle this mess, but the failure would've been personal. If I had ruined things so thoroughly so early on in our nonrelationship, then I would've taken that guilt to the grave.

I handed her the flashlight. Then I put a knee on the bed and picked her up like the precious cargo she was. Once her weight was in my arms, the dread inside of me diminished. "Aim the light ahead so I can see."

"You can't carry me. Just get me my shoes."

I ignored her and kept walking. She dutifully wielded the flashlight so I didn't run us into any doors. When I passed the busted doorframe, she didn't say anything. She had to have heard me crash my way into the house.

"I've got the pickup running, and the heat's going full blast." I held her tight. Her feet were bare, but I couldn't rush across the crunchy sidewalk in case I hit a patch of ice. Instead, I smashed through the same path I took from the road to the house in the snow that had piled up and only half melted before the cold front came through.

Carefully, I opened the door of the pickup and set her inside. I buckled her in, and she let me. The glow of the dashboard made the glassiness in her eyes worse. She was stunned and scared.

"What do you need from the house?"

"Nothing." She said it as if she didn't want to be a bother again.

"I'll be back." Gently, I took the flashlight from her and ran back inside. First, I went downstairs and found the shut-off valve for water into the house. Then I flipped all the breakers. That was all that would be done with the mess tonight.

For the first trip, I left anything that was in a bottom drawer, unsure of how high the water got or if it'd wicked its way up the particleboard of the dresser. I gathered as much of her clothing and shoes as I could.

On the next trip, I got her toiletries. Cold water flowed over the toe of my boots as I splashed my way in and out. Before I left, I grabbed her crochet basket and the throw she'd made off the back of the couch.

I tossed everything in the back seat and found a strap in the box of my pickup from when I moved furniture. I went to the busted front door and secured it as best I could. I got behind the wheel. My fingers were frigid and losing feeling, but I didn't care.

Her wide gaze was on me in the dark. Not much of her face stood out, and the rest of her was swamped by my jacket. "You didn't have to get all that."

Yes, I did. "Call the landlord on the way home."

"It's the middle of the night."

"And his shithole of a house just made you homeless. Let him know I shut the main water supply off."

She nodded, and determination filled her face. She called. "Um, hi. This is Violet Duke. Something... happened...with the plumbing in the house and it's flooding. It's flooded. The water supply is shut off. Call me when you get this. I won't be at the house. Thanks. Bye."

"You were entirely too polite." I would've started with *Listen, fucker*.

"I'm tired."

Guilt wound its way around my temper. "I know. You can take the bed, and I'll sleep on the couch."

"What about the guest room?"

"It's...there's no bed in there." That was all part of the conversation I'd planned to have with her this weekend. But it'd have to wait. She was tired and majorly stressed.

"Oh."

The rest of the drive was quiet. I didn't know what to say. I could tell her it would be all right, but she'd drive herself crazy wondering how.

I pulled up to my house. She unbuckled and moved to open the door.

"Don't," I ordered.

She stopped. "Oh, right." She tried to twist around, but she couldn't reach the back seat. "You packed my shoes."

"Nope. I'll be right there." I got out and jogged around to the passenger side.

"You can't keep carrying me," she said as I did just that.

She sighed and sank against my chest. Her exhale wasn't frustration with me. Violet was logical. All the issues that the busted plumbing caused were likely streaming through her mind. She was probably worried about missing work. Wondering how to get her car. Thinking about inventorying the belongings I had grabbed and planning how to replace the rest.

And then there was finding a new place. While she was in the house she was determined to let go.

I took her inside, flipped on the hallway light by tilting both of us until I could reach the switch, and took her right to my bedroom. "Just rest for now, okay? I know you might not be able to sleep, but get some rest." I set her down on the edge of the bed.

She nodded. "Evander…"

I tilted her chin up. "Not tonight. Everything can wait until you get some rest. And do not worry about that house. For once, the landlord is going to have to take care of it."

Some of the stress leaked out of her expression. Her shoulders hung, and she worried her lower lip. "I just need to use the bathroom."

"While you're in there, I'll grab your stuff and put most of it in the corner. Tomorrow, we can find a place for it."

She nodded again, closed her eyes, and took in a long, shallow breath.

"As long as you need, Violet. You stay as long as you need."

"My aunt—"

"Will have to understand. You lost your home. You're pregnant. She might even know how shitty that landlord is."

"Chad is kind of shitty."

Fucking Chad.

"He sells insurance in town, apparently," she said bitterly.

The asshole would make sure he was covered. "Keep bugging the hell out of him if he doesn't return your call at the crack of dawn." Or I'd track him down.

"Okay." The heaviness surrounding her eased. "Thank you."

"Nothing to thank me for." In case she wanted to disagree, I walked out.

When I returned with the first armload, the bathroom door was closed, and a crack of light from underneath speared into the hallway. She was still inside when I carried in the second load. I set her items in a neat pile and left her toiletries on top of her clothing. The crochet basket was holding everything up. If it wouldn't take so long, I'd hang all her clothes up. I had yanked them out of the closet on hangers. For now, this would have to do. If I did more work, she might think she had to pitch in.

I passed the bathroom door and heard her murmuring inside. As tempted as I was to linger, I kept going. If she wasn't talking to fucking Chad, I'd be too tempted to find his address and be on his doorstep in a half an hour.

I was making up the couch for whatever sleep I could capture before morning when she came out. Her bare feet stuck out from underneath cozy-looking pale-blue pajama pants.

"Chad said as long as the main valve is shut off, he'll wait until morning. He thought the temperature should hold to keep everything from freezing too bad, and he wants me to meet him there at nine."

Nine wasn't that far away, but it wasn't like either of

us would be getting much sleep. "I'll go with you, and we can pick up your car."

She hugged herself.

"Go to bed, Violet." I stayed right where I was. The temptation to tuck her in was strong, but I wasn't crossing her limits when she was so emotionally raw.

"Good night, Evander."

"Night, Violet."

Violet

"Hey," a deep, pleasing voice said.

"Mm." I snuggled farther into the covers that smelled like the best dream ever.

"Hey." A big hand jostled my back.

"What?" I said on a groan. "I'm sleeping."

"I know, wildflower, and I let you sleep as long as I could. Chad can suck it and wait a little longer."

Who was Chad? I blinked my eyes open. Darkness surrounded me with light toward the top of my head.

"We should get going as soon as you're ready."

The events of the night rose in my mind. Flooding. Evander. Dependable, handsome, heroic Evander, rushing to my rescue.

In the end, it'd only made sense to call him. The logical choice. I wouldn't be waking up kids, and he had room for me to stay over, or he'd have made sure I got checked into the motel. I'd needed him, and he'd been there. For once, I didn't care what his motivations were.

I flung the blanket off my head and sat up. "What time is it?"

"It's eight thirty." Evander hovered by the edge of the bed. He wore a tight, long-sleeved gray shirt and dark-gray cargo pants. A ball cap was on his head. He was ready to go.

"Oh shit." I wiggled to the edge of the bed. My shirt was twisted under my boobs and stretched wide over my belly. He looked like an outdoor activewear model, and I didn't feel like more than a lump of modeling clay.

"You're not rushing for that jackass. Take your time, and we'll get there when we get there."

He walked out, his ass on display. He hadn't turned on a light but had raised the blinds.

The man was so considerate I could melt. I scrubbed my face with my hands and blinked as much of the tiredness away that I could.

I couldn't believe I had fallen asleep, but exhaustion had overtaken me. Fatigue and Evander's fresh linen smell surrounded me. Last night, when panic would rise, I'd take a deep inhale of that scent. It was the only way I'd fallen asleep.

I could've gotten a lot worse of a baby daddy. I reaped the benefits of Evander trying to make sure his kid was cared for.

My gaze landed on a pile of my things. Oh, my toothbrush. I stood and flexed to each side, stiff and sore from huddling while waiting to be rescued. Relief flooded me when I saw all the main clothing I wore was in the bedroom. He'd really cleaned out my closet. A suitcase that I had kept at the top of the closet was next to his dresser. Curious, I opened it. Underwear and bras filled the inside.

He was so damn thorough.

I selected an outfit and took everything to the bathroom. I didn't see him on my trek between rooms, but I spotted the closed guest room door.

What was he doing with that room? Why was the bed gone? Was he moving out? Moving someone in?

I dropped my items on the bathroom counter and stared at my pale complexion in the mirror. *Not today, Violet. Table all those concerns until you figure out your own living situation.*

I didn't have the energy to figure out my near future. I knew what I wanted. I just didn't know if I could have it.

After I cleaned up and dressed, I found Evander in the kitchen. He was at the stove. "Want some eggs?" he asked, looking over his shoulder. His gaze dropped down my body and back up. There was no smolder, just concern.

Lily might've been right. He had looked at me differently. But now he was back to having his emotions locked up around me. I had deliberated too long.

I tugged at the hem of my long shirt that mimicked a soft green empire skirt. The top was long-sleeved and comfy. A pair of leggings in the same material completed the look. Dressy but practical. I would wear something like this every day if I could; I just couldn't wear it in the lab. Might as well wear it to see and hear how my home was destroyed.

"Eggs sound good." We had only ten minutes before we were supposed to meet Chad.

I sat at the spot at the table I had usually sat in. A

plate was already there with toast. Evander turned the stove off and scooped some eggs onto my plate.

We ate quickly—he was done first, as always.

I put my plate by the sink. He beat me to the door and had my winter coat ready. My shoes were on the black mat, and my purse was on the little table next to it.

He'd really thought of everything.

"Thank you again. For grabbing all this." I held a hand up when he opened his mouth and shook his head. "Thanks are deserved. It was the dead of night and fifteen below zero."

He just shrugged. "It's supposed to warm up a lot today. We'll get back to more seasonal temps."

Outside, clouds covered the sky, but the snow on the ground reflected the light and made the day brighter. A fluffy kitten was curled on the step.

"Flo," I cooed and bent to pet her. "You've gotten so big."

She mewed and bumped her head against my hand. My heart twisted a little at missing months of her growth. Poly bounded up the porch and greeted me.

I laughed, and wasn't that the last thing I thought I'd feel like doing today?

Evander didn't rush me, but I pulled myself away from the kittens. "Okay. I'm ready to face my landlord."

On the drive, I ran through scenarios. I could find another place. I had saved some money, and Chad should give me back my deposit. He should also let me out of the lease. He'd have to.

Then there was work. I had already rearranged and shifted as much as I could. I had another doctor's appointment in two weeks too. What about a nursery?

Panic shot through my veins. My chest constricted.

"Oh, god. The nursery. I don't have anywhere for Bud." The furniture was the type to soak up water, not repel it. I didn't want to flirt with mold around a baby.

Evander didn't flinch at my outburst. "One thing at a time, Violet. Seeing how Chad deals with this is our first priority now that you and Bud are safe."

I took a calming breath. He was right. Chad first. Housing second. Nursery third.

But time was running out. I had a little over two months to get everything ready. Each day my mobility was affected a little more. I'd quit untying my shoes. They'd turned into slip-ons.

A gleaming red pickup was in front of the house when we pulled up. Evander didn't park in the driveway, probably so I could leave with my car.

The door was hanging open. Chad peered out. He was closer to Evander's age and wearing fishing waders over a heavy cream sweater. His blond hair was combed to the side, and disapproval lined his face.

"Who broke the door?" he asked without greeting either one of us.

Evander drew himself to his full height. "That was me."

Chad frowned as he sized up Evander from inside the door. "You should've waited for me to come with the spare key."

"When would that have been?" Evander asked, his tone deceptively even. "Besides, I was the one who fixed it last time when Violet had to body-slam it to lock it." He smiled tightly. "I guess either way, you were meant to repair the frame yourself."

Chad's frown lines deepened, but he moved out of the way so we could enter. The cold kept the smell down.

Still, the mustiness was cloying. The carpet might be new, but the smell of wet fabric was ripe in the air.

Chad propped his hands on his hips. "So, I had a look around. The bathroom and the spare room got the worst—"

"That's the nursery." My heart thudded. Evander might've said not to worry yet, but I did. The nursery was even worse than my bedroom.

"That sucks," Chad said as if he didn't care how high the suckage rated. "But, uh, it's clean water. A good shop vac and some fans will do wonders. I think if you get started today, you can probably be back in by—"

"Whoa." Evander put his palm up. "What are you talking about? You expect her to do the cleanup?"

Was Chad for real? Even if I wasn't seven months pregnant, his attitude would be insane.

Chad shrugged, his expression affable like he was going above and beyond. "I can take some off the rent, of course, and then there's the door—"

"That you never fixed." I planted my hands on my hips, mirroring his power move. This guy had a tone like Willis's, and I was not having it. "Along with the garage door opener, all the cabinets, half the lights—need I mention the plumbing?—and the oven!"

Evander snapped his head toward me, shock in his eyes.

Chad recoiled. "I had all those arranged to get repaired. All I asked for was patience."

"Patience?" I snapped. "All I asked for was a safe house to rent!"

Chad put his hands up. "Now, listen—"

"Shut up." Evander didn't raise his voice, but he edged over until he was between me and Chad. "You screwed her over because you thought you could. Guess what? You can't. This place is your problem. *You* get the goddamn shop vac. *You* run the fans. *You* give her the deposit back and all her rent for the month. *You* are going to pay for the damages to her items—"

"If she had rental insurance—"

"Don't fuck around, Chad, or you're going to find out."

Chad's mouth dropped open. He stepped back. "Are you threatening me?"

"No," Evander said, still not raising his voice. "I'm telling you what you're going to do. Just like I'm going to tell you that if you don't, I've got the time and money for a lawyer. I've got all the days in the world to tell everyone about how a local boy took advantage of a single pregnant woman. I've got plenty of family who can tell the stories far and wide. Rentals aren't your only business, are they, Chad? I mean, the Barrons have made a lot of enemies in this county, but I think people will empathize with a soon-to-be mom who moved to town to give herself and her baby a better life. Can your businesses withstand that?"

If I thought Evander couldn't get hotter, I'd been wrong.

Chad's eyes flared when Evander revealed his last name. "I see," he said tightly. "I didn't recognize you at first, Evander."

"Shouldn't have made a goddamn difference. If the money isn't in her account by the end of the week, you'll be hearing from me." Evander took a step forward. "How long was she without a water heater?"

Chad's gaze lifted to me. I stared at him square on,

challenging him to answer honestly or I would. "About a week," he finally said.

"It wasn't working well for two weeks before that," I added to be petty.

"And the motherfucking oven?" Evander stabbed his finger toward the kitchen wall, not waiting for a response. "Do you realize what a goddamn safety hazard that garage door is? And you expected to stand by while she struggled to not have it fall on her? All while cashing her checks? You know what? That money better be in her account fucking Monday, or I'll have a nice long talk with Cameron and Naomi about what our options are. I'm sure they have a good lawyer for me to contact."

Blood leached from Chad's expression.

"Now I'm taking Violet somewhere warm and safe," Evander continued. "You can reach her by phone, but you shouldn't have to. She's done with this place. Right?"

Chad's jaw worked, but he didn't say anything. He nodded.

"And you're going to pack up all her shit and take it to my dad's place. He can store it in his shop. I'll text you the directions."

Chad's jaw flexed harder. "I know where Bruce lives."

"By the end of tomorrow. Money by Monday." Evander turned. His demeanor immediately softened when his gaze landed on me. He steered me around and out the door.

Chapter Twenty-Six

Violet

Evander and I arrived at his house for the second time in not many hours. He'd driven, but I felt like I was floating. I had gratefully let him lead me out of the rental house after he told Chad off. He'd made my landlord face a reckoning, and god, that was *hot*. Evander had laid into him without violence. He hadn't had to boast to make others think he had more influence or power. He'd stated facts and outlined what he expected Chad to do.

Willis would've stood back and made me handle it all. Then he would've critiqued how I did while taking all the credit. He wouldn't have changed for a kid.

When it came to parenthood, I was secure. Evander would be a good partner.

Longing bloomed inside of me. I wanted him as more than a co-parent.

He put the pickup in park. "I need to go check on Mom and Dad. He needs a hand with the fencing around the winter pastures while the temperature climbs above freezing." He leaned over the console. "Get some rest. You've dealt with enough. That jackass can do all the work he never did for the last four months."

I nodded, numb, except for that yearning. A million tasks filtered through my head. I didn't have a home. Again. I had a job, so there was that.

Oh no. The nursery. "Do you think all the furniture got wet?"

He shuttered his gaze, and that told me everything. "We'll have to see."

Tears gathered in my eyes. "That wood is too cheap, and it's been wet now for hours. I'll never be able to get it clean enough." Between the moisture and the damage to the base that supposedly supports it all? I'd never be comfortable with its safety. "You and Dad did all that work for nothing."

"It was a good bonding experience." He gave me a slight smile.

I basked for a moment under his attention before the despair crept back in. My vision went cloudy.

"Hey," he said softly and captured a tear that ran down my cheek with his thumb. "It'll be okay. We'll get you back on your feet."

On my feet. By myself again. Because I turned the best guy away. For what?

Miss Independent?

I was really fucking dependent right now. I struggled to gather myself. He didn't need to baby me. His parents were waiting for him. "I'd better let you get going. I've got to look for open rentals."

A flash of something flitted through his eyes. Disappointment? Or was he hiding his relief that I wasn't going to infringe on his bachelor pad again?

The stress and weariness caught up to me. I yawned widely, covering my mouth. My whole body shook.

"Let's get you in." He hopped out and came around to my side before I climbed all the way out.

We went through the side door this time. In the light of day, the work he'd done on the mudroom was easier to see. He'd painted the space a light and welcoming gray. A new coat rack and bench seat ran along one wall across from the washing machine and dryer. The torn-up linoleum had been replaced with new stone-patterned flooring. Durable enough for a mudroom but nice enough to complement the hardwood.

"You've redone this whole space," I said as I shrugged out of my jacket. I hung it on a hook. Wistfulness washed through me. This small room was more inviting than my entire rental had been.

"I like to stay busy."

I could've kept him busy. *You had your chance.*

I turned my back on him and blinked back tears. "I'm going to go lie down." In his bed. Surrounded by his scent. All my items sat in a pile on his floor. Temporary. Just like last time. A consequence for being too proud.

"I'll call you when Chad delivers your things."

"Thank you."

The door opened and closed. He was gone, and I was alone in his house.

I didn't get a chance to see the interior when he carried me in last night, but he'd made some changes. My heart sank further as I noted each one. The walls were still bare, but he'd removed the big coffee table. An end table was also gone, and the glider rocker no longer stood in the corner. My throat burned.

The acid seared hotter up and down my esophagus. I veered back into the kitchen for a glass of water. After a moment of admiring even cabinets with doors that closed all the way, I opened a cupboard. It was half-full of dishes. Enough for more than one person.

A tear rolled down my cheek, and I sniffled. If my house hadn't flooded, I'd be oblivious to this. Nothing like salt on a gaping wound. The urge for water gone, I trudged past the closed guest room door and paused. What changes had he made in there?

I scratched the back of my neck. If he was moving another woman in, wouldn't she go in his bedroom? It'd only been almost a month since I turned him down, but maybe things went hot and heavy. Maybe I was the "Good Luck Chuck" of relationships. Men had to deal with me before they met the loves of their lives.

Ugh. I was working myself up while fatigue was pressing me down. My hips ached, and my pelvis threatened to crack apart like a wishbone.

I went into his bedroom. The smell of him immediately massaged away some of my anxiety when it should be doing the opposite. I nestled in the covers, but my mind refused to shut off.

After two hours of dozing on and off, I dug out my phone and called Lily.

"Hey," she answered. "How ya feeling?"

"Itty-bitty," I confessed and told her everything.

"Oh my god. You're okay?"

"Yeah." No. "I have to find somewhere to live. Think I'll be able to see some places this weekend?"

"I'm sure you can, but there's no rush. You're with Evander, right?"

Hadn't she heard a word I said? "Yes, but he's sleeping on the couch. And he might be seeing someone else."

"From everything you said about him, he doesn't strike me as a guy who moves that fast."

"Willis is married."

"What?" An indignant gasp echoed over the line. "That bastard. Don't get me wrong, I'm glad you're not married to him, but he played games with you. Honestly, he probably still is."

Her insight helped a little. I had to quit letting him get to me. I had to quit using him as an excuse. "Maybe I'm a good luck charm. Once Evander was free of his obligation toward me, he could find someone he really clicked with."

She made a tsking noise. "You're putting a lot of thoughts in a man's head. Does he know all this?"

"It's not my business."

"Look, I get the whole pregnancy paranoia. I don't think I would've caught Carter cheating on me if I wasn't pregnant at the time. Already, I can tell I'm worried Eliot's going to wake up one day and tell me, 'Welp, that's all for us.'"

"That man will never betray you."

She giggled. "My point is that I've already talked to Eliot. My first marriage absolutely dissolved after I learned I was pregnant with Kellan. I'm at about the same stage as when I had to move back in with Mom and Dad. Eliot wakes up every day, tells me how much he loves me, and tells me his plans for every second of the day. I didn't ask him to, but I talked to him about my fears. Have you talked to Evander?"

"You and Eliot are married."

"And you're in love with Evander."

I snapped my mouth shut. My pulse spiked, my heart throwing itself against my sternum. "I'm not."

"I think you have been for a while." She was almost apologetic. "You just haven't admitted it to yourself."

No. I hadn't. I was in love with Evander. And it had scared me. Each breath was like sucking through a straw. I loved Evander.

"It's too late," I said, miserable. "I swear he's moved on. If there's no one else, he's still just as far away. He's doing all this for the baby."

"Just maybe he's doing it for you too."

"How will I know?" My chest ached for Lily to be right. "I was so wrong before, and I wasted years of my life."

"You did it because no better option presented itself. As soon as you saw an example of what you wanted, you went for it. Then you stopped because you'd been hurt before."

I'd been terrified. "What if he's not really—"

"What if he really is? What if he feels the same way about you?"

I pursed my lips. "So I'm guessing you're not going to tell me if you know of any open rentals in town?"

"I actually know of one. One of the vets at the clinic, Doc Julio, owns an apartment complex by the pool in Crocus Valley. Can you talk to Evander?"

"We'll see" was all I could give her. Evander and I were on a good path for parents who weren't a couple.

Would I ruin it if I told him that I wanted take backs? I'd turned him down and then changed my mind?

After she hung up, I stared at the shadowed ceiling. The phone buzzed. Buzzed again.

Did Lily know more than one rental place? I squinted at the screen. A series of pictures came through from my landlord. **Please send receipts so I can reimburse you.**

Horror filled my gut as I looked at the images. A picture of the changing table. The squared-off bottom was already warped. I had chosen that style not because it matched the crib, but because I thought the design would be sturdier for when the baby got older.

The crib was better, but the legs I could view in the picture looked the same as the crib. They'd been wet for too long. The moisture had crept through the finish.

The cheap rocker that Dad and Evander had assembled was in another photo. Chad had tipped it on its side in the driveway. The runners were made of better wood. It could probably be rescued and sanitized.

Next were pictures of the couch and loveseat Alder bought. The bed, which had been on a metal frame. My dresser. Some I could save, some maybe not.

I sighed, clicked the screen off, and put the phone face down on the nightstand. Pressure was building behind my temples, and I didn't care to make more decisions today.

I sat up and swung my legs down. I was not going to get rest while my mind tumbled like it was. I opened the blinds a few inches to let in natural light. His room was painted the same light gray as the mudroom. His black and charcoal gray bedding fit the rest of the vibe of the house.

My clothing taunted me. I checked the closet. Room

could be made for my things, but it seemed invasive. Lily was right. I needed to talk to Evander. How would I even start? *Guess what? I changed my mind!* I'd be the manipulative woman he feared.

My mind circled round and round. I needed something to do, or I'd cry all afternoon.

I sorted through my clothing, mentally noting everything that needed a space until I found another rental. I unearthed my crochet basket and the blanket that had been draped over the arm of the couch. I ran my hand over it, touched he'd taken the time to grab it.

Did he know that blanket was for him? The gunmetal gray was a few shades darker than his couch and would pair nicely with the throw pillows.

Why had he grabbed those? They weren't essentials.

He'd done it for me. Because I'd made it. He didn't have to tell me in his deep voice.

The contents of the small basket on top stopped my world from spinning. Inside were coloring books, colored pencils, pens, and markers. The designs in the books were flowers.

My crochet supplies were there too. He hadn't needed to rescue any of that. But he'd come for me.

After I had moved, he'd brought the kittens to visit me.

A whole line of cars for the pumpkin party, but he'd left my spot open. The chocolate silk pie. If I looked in the fridge, would I find it chock-full of milk and orange juice?

All along, he'd been caring for me. He'd been considerate of me. Outside of being the baby's mom, he'd seen me. I'd soaked it all in and made excuses.

Yet he'd still put himself out there. For me.

Tears streaked down my cheeks.

He'd shown me who he was, and I'd pushed him away. And now I was afraid it was too late.

***

Evander

Violet wasn't answering her phone. She must be resting. I quietly let myself into the house. Her landlord said he had sent her pictures of all the water-damaged items in her house, and he hadn't heard back.

If she'd seen them, she was likely upset. I didn't want to risk making her feel worse with what I had to talk to her about, but it was all related. I told Dad I had to knock off early. The rest of the week was supposed to be slightly above freezing. I'd help with the fence then.

Moaning sobs reached me. Alarm pumped through my blood. I didn't bother with my boots.

Darting through the kitchen, I followed the sound. "Violet?"

She was in my bedroom, sitting on the edge of the bed, hugging the gray crocheted blanket I'd grabbed from her crappy rental.

"What's wrong?" I dropped to my knees in front of her. She sobbed harder.

Was it the stress? All the ruined furniture? If it was something else, I'd take care of it.

I wrapped my arms around her. "Talk to me, wildflower."

"I-I'm sorry," she said with halting gasps. "I'm so sorry. I-I messed it all up."

"What do you mean? How?"

"You're perfect, and I rejected you."

I gently eased her hands away from her face. Watery blue eyes met mine. "What in the world are you talking about?"

"The cats. This blanket. You don't laugh at my crocheting. You put my cat couches in their shed."

"You made them."

"Exactly!" More tears spilled out of her eyes. "And this!" She flung her hand toward the phone sitting next to her. "You sent me pictures of the sunset."

My concern was giving way to confusion. "Is that bad?"

"Yes. It means I'm an idiot." She pressed her palms to her eyes. "I convinced myself you were doing everything for the baby. That you could change your mind, that you have, and moved on."

"Moved on where?"

Her body shuddered. "Not where, who. Like whoever you're redoing your guest bedroom for."

Shock squashed the confusion swirling in my brain. "You think I'm getting the guest room ready for a woman?"

She nodded, her pretty face red and blotchy.

I gawked at her. "Why wouldn't I put this other woman into my bed if I was moving on?"

"It could be an office. Or a craft room." She sucked in a shaky breath. "I don't know why guys do what they do."

Her tone was loaded with hurt and betrayal. The way that asshole had treated her left her scared, just like what I had been through had left me jaded. But Violet had made me work through it because she was worth it. I'd do the same for her and work like hell to be worth it for her. "Violet, there's been no one but you since before you."

She screwed her face up. "Really?" She started sobbing again. "Willis got married, and his wife made sure to send pictures to our friend group. I'm sure she *forgot* I was still in the group," she said bitterly. "I thought if he could move on so fast, you could too."

That dick. Was there time to drive to California and kick his ass and slap the camera out of his wife's hands?

I lifted her chin and waited until she caught her breath. Tears continued to flow down her face. I swiped at her cheeks, but it was like a twig stemming a broken dam. "Really." I caught a tear with my mouth, and her lips parted. "I want to show you something. I wasn't sure if it would upset you or if you'd think I was being pushy. But Mom said I had to decide what I wanted to do about my feelings for you. So I did."

She blinked and sucked in a shuddering breath. "Did what?" she asked, sounding all cute and stuffy.

"I decided to give you as much time as you needed to trust me. I'd stay in this house until I finally won you over, and if it wasn't before your aunt had to sell, then I'd buy it. And keep waiting."

"That's years away."

"I'm a hurry-up-and-wait kind of guy."

"Oh, Evander." She ran her hand over my cheek, and her palm brushed down my stubble. "I've fallen so in love with you."

The world started spinning again. Everything I wanted just happened. Violet Duke said she loved me. The smartest, most stubborn woman I knew fucking loved me. I had gotten up this morning hoping to make her day easier, to help her stress less and get her on her feet.

Instead, she had made my goddamn day. I placed a hard, quick kiss on her mouth and rose. "Come on." I held my hand out to her. "I want to show you what I did for the woman I'm in love with."

"Evander..." She stared at me, then her gaze dropped to my outstretched hand. "You love me?"

"So damn much. Let me show you."

She slipped her soft fingers through mine and stood. This was the moment we were on the same page for the first time. We were together. She wanted me, and I wanted her. Nothing more. Nothing less. Everything else was a bonus, and I had a gift I'd been working on here. For her. For the baby. For all of us.

Chapter Twenty-Seven

Violet

I want to show you what I did for the woman I'm in love with.

Evander loved me. *So damn much.*

I hadn't ruined us. Evander understood. He got me, and I'd never had that before. Now I had him.

He led me to the closed guest room door. He kept his hand wrapped around mine as he tipped his forehead toward the doorknob. "Open it."

The curiosity inside me grew. What had he been doing with this room?

I put my hand on the cool knob, twisted, and pushed the door open. His hold tightened on me.

I took in the room. My soft gasp echoed between us.

This was no longer a guest room. He'd moved the bed and dressers out. He'd painted. He'd even replaced the blinds. None of it in the way I had feared. This wasn't going to be an office or a craft room.

The walls were the softest yellow. The blinds were now room darkening and a comforting gray that paired well with the paint color and tied the room in with the rest of the house. On the walls were...

"Oh my god." I wandered inside, towing him behind me.

Instead of animal drawings, the walls were decorated with hexagonal structures that had little *H*s and *O*s coming off them. One of them tickled my brain, and I studied the drawing. Two different sugars linked with a bond depicted as a sharp zigzag. No...

"Lactose?" A maniacal giggle burst out of me. Next to the chemical structure was a colorful canvas with the words "Be a proton in life." Positive signs were scattered around the letters.

My gaze jumped over the sturdy crib, a five-drawer dresser already anchored to the wall, and a changing table, all matching. A plush glider rocker sat across from the crib. All of the furniture was very familiar.

This was the same set I had admired when I had been with Alder to get the cheap items for the rental. I did a small spin, and my attention landed on the end table.

A choking sound left me. Tears flooded my eyes. The end table with the welding that reminded me of the chemical structure for acetylene.

Evander had designed a nursery straight from my imagination. All because he paid attention. To me.

How did he know I had pinpointed that piece out of everything?

"Evander," I whispered. "This is amazing."

"You like it?"

I spun to him, letting go of his hand to grip his shoulder. "I love it." I put my palm on his cheek. "I can't believe you did all this."

"Ever since I saw you at the bar that night, I knew you were special. I was too damn afraid to admit how much."

The initial connection between us was undeniable. So strong that neither of us had the courage to believe it. Except that we had, or we wouldn't be together right now. "I thought no guy could be that good in bed and then be a decent guy. When you opened the door that day, I just assumed that, yep, everything was too good to be true. I thought I'd just fool myself again." I rested my head on his chest. "Only I almost fooled myself out of the best thing that ever happened to me."

His strong arms came around me. "I wasn't going to let you do that. I was ready to take a million pictures of the sunset or find more kittens to rescue."

I smiled and listened to his steady heartbeat as I looked at as much of the room as I could see. "How did you know? All this? It's perfect."

"Hattie told Liam about someone admiring his end table, and he figured it was you. There are not many people running around complimenting furniture on its chemical structure. I asked her what else you had liked, and she was happy to help. The furniture set had sold, so Hattie had to track down another set and get it shipped."

I pulled back. "You did all that?"

"I wanted to get what you liked."

My gaze landed on the furniture I had thought was so far out of my budget I had forgotten all about it. "That's what you had in the back of your truck when you gave me a ride to my car?"

"Yes, and that ride was an excuse to get closer to you. I didn't want you to know what I was doing until I was ready to talk to you. That's why I was keeping my calls and texts private. I didn't want to pressure you."

The man absolutely humbled me. "All I did was crochet you a blanket."

"You made me a blanket?"

"It's the one you brought from the rental, but I was too afraid to give it to you. Wait here." I untangled from him and went to his bedroom. I returned to the stunning nursery with the blanket and handed it to him.

His brows drew together, and he ran a hand over it. "Other than a quilt from Mom, no one's ever made me anything."

He said it in a reverent way that made me feel like he really treasured my gift. "I'll make you another."

"You don't have to unless you want to. I'll take anything you give me." He tugged me to him, crushing the blanket between us. "But, Violet, I'll move heaven and earth for Bud. But I'll never leave heaven or earth without you. I'm gonna be right here, buying you yarn, telling you to come outside for sunsets, and watching you cuddle cats and our baby on the porch."

"Oh, Evander." Everything inside of me melted. I was utterly smitten and deeply in love. Small thumps hit the inside of my belly and kept going. I smiled and took the blanket from him and draped it over the edge of the crib. Then I grabbed his hands to rest them on my belly.

Tiny thumps resonated through me and into him. Astonishment lit his eyes. "Is that..."

"Bud's saying hi."

He lowered himself to his knees and touched his forehead between our hands. The bumps lessened until they stopped. He gazed up at me. "I want to spend my life with you, Violet Duke. I can wait for a decent proposal, but I have to let you know."

His life. My life. Our life. I feathered my fingers over his head. "These last few months, with what little of you I allowed myself to have, have been the best of my life. I'm tired of waking up every day and not seeing you."

"I want to see you in my bed every goddamn day. I hated having to leave every time we were together. I love you, wildflower." Love welled in his gaze, along with heat, tenderness and affection.

I'd had what I wanted all this time. "I was single at the brewery because I saw Lily and Eliot, and I had to get away. I wanted a guy to look at me that way, and I never thought it'd happen. I didn't even believe it when she said you already did." I'd wasted weeks. No more. "I love you so much."

He rose, that exact look in his eyes aimed directly at me.

He kissed me. Salt still lingered on his lips from my tears, but he was nothing but hot and sweet. I licked out my tongue to meet his and gripped the back of his neck. Carefully, he moved until he was between my legs. Even with my stomach between us, this position was perfect.

"Tell me," he growled against my lips, "how far can we go?"

With him? "I hope all the way."

Evander

. . .

I held the world in my arms. Violet fucking loved me. Her reaction to the nursery was more than I could've hoped for. More than that, she'd been thrilled about it after trusting me. "I'll be careful."

She sucked on my bottom lip. "Not too careful."

Fuck, this woman. I picked her up with an arm around her back and one under her legs.

She yelped, then laughed and clutched my shoulders. "I can't believe you can do that."

"Believe it. I'll be doing this when I'm ninety." I'd never been more sure of anything. I gingerly maneuvered through my bedroom door.

I laid her down and spotted her phone on the nightstand. I grabbed it, handing it to her. "Pull that thread of Vasectomy Willis and Rebound Wife."

She frowned but did as I asked. I snatched the phone and leaned close to her, putting our heads together. Her hands fluttered to her belly, smoothing the material of her shirt over the mound, showing how obviously pregnant she was.

"Smile and say, 'We're expecting,'" I said.

She laughed. "Won't that make me as petty as them?"

"Abso-fucking-lutely. I don't want that asshole ex of yours to think he's bothered you for one second." I chose video and hit record.

A sly grin graced her face. In unison, we shouted, "We're expecting!"

I clicked and sent the image showing us smiling and in bed. Once that was done, I didn't waste time. I'd been waiting for her for too long.

"I can't believe you did that," she said. "I love it."

Anything for her. Dragging her black leggings down,

I made sure to get the underwear too. "This dress has been driving me crazy all day."

"Like the way you told off Chad did to me?"

"I should've done it from the beginning." I grabbed a pillow to put behind her. "Now lean back and spread those legs, Violet. I'm a hungry man." She clamped her lower lip between her teeth, but she did as I asked. "You're soaked for me, aren't you, wildflower?"

Her knees trembled. Perfect.

I draped myself over the bed and dove between her lush thighs.

"Ev—" she groaned and arched into me.

Her body was slightly different at this far along in the pregnancy, and I loved every part of it. I hated that I missed so much. Never again. I would make sure that she always wanted me close to her.

Violet was arching off the bed within seconds. I didn't even have a chance to push a finger into her tight pussy.

"It's never been this fast before—oh! Evander!" Her knees fell open, and she rocked into my tongue over and over. "Yes, yes, yes!"

There it was. My answer. She was mine.

I could keep lapping at her, get her off again, but I'd been without too long. I rose enough to rip my fly open and free my erection. Since I wasn't wasting time for this first round, I notched myself and slowly pushed in, staying on my knees to keep pressure off her stomach.

This had to be as good for her as it was for me. She clamped her legs around me. When I was fully seated, I paused. The first time I'd been in her, she'd rocked my world. This time, she'd given me the damn universe.

She adjusted with me and groaned. "So full. I missed this."

I pulled out and took my time thrusting back in. "Fuck, Violet. We're not leaving this bed for the rest of the day." I fell forward, catching myself with an arm, my hand planted by her head.

I rested a finger on her clit.

"I can't come again. That first time was too strong... ungh." Her eyelids fluttered. "You always prove me wrong."

"You did it first. I'll always be trying to catch up." I increased my rhythm.

"Those chemistry decorations? Those are going to get you laid for a long time." She unhooked her legs and hitched them to the side. The bed rocked with my thrusts. "So fucking good."

The best. My desire would explode or implode if I didn't come soon, but I needed more time, just a little more of us together. Connected. "I'll paint this whole house full of chemistry equations to get you under me."

She gripped my shoulders and held on for the ride. "You got me under you long before that."

My balls tightened. I couldn't hang on. "Come for me, wildflower."

Her walls clenched around me so fucking tight I barely held on until she cried my name. Then I let go, kicking my hips and shaking until I spent everything inside of her. This time, she was mine. I wasn't leaving, thinking I'd never see her again. I wasn't trying to act as if we were nothing but an "expecting parents with benefits" situation. Violet Duke was mine.

She held on to me, her chest heaving, her stomach brushing mine. I pulled out of her and rolled behind her, curling her into my front. I was still dressed, but I didn't want to leave her long enough to take my jeans and shirt off. Not yet.

"Mm." She snuggled into me, her ass wiggling against my still-hard dick. "I think I could sleep now. I tried to earlier, but I just tossed and turned."

"In that case, wait here." I got up and stuffed my obnoxious hard-on back into my jeans. I went into the bathroom and returned with a damp, warm washcloth.

I handed it to her, and while she cleaned up, I changed into sweats. Then I got her under the covers and wrapped myself behind her again. This moment was more perfect than I could've imagined. "Get some rest."

"You seem to be saying that a lot lately."

"I like seeing you in my bed, and that beautiful mind of yours is keeping you awake."

"I was so worried after I saw the pictures of the nursery equipment." She yawned.

I pressed a kiss into her hair and draped an arm over her abdomen. "Dad thinks he can cut off the damaged parts and repurpose it." My parents were excited and wanted to help. Instead of thinking the worst, I liked seeing their enthusiasm. I appreciated it and them.

"That's sweet of him, but we don't need it now."

"Then I'll tell him to go ahead and do it for their place after the baby comes. It'll keep him from trying to fix the fence on his own."

She traced lazy circles over the back of my hand. "What are you going to do?"

"I'm going to marry you, we're going to get this house, and I'll grow goddamn pumpkins until I take over for Dad. I already talked to Stetson, and he brought up the idea of separating the ranches into individual businesses first. It's a lot for him to oversee."

"You're okay being a farmer and rancher?"

"I don't care what I am as long as I'm with you." I splayed my hand over the swell of her stomach. "But just so you don't worry, yes, I'm more than okay with it."

"I love you," she murmured. A heartbeat later, her breathing evened, and she went limp.

"You're my world. You're my beautiful wildflower."

Epilogue

Violet

"Well, Bud no longer fits." I cradled my newborn daughter in my arms. My body ached and the fatigue was staggering, but I was so damn happy. "We got so used to calling her Bud that we never did come up with a name."

Evander sat on the edge of the bed. We were going home soon, and we had all the paperwork to fill out.

He ran a finger down her nose. Her little mouth worked like she had an invisible pacifier. "Willa Annie Barron. If you're sure about using Annie."

"I can't be upset with Grandma Annie since what she did made sure I could find you again." And Willa was an ode to his sweet mom. He never said, but I knew it was important to him to honor her. I handed Willa over, and he carefully accepted her. I would never tire of watching his big frame snuggle a tiny little baby. "Willa Annie Barron. She'll be the prettiest guest at our wedding reception."

To be compliant with the trust, we'd had to get married at the justice of the peace so I could live with Evander. My aunt had been apologetic, but I didn't care. If I had married him then or in six months or in six years, it didn't matter. Evander and I would be together.

But since we had to say our vows early, the house would be officially ours earlier.

"A beautiful July reception for my beautiful girls." He leaned forward and kissed me. "I might get the siding replaced before then. You can be the foreman," he said to Willa. "Make sure I'm doing it right."

This man. He made every day special. By the time I woke for work, he was up and had breakfast waiting. When I got home, he had a meal in the oven. I got foot rubs, back rubs—anything rubbed.

Some nights, I sat in the nursery and admired the love put into the decor. When I mentioned that there was nothing in the room that gave a nod to his army time or ag background, he'd painted the two other walls. A baby bear with an army uniform on one wall and a pasture full of sunflowers on the other. *Colorful and stimulating*, he'd said. *Good for Bud's brain.*

In July, we'd have a small reception with just family amid the second annual goddamn pumpkin patch. He'd even named his side hustle GD Pumpkins.

"I have my two girls to myself for the next three months," he said. "I'm going to take good care of you both."

My eyelids were getting heavy. "You already have."

When I woke up, he'd be there, caring for Willa and me. And he'd have that look in his eyes. The one that said we were his world. His everything. Just like he was mine.

. . .

Alder got his life on track and he's ready to take the reins of CEO. But it includes a move to Coal Haven, and when he learns his ex-wife, Daisy, and her daughter need a place to stay, he makes an offer. Marry him one more time, and she can stay in the house for a year until the inheritance is official. The only problem is...he has to live there too. Read Alder and Daisy's story in Daisy Whispers.

Thank you so much for joining Violet and Evander! You're cordially invited to attend their wedding reception with all the Dukes and the Barrons in their bonus epilogue, available when you sign up to my newsletter on mariejohnstonwriter.com.

Marie Johnston writes paranormal and contemporary romance and has collected several awards in both genres. Before she was a writer, she was a microbiologist. Depending on the situation, she can be oddly unconcerned about germs or weirdly phobic. She's also a licensed medical technician and has worked as a public health microbiologist and as a lab tech in hospital and clinic labs. Marie's been a volunteer EMT, a college instructor, a security guard, a phlebotomist, a hotel clerk, and a coffee pourer in a bingo hall. All fodder for a writer!! She has four kids, cats, lots of cats, and a corgie.

mariejohnstonwriter.com

Follow me:

King's Queen

King's Queen